RED ROSES

TASHA HUTCHISON

RUNNING WILD

Published in North America, Australia, and Europe by RIZE.
Visit Running Wild Press at www.runningwildpress.com/rize, Educators,
librarians, book clubs (as well as the eternally curious), go to
www.runningwildpress.com/rize.

ISBN (pbk) 978-1-960018-36-6
ISBN (ebook) 978-1-960018-30-4

I dedicate this book in fond memory of Johnnie & Lillie Henderson and Jerry Hutchison.

ACKNOWLEDGMENT

To my husband, parents, siblings, and friends, thank you for all
the encouragement over the years. Especially my dear mother;
if not for you, I am not sure if I would have ever tapped into my
gift of writing.
You challenge and inspire me.

I love you all.

1
IT'S WINE O'CLOCK

Not having to spend a Friday night in the summer with a dead body felt unreal. It's almost unheard of as a Chief Forensic Pathologist. We were long overdue for a girl's night. So, I invited my best friends; Brooklyn Rahimi, Tammy Avalos, and Lorraine Collins. It was also the perfect time to unveil my renovated wine cellar. A stress-free night of conversation and dancing with my girls was music to my ears. The wall of wine is only a cherry on top.

Brooklyn's outfit gave me an eyegasm. She loved fashion as much as I did. We've fought over fashion and bonded over it many times. Tammy is a free spirit. Her dating card has been full since her divorce. It's a miracle she has time to hang out with us. Poor Lorraine hates it. She's always nagging Tammy to settle down. But, everyone isn't like her. She's a true romantic. Even after all the drama with her daughter's father. Anyone else would've given up on love. But Lorraine's fire for love is as red as her hair.

We were all kid-free for the night. Well, all of us except Tammy. She hates to admit she's the grandma of the group, or as she calls it, Gigi. While the fathers are on daddy duty, we were going to do our best to challenge our almost forty-year-older livers to a duel. Except poor Tammy. Her liver is going on fifty. But, she can hang with the best of them.

When the girls arrived, I gave them each a bouquet of my favorite flowers—red roses. I knew they'd come locked and loaded with gifts to break in the wine cellar, and they didn't disappoint. Lorraine gifted me six large candles. Tammy gifted me a dozen bottles of wine to help stock my wine cellar, and Brooklyn gifted me the most beautiful white marble tabletop wine opener with a gold handle. It even had my name engraved in gold on the base–Iris Reid. That's what I love about my girls. They're classy and thoughtful in every way.

After years of my basement being a disaster area, I buckled down and hired a contractor and a decorator from Highsea. I told them I wanted it to look like it jumped right out of a page of a design magazine, and into my home. They exceeded my expectations. The decorator went with a modern white and silver color scheme to match the rest of my home.

Four white faux leather chairs with silver arm accents sat in a circle in the center of the room. Small silver tables were placed between each chair. A silver abstract chandelier with bright white lights hung over the circle of chairs. The decorator described the chandelier as unique. I called it chaos. But what did I know?

Whenever we got together, the first few minutes of conversation were the same as the chandelier; chaotic. We're all so eager to catch up; we usually end up talking over each other combined with hugs and kisses. We pretty much play Double Dutch and jump into the conversation when we can.

"Iris, I really hate the idea of you living in this big beautiful house alone." Lorraine shrugged, eyeballing every inch of the house within her peripheral as if it were her first time visiting. But she remained within her wheelhouse. Lorraine wouldn't be Lorraine if she didn't urge us to attach ourselves to a man in order to have a happier life. As if men were the be all and end all.

I knew where she was going with her comment. Heck, we all knew where she was going with it. "I don't live alone," I explained with a smile wide enough to show all my pearly whites. "I have my son."

"That's different, and he's a teenager now. He's going to have his own life with sports and friends." Lorraine glanced at each of us before mentioning my ex-boyfriend and father of my child–Rodney. The same man who'd break out in hives whenever I'd mention marriage. It's like he was allergic to the very thought of commitment. I guess that's asking for too much in his eyes. "You should get back with Rodney. You guys co-parent so well. It's a shame you aren't together."

"I want love. I welcome love. But I need more than love right now. I need to find myself." I waved my hands to move on from the conversation all while silently wishing and praying this would be the one and only time she'd bring him up. "That's not what this night is about."

"Yeah, let it go," Tammy yelled. "Alexa, play Buy me a Drink by T-Pain." She broke out her best dance moves, as she glided across the room, twisted, turned, and dropped it low, all with a carefree smile.

"Ooh, that's my song." I ran over to dance with Tammy. Neither of us had any rhythm to save our lives. But we didn't care. We were going to have a good time if it killed us. Plus, as long as we danced, Lorraine wasn't preaching.

"Let me show you how it's done." Brooklyn raced over with a full glass of wine in hand. Thankfully I had marble floors. It's easier to clean because the girls are always wasting good wine.

"You have to swing your hips like this." She moved like a sexy snake. "Yeah Iris, you got it. You got it."

"What about me?" Lorraine asked, rolling her body to the beat.

"It's a little nineties, but it's giving what you're trying to give." We all laughed and danced until the song faded.

Whenever I spent time with the girls they had a way of helping me get out of my funk from a long week from performing back to back autopsies. Genuine friends are not overrated. My girls are the best. Though, I could be biased from my deep affection for them.

After Brooklyn finally let Tammy and Lorraine know about her having Huntington's disease, it allowed us to bond in unimaginable ways. Now seven years later we were a family—sisters, if you must. It's true what they say. Friends are the family you choose.

I can depend on the girls in every capacity of my life. They're a shoulder to lean on, counselors, and even babysitters before Junior began throwing fits about being old enough to be on his own for a few hours. There's something about teen years. The moment kids turn into teenagers they want to do everything on their own in their own way.

"You guys have no idea how much I needed this," I sighed, fanning myself with a linen napkin. "I had to perform an autopsy on a ten-year-old girl a couple days ago. I hate it whenever a child lands on my table. I can't escape the visions of them laying there lifeless. It consumes me. The shit is unnatural."

"What happened to her?" Tammy asked with wide eyes.

"I'll share this one time, and only because I brought it up and you're all my sisters," I explained. I made sure the girls knew why I never talked about my cases years ago. I take my position seriously. It's a private matter for families that should be handled with respect in every way possible. It feels like gossip to discuss their cases in casual conversations, so I try to avoid it at all costs. But I couldn't stop thinking about a recent case. It clinged on me like a wet bathing suit on a windy day at the beach. "A thirteen-year-old girl died from asphyxia due to an opioid overdose." I gulped my wine and poured another glass right away. "When I explained my findings to her parents they told me how badly the other kids bullied her. When she was two-years-old, she grabbed a pot of boiling water from the stove and burned herself pretty badly. She had scarring on the right side of her face, shoulder, arm, and hand. The kids had been taunting her for years. I mean, who could endure eleven years of constant bullying and not develop mental and emotional issues?"

"I know I couldn't." Brooklyn raised her hand. "Some kids are savages."

"It starts at home," Tammy said, pointing matter-of-factly with a nod.

"Why are the parents always to blame?" Lorraine butted in. "Jeffrey Dahmer's parents didn't teach him to eat humans. And still he indulged on sautéed heads, fingers, and toes like a delicatessen."

"You don't know what his parents taught him," I interjected.

"I stand corrected, I would hope his parents didn't teach him to eat human flesh," Lorraine giggled.

"Why do you always go so damn dark?" Tammy asked Lorraine with scrunched eyebrows.

"Yeah, and please don't get started with the black-eyed children nonsense tonight," Brooklyn gave her two cents while polishing off another glass of wine. "I can't remember a time I've known you and you haven't talked about the black-eyed children conspiracy theories."

"Fine, I won't talk about it." Lorraine shrugged. "But don't come crying to me when one of those freaky ass kids ends up in the backseat of your cars."

"We won't," the three of us replied simultaneously with stomach curdling laughs.

Brooklyn walked over to the wall to pull a bottle of Red Opus One. Rodney gifted me a six-bottle wooden case to commemorate my wine cellar the day of the big reveal with the interior designer. The man had taste and he wasn't stingy with his money. I'll give him that much. "Seriously, you need to do better with your mental breaks, Iris. It's been four years since you've taken a vacation."

"Five years," I corrected her.

"Damn," Tammy squealed, gulping the last of her wine to make room for a glass of Opus One. "Lorraine can cry all she wants. But when it's time for my vacation, I don't care what she says. Mental health is self-care, and vacations fall under that umbrella. I need my time away on a tropical island every summer like clockwork to function in life."

"That's Lorraine's problem. She thinks of herself as the sensible one in the group. Everything has to make sense, and if you don't understand it or see it her way, she'll make you see it," I explained.

"First, Iris, I'll bet that's why you don't have a man." Lorraine pointed at me. "You don't make time for one. You can't be happy living alone without having a good man to come home to talk about your day and make love to at the end of the night. Secondly, I am the sensible one. I keep all you in order in a respectable way. Otherwise, you'd self-destruct." She hurriedly looked away the moment the words left her mouth.

"Yeah, you better look away," Tammy chastised. "You of all people know better than to equate happiness to having a man. Michael put you through pure hell, and made you a single mother because you were so hell-bent on making that messy

6

relationship work when you knew you should've walked away a long time ago before you had a child with him," she explained. "And lastly, don't flatter yourself. We are intelligent and capable women. We don't need a babysitter. We keep ourselves in order."

"Screw you, I love my daughter," Lorraine yelped, marching across the room. "Violet is the best thing that came out of that tumultuous situationship. Talk about Michael all you want. I don't care about him. But leave Violet out of it."

Michael was Lorraine's worst decision whether she wanted to admit it or not. The moment he came into her life, her world turned upside down, and every time she thought it would get better, he flipped it again. But I can relate to Lorraine in that way because all she wanted from Michael was a commitment he was never willing to give. Rodney was the same in that regard. So, I know how it feels to hold on to a dream with someone who's not capable of giving you what you need and desire in a partner.

"Hey, hey, hey, ladies," I interrupted before it turned into a full on catfight. "Violet is an amazing little girl. I love her with all my heart. Tammy deserves a vacation. She works hard." I held my glass in the air. "Here's to our amazing kids and self-care."

"Here, here." We toasted with a big sigh of love. Blood relation doesn't negate the fact that we were sisters. We're always together. We uplift each other. Sure, there's drama, but we resolve it in love, and most of all, we chose each other.

Tammy eased over to hug Lorraine. She accepted with no qualms. At the end of the day, they loved each other. Siblings fight every now and again, then come back together with resolve and move on like it never happened. The best thing about us is we don't sweep things under the rug. We face it and work through it.

"We should take a girl's trip. If nothing else, we could do it in the name of love for poor old overworked Iris." Tammy snapped her fingers. "I have an idea. You three should come with me to La Isleta Sanguinea. You have three months to plan and get your affairs in order. That's more than enough time."

"It may be three months in advance, but I can't take off. My work is too important," I explained.

"We know you're an important person, Iris. But your mental health trumps all. If you're carted off to a padded white room in a straitjacket, they'll replace you within a couple of days." Brooklyn touched my arm. "At least give it some thought before you decline. It's March, you have time to get your affairs in order."

"Well, I can't go. One of us should be at the office." Lorraine crossed her legs in a huff.

"We hired people who are more than capable of running the business without us having to micromanage them. You're as bad as Iris."

"I'll think about it," I assured her.

"While you're thinking about vacation nonsense, I have something else for us to do," Lorraine explained with jazz fingers. "Iris, remember when you said you needed more than love? That you needed to find yourself? Well, I have the perfect remedy for that." She took four boxes out of a shopping bag. "I thought it would be cool if we took Ancestry tests to discover some interesting facts about our family history."

"Ooh, I've always wanted to take one of those. Give me that." Tammy snatched one of the boxes from Lorraine to examine it.

"No way, I'm adopted. It was hard enough to build a relationship with my birth father. Adding more to that makes my head dizzy." Brooklyn winced.

"Yeah, and I've never met or known any blood related

family outside of my parents," I explained. "No extended family ever called, came for visits, sent letters or anything. I used to wonder why. I even built up the courage to ask my mom once. But I left it alone when she became defensive and evasive. When they died in a car wreck, I figured I may as well leave it alone. It's a can of worms I don't want to open. I lost them when I was twenty-two years old. I'm with Brooklyn on this one. I'll pass." I waved Lorraine away.

"So you mean to tell me you aren't the least bit curious?" Lorraine asked with a mischievous look plastered on her face.

"I'm thirty-seven-years-old. I got over my curiosity a long time ago," I said, pouring a glass of wine to wash away the bad taste in my mouth from talking about this sore subject. I've gone through all the stages—curiosity, anger, sadness, and now acceptance.

"How could you say that? You can't know who you are as a person if you don't know where you come from." Lorraine smoothed her yellow silk skirt. She'd gone the Ronald McDonald route.

"It's pointless," I replied. "I'm too old to care now. What kind of authentic relationship could I have with them?"

Tammy ripped the box open and quickly swabbed her mouth. "Here's to finding a rich uncle with no kids."

"I can't deal," I chuckled with my hand covering my mouth.

It wasn't often Tammy butted into conversations, but she had perfect timing when she felt things were getting too heavy. Oh how I wished she had the same timing when she and Lorraine were having one of their many squabbles.

Lorraine ripped open her box and swabbed her mouth. "Two down and two to go."

"Forget it, I'm not doing it." Brooklyn sat the box on the table and leaned back in her chair with her arms folded over her chest in a huff. I could see the confusion in her eyes because I shared the same confusion.

"What's that look?" I asked Brooklyn.

"I want to know but I don't want to know," she explained.

"I get it and I'm with you. I'm not doing it either." I followed Brooklyn's lead, stubbornly folding my arms over my chest.

"You two are the main ones who should take the tests. Brooklyn, you're adopted. You've met your father, and you two have created a pretty good relationship. Think about the rest of your family that's out there," Tammy explained. "Iris, you sat there and told us a long story about how you always wanted to know your family but your mom was a brick wall. Lorraine may get on my nerves, but she's right this time. Neither of you will ever know who you are until you know where you come from. Now swab your damn mouths." She held two boxes in front of us with the mom-eyes, practically reducing us to a couple of bratty teenagers.

"Come on, Iris," Brooklyn said. "We may as well do it to shut them up." She took the boxes from Tammy and passed one to me.

I pushed it away, sticking to my guns. She may have folded, but I stood strong on my decision. "I know I have family out there. But those people may not want anything to do with me. I'm not ready for that kind of rejection. I have all the family I need right here with you guys. Why fix something that isn't broken?"

"You're not going to like me after I say this," Tammy spoke frankly.

"Then don't say it." I shoved my hair away from my face. The room suddenly became hot. Nothing another glass of wine couldn't fix.

Down the hatch.

"You're an accomplished woman. You help bring closure to family and friends. Now add being a single mother to the mix. Yes, Rodney is active in your son's life, but Junior lives with you full-time. That is a job in itself. Now sprinkle how much you help Brooklyn when it comes to her having Huntington's disease into the mix." She walked over to put her arm around Brooklyn's shoulders. "You're superwoman, but it's time for you to put all your focus into yourself. This has the potential to change your life in a good way." She shook the box. "A person could never have enough family and love in their life. Yes, we're friends who've become family. But, these people will be your blood family–your tribe. Take the test."

"You don't know if this *tribe* wants me in their life, much less to grow to love me."

"You don't know either," Tammy replied.

"There's one thing you got wrong," I said.

Tammy asked, "What is that?"

"You tell me, since you know it all." The temperature in the room rose about ten degrees. Perhaps I could blame it on the wine. We'd had enough.

"You've mastered wearing your hard shell. But I know you, and I'll bet my life you have questions about your past and your family. All it takes is a simple swab. Stop being a baby, and do it." She ripped the box open and held the swab to my face.

I stuck to my guns and pushed it away.

"Let's say your family doesn't accept you. That'll be their loss. But the three of us will be here for you in any way you need. Now swab your mouth." This time she opened the box and put the swab in my hand.

My back was against the wall, and all eyes were on me. They'll say I'm the difficult one if I don't do it. Peer pressure should not exist in friendships of middle-aged women. "Fine, but if this blows up in my face, I'll be sending you my therapy bill."

"I'll do you one better. I'll pay for it and drive you to your sessions. Then I'll take you out for a nice dinner and drinks afterwards." Tammy smiled.

"Fine." I swabbed and shoved the stick inside the plastic container while Tammy filled out my information on the paperwork.

Brooklyn held my hand with an enduring smile. If no one else understood my plight, I know she did. Heck, Brooklyn more than understood. We had been in our dorm room at Pinemoor State College writing essays when a knock on the door interrupted us. It was a police officer. The moment the words rolled off his tongue about the death of my parents I instantly morphed into a zombie. Brooklyn, being the kind-hearted person she is, took control. She and her mother made sure my parents had a beautiful home going. Brooklyn rallied our friends to make sure I maintained my perfect GPA. She even made sure I ate and took care of my personal hygiene. So when Brooklyn went through a difficult time with her illness, I happily dropped everything to be there for her. It's the least I could do. We'd been by each other's side for many life-changing milestones while in college. She was nineteen when she learned she had Huntington's disease. I was twenty-two when my parents died in a car accident. We were each other's rock. So, I had no doubt that whatever came of this, she'd be there for me just as she always had.

"I'm mailing these out first thing in the morning." Lorraine made the boxes dance as she packed them back inside the bag. "This is so exciting."

I rolled my eyes and began cleaning up the empty wine bottles. "You three know the routine. Whenever there are two or more bottles empty, find a bed for the remedy."

Tammy walked over to me with puppy dog eyes. "I hope you're not upset with me. I know I can be a bit pushy sometimes. But I don't want you to have any more questions about your family. It's time to face it once and for all."

"I'm not upset with you. But you need to have some consideration of how this could affect me. I'm not good with rejection, and I have a sneaky suspicion that's exactly what's going to happen if I contact them." I went on to explain, "Growing up, I thought it was normal not to have family outside of my mom and dad. But as I got older and heard my friends go on and on about their cousins, aunts, uncles, grandparents, and so on, I knew there was something wrong. But, I could never get an honest answer from my parents until they totally shut the conversation down once and for all. When they died in the car accident, I took that as a sign to leave it alone. I don't know who those people are and why there is separation. But, I trust my parents. They must've had a good reason to keep them at bay."

"I hear everything you say. Truly, I do. But, you spend your days bringing closure to families and friends. Now it's your turn to bring closure to your own life. Who knows? This may be the start of a new chapter. You've been around Lorraine far too long. You're going dark when you don't know if this situation calls for it." Tammy shrugged.

After I went back to school to become a Forensic Pathologist, it challenged me in many ways. It's like a puzzle, and I'm the only one who can find the final missing piece to complete it. But it's easy when it's someone else's puzzle and not my own.

"Maybe you're right." I shrugged.

"At least you won't have to do this alone," she paused, sighing deeply. "At thirty-five, I found my father. Our reunion wasn't all rainbows and kittens. He was a tough old man, stuck in his ways, and didn't see anything wrong with running off to chase his dreams even though he had a kid. He said he only had one life to live and he wasn't wasting it by being held down with responsibilities he never asked for."

We all held our breath on the edge of our seats as we listened to Tammy share this part of herself she'd never shared with us. It helped me understand her more. Even though she hasn't verbalized it, I wondered if this factored into her dating life. Oftentimes she'd have three dates in one day for breakfast, lunch, and dinner. Mind you, she's forty-seven-years-old with no plans of slowing down.

"That's terrible. How's your relationship with him now? You never talk about him," I asked, touching her hand. You couldn't see with the naked eye, but once I touched her hand, I could feel her shaking. It affected her more than she let on. I held back my tears. She's my sister. I wanted to comfort her, but I didn't want to infringe if she wasn't ready to share.

"I tried the father-daughter bit, but after a while I chose to cut the cord. I had all the answers I needed. With a ton of counseling, I no longer wonder why he wasn't there or if I wasn't good enough. Do you remember how I was when you first met me?"

Brooklyn and I met in college. She knows why I'm guarded and why it's hard for me to welcome new people into my life. So, she invited me to dinner to meet Tammy and Lorraine. Albeit, it wasn't a regular dinner. Tammy double booked us with two dates. One before our dinner and one after our dinner. To say I was impressed with how she juggled us with her dates without making us feel like we were in the way is an understatement. The woman has it down to a science.

"Yeah, you were booked and busy that night."

She playfully tapped my arm. "I didn't realize it then. But I was searching for my dad in every man I met. I believe you keep people away because you've operated so long without family. You owe it to yourself to make the most beautiful life possible."

"Are you okay," I touched her forehead to see if she had a fever. "I've never heard you go this deep before."

"I'm fine," she laughed. "Go on this journey and get to know yourself, and you too could one day become as deep as me." She snapped her fingers with a grin and twisted her hip.

Perhaps Tammy's observation of me hit the mark this time. I'd built a wall no one could get around because of my isolated past. I've lost more than a few love interests and possibly great friendships. Then I blamed everyone else for not seeing the good in me. When more than likely I never gave them a chance.

"I'll think about it. Go get some sleep, old woman. I'll see you in the morning."

"This is the second time one of you has referred to me as an old woman as if I couldn't run circles around each and every one of you." Tammy kissed my forehead and sauntered upstairs.

Without a doubt I knew I made two great decisions even with my issues. Having my son, and lowering my wall enough for Tammy and Lorraine to be in my life. But this wasn't the relaxing evening I had in mind for our girl's night.

Thanks Lorraine.

2
DECISIONS, DECISIONS

Two weeks passed since Tammy practically forced the swab in my mouth. To say my nerves were running amuck was an understatement. Even when I actively thought of other things, the Ancestry test found its way, front and center. It lingered in an abyss of ominous darkness within my soul.

When my parents died I never addressed the pain it caused me. With no extended family to lean on, it birthed mental and emotional issues. I put my feelings away to focus on other things outside of losing my parents. Thinking about them made things worse. It only reminded me how alone I felt without them.

I'd gotten lucky to function enough to date Rodney for as long as I did and we created an amazing kid. But, he has as many issues as me. His biggest issue is him lacing up his shoes and running like an Olympic Track Star away from commitment. Like clockwork, I'd be ridden with emotional pain. That's when I'd rather be alone to drown myself in work to push through those feelings.

The girls and I planned to meet at Lorraine's house to read our results. God knew I'd need their support. Still, there's a part of me that didn't want to know the truth because it would undoubtedly change my life.

Am I ready for that kind of change?

I knew I'd get a slew of matches. But thanks to my parents, I wouldn't recognize any of the names. Not a grandparent, aunt, uncle, or cousin.

For the better part of the day I rested on the sofa with my leg kicked over the back. I sprinkled rose oil around the living room. It's supposed to soothe emotions that come with depression, grief, apathy, and stress. It did as much as it could although it wasn't enough to totally relieve me of stress while I waited for Rodney to bring Junior home. You'd think the rain tapping against the window would help calm my nerves. But nope, my nerves were on a warpath. I was afraid nothing would help and I'd eventually end up in a padded room being fed soupy jello while strapped in a straightjacket.

It's quite difficult to not feel upset and frustrated at my birth parents for their decision to create a cloud of mystery around our family. It left me at a disadvantage. If I move forward and reach out to them, how would I ever know if they tell me the truth about their absence in my life? I could only take their word for it.

Going through life without knowing about my roots left me with a shifting sense of identity. For nothing else, that's a good enough reason to reach out to my family. On the other hand, it could've been them who didn't want any contact with us.

As a mother, it's my job to at least try to give my son a life better than what I had. My friends have become family, but my son needs more than just friends. Humans are capable of surviving on our own. But as Tammy said, why should we walk alone when we're born into a tribe of people who could love and protect us, and even when they can't protect us, they'll help us through any obstacles.

At twenty-two, human brains aren't fully developed. I often wondered what kind of woman I'd be if I hadn't experienced trauma at such a young age. I find it painfully difficult to be vulnerable when the moment calls for it. But even still, I made it without my tribe. They never tried to reach out to me. So they more than likely don't want to get to know me, much less meet me.

Sundays were usually a day of relaxing. Before Rodney brought Junior home from their weekend together, I'd spent the day lounging in my silk pajamas, cucumbers on my eyes, feet up, with a glass of wine while true crime shows played in the background. Not so much this time. This Sunday came and went in the blink of an eye, and before I knew it, they were at the door.

Boy, were Rodney and Junior a sight to see. I couldn't help but erupt in a fit of laughter at the sight of them. They were dressed in matching gray slacks, white button down shirts, gray bow ties and suspenders. A thirteen-year-old kid, dressed like his old butt dad. The sight of them sent me into hysterics. Just what the doctor ordered.

"Mom, please." Junior rolled his eyes in a huff. "It's not funny."

"You do know Junior is too old for you to continue dressing him like he's your Bobbsey Twin." I needed to say something. I could see disdain written all over Junior's face. I'd been doing my best to teach and encourage him to find his voice and express his feelings. But he often stuffed them away to avoid conflict. It's not a trait that will serve him well in the long run.

A docile person is the most mistreated person on earth. It's okay for Junior to pick his battles but at least pick them. He needed to speak up about his feelings. Let people know what he accepts and what he won't accept. That includes his parents. Otherwise be prepared to live an utterly unremarkable life.

"You don't have to say it. You know we look good. Did we wake you?" Rodney tugged on the collar of my pajama shirt and marched inside the house, flipping on lights as if he still paid the bills.

"I wish I could sleep. I have too much on my mind." I kissed Junior on the cheek. "Did you have fun? I missed you."

He looked up at Rodney and exploded in laughter. "We went to the amusement park with Uncle Frank Saturday."

"What's so funny about that?"

"Dad got on a ride."

"I see where this is going. What happened?" I asked.

"Dad rode one of the biggest rides at the park. He got off holding his stomach and threw up in front of a crowd of people." He clutched his stomach, mimicking his dad.

"Now why on God's green earth would you get on the biggest ride in the park when you know you're afraid of heights."

"We were making memories. I wanted to participate instead of standing around like a loser." Rodney waved his hands with a look of embarrassment. I took it easy on him because I know his ego is fragile. At least he accomplished what he set out to do. He made memories with our son.

"You should've seen it, Mom. Some guy saw dad throw up and he threw up too."

"Oh no, the domino effect."

"Yeah, I got it on video." He whipped out his phone.

"Hey, hey, hey, who are you? TMZ? Go take a shower." Rodney rushed Junior away while he rolled his luggage across the room.

I grabbed Junior before he got away and whispered, "I'll watch the video later." He gave me a nod with a chuckle.

"You look like hell. What did you do this weekend?" Rodney asked, flicking my silk collar.

"It's a long story," I replied. "Are you hungry? I made chicken enchiladas."

"*You're* offering me dinner?"

"I think that's what I'm doing." I walked towards the kitchen.

"Why couldn't you be this nice while we were together? I had to rough it most nights."

"Oh ha-ha-ha, you're a comedian now," I replied. "Do you want a plate or not?"

Rodney made a beeline to the kitchen, rubbing his hands together. "Hell yeah, I'm not turning down your chicken enchiladas." He sat on a barstool by the island. "You can tell me your long story while I eat."

"The girls came over to celebrate my new wine cellar. Then out of nowhere Lorraine pulled the most random stunt ever."

"What?" He asked with raised eyebrows.

"She brought Ancestry tests for us to take." I sat his dinner in front of him. He practically salivated at the sight of it.

"I mean, it's not that random. She knows you and Brooklyn don't know your family," he replied, studying his plate of food. "Boy do I miss your cooking. Thank you."

"You're welcome," I replied, getting him back on track with my issue at hand. There aren't many people I trust, but Rodney tops the list. He repeals commitment, but the man sure knows how to give solid advice. "Okay, so what's the point in trying to know who they are after all these years? I'm closer to being over-the-hill now. Isn't it too late?"

"Doesn't matter how old you are. Family is family," Rodney

replied, totally undermining my contempt. "Did you take the test?"

"I didn't have a choice. Tammy practically forced the thing in my mouth."

Rodney patted the stool next to him, motioning for me to take a seat. "Do you remember when we first met?"

"How could I forget?" I laughed. "Me and Brooklyn were drunk at a bar. You were nice enough to make sure we made it home safely. Thank you a million times over for that."

"You and Brooklyn were the most attractive women in the bar. Those men were looking at you two like a pack of hungry wolves. I couldn't let you leave alone in good conscience." He brushed the hair away from my face. "It wasn't easy getting you guys home. I swerved all over the highway because you and Brooklyn wanted to hang out the window singing, *I will survive*," he recalled.

"It's a song of healing for us."

"Of all the songs, why that old one?"

I hopped from the stool, swinging my arms, dancing and singing the chorus of the song. "Whenever one of our relationships ended, we'd play that song. Then we'd drink wine until we were plastered enough to forget about the jerk the next morning. It just so happened we decided to go to the bar that night." I touched his arm. "You earned my respect forever that night. You didn't take advantage of us or turn into *the killer*. We never did that again."

"You better not ever do anything that stupid again." He polished off the last of his dinner. "That was fantastic. Next week, I'd like to request your famous Birra Tacos?"

"If you're a good boy, I'll think about it," I joked, cleaning his plate.

"Did you and Brooklyn play the song after our break-up?"

"To the maximum volume."

"Wow, I'm sorry I hurt you," he apologized with the saddest eyes I'd ever seen.

"Water under the bridge."

"You keep thanking me for watching over the two of you. But I should be thanking Brooklyn," he explained. "When I got you home, she whispered your phone number in my ear and told me I better call you in the morning."

I held my stomach in laughter. That's Brooklyn to the core. "We owe her the world. Thanks to her, we made a beautiful little boy."

"That we did, and he's growing into an amazing young man. I'm so proud of him." He drove the tip of his finger into the counter. "After a week, you had me hook, line, and sinker. I'd never met anyone as fiery, outspoken, beautiful and intelligent as you. But even with all those qualities, something kept holding you back from me. You've been running from your past for too long. It's time to face it."

"I know I should, but..."

"Look at me." He held my hands. "As incredible as you are, you have issues. You're extremely guarded. I begged for you to let me into your life, and after all these years, I could only get so far. We share a kid together. You don't see anything wrong with that?"

At that very moment, I finally understood why he never made a commitment to me. How could you commit to someone who won't let you in? Just like all my relationships–platonic or romantic, I kept him at bay. "Where are you going with this?"

"You say you'd be alone if it wasn't for Brooklyn and her parents. But that isn't true. You have a blood family out there. Maybe your parents kept you away for reasons you may never know or understand. But they're gone now. At least try to get the answers. You never know. It could open up a whole new world for you."

"What reasons would my parents possibly have to keep me away from my family?"

"I don't know. That's for you to figure out."

"Don't you think I'd be opening myself up for pain and disappointment?"

"Sweetheart, life comes with pain and disappointment. I know you've tried your damnedest to avoid it—protecting yourself from all possibilities of being hurt. But it's life. If it happens, you deal with it the best you can and if your best isn't working, you seek professional help."

"See how well that worked out."

"I've apologized a million times for hurting you."

"Well make it a million and one in counting."

"I thought you said it was water under the bridge?"

"I stand corrected. Now go on," I urged.

He kissed my hand. "The only reason you became friends with Tammy and Lorraine is because they were friends with Brooklyn. Otherwise you wouldn't have ever given them a chance. You don't know yourself as much as you claim, because if you did, you'd see the woman I see."

"What do you see?"

He clutched my hands tighter and stared into my eyes with such intensity it made me want to rip his clothes off. "I see a gorgeous, intelligent, funny, charismatic woman who has no idea of the beauty of her strengths. Whatever you learn from this will only enlighten you."

"Why couldn't you be this sweet while we were together?"

"Touché," he chuckled, wagging his finger with a sly smile. "But here's the million dollar question." He walked towards the living room. I stayed close in tow to hear every word Rodney spoke. I'd become invested at that point. "What are you prepared to do with the results once you have a way to contact your family?"

"Do you want the truth?"

"I don't want a lie."

"I'm terrified." I showed him my trembling hands. "Do you see what this is doing to me?"

"Oh I see." He touched my face. "Two things could happen. They could remain strangers or they could become a huge part of your life. Either way, you'll gain something from it —knowledge of self." He kissed my forehead. "But it's time to deal with it once and for all."

"I don't know," I sighed, hanging my shoulders feeling defeated in every way from my emotions taking over. I've never operated well when I am unable to control what is happening around me. This could be catastrophic, and that terrified me.

"If you decide to see this through, don't worry about Junior, I'll take care of him. It'd be nice to have my little man with me one on one on a daily basis for a while."

"Well aren't you full of surprises? Are you trying to win me back?"

"You and I both know you don't want that."

After our break up we began to do this little dance of one of us wanting to rekindle the relationship while the other totally repelling it. I'd been giving him hints of wanting to try to make the relationship work, and I knew he picked up the hints because he'd make it clear that it's not something he wanted.

I dated Rodney for eleven years. We had a great relationship. Then on our eleventh anniversary, I told him, *it's time we make it official.* He stumbled over his words, sweated through his clothes, and only a few months later; he cheated. Rodney loved to give advice, but he couldn't seem to take his own, which is terribly disappointing. Between the two of us, we could run a successful magazine with all our issues.

"Maybe I'm ready to give us another chance. It's been eight years since we were together. Maybe we've both grown."

"I'm not ready to buy a new wardrobe," He replied, referring to the night I destroyed his clothes. He betrayed me and I reacted. Poured bleach all over his designer labels and cut the tongues out of his dress shoes. Albeit, I didn't feel any better afterwards. It made me feel like a bad person. Nothing is solved when you both are hurting each other, and we had a kid to raise.

We shared a laugh before Junior busted up our party.

"What's for dinner, parents?" He stood in the doorway with a big smile that lit up my topsy-turvy world.

"I made your favorite, chicken enchiladas."

He rubbed his hands together with a big smile. "Thank you." He wrapped his arms around me, resting his head on my chest. "Dad should take some cooking lessons from you."

"You didn't like my food?" Rodney asked with raised eyebrows as if his Ramen noodles could stand against my homemade chicken enchiladas.

"All I'm saying is, I'm starving." Junior bounced off the walls.

The three of us spent the rest of the night together as a family. Part of me wished we could have this togetherness every day. The joy on Junior's face whenever we were together is always priceless. But right now, the perfect family isn't included in our story. We may not have worked as a couple, but we're a great team when it comes to our son. Somehow we mastered putting our crap aside to give Junior the best environment to grow and learn.

We laughed and told stories until Junior fell asleep. Then Rodney showed himself out and I had an epiphany. Family is necessary. I took his advice to mentally prepare myself to face my fears while soaking in a warm milk and honey bath. I hated to admit it, but the thought of opening my heart and mind to the possibilities felt great.

My family could never want anything to do with me, and that would be okay. At least I'd be able to finally close that chapter of my life; of course with extensive counseling on Tammy's dime. On the other hand, my family could love me. Then I could give my son something I never had—blood relatives. People he could make memories with as he grows up. It's far more valuable than any tangible thing I could give him.

Growing up, I'd listen to my classmates go on and on about their weekends with their family. Then I daydreamed of one day spending time with my grandparents, aunts, uncles and cousins. I imagined sitting on the floor while my grandmother brushed my hair. I imagined her giving me soft kisses on the cheek afterwards. My aunt would sit next to my grandmother and tell stories about her colorful life. I imagined having over-protective uncles who'd give any man in my life the third degree. Rodney would've gotten a kick out of that. Then there's my cousins. They'd be the closest thing to having siblings.

None of those dreams ever manifested. But once I moved away to college and met Brooklyn, I no longer daydreamed. I began making memories of my own. I made some great friends and a good life. I didn't live in a shell anymore. It was the best time of my life. Though, deep down I wanted to know my family. But dreams are just that. They're only dreams, and I live in reality.

If I meet my family, I could be opening the door to chaos. Then again, I could find all the missing pieces to make sense of this crazy puzzle and rebuild my past brick by brick. Every layer would help me to learn more about what made me who I am. That level of knowledge about self is enough to make anyone a powerful person.

I aspire to embody that kind of power.

3
WHERE TO GO FROM HERE

The time had finally come for us to read our Ancestry results, and I still had no idea if I wanted to know mine. We'd been experiencing stormy weather for the last few days. But even though the rain had cleared, and the stars were abnormally bright, a storm brewed deep within me.

I'd lost count of how many times I thought about turning around and going back home on the drive to Lorraine's house. But, I knew better. She, Tammy, and Brooklyn would only come to my house locked and loaded with their laptops, demanding I let them inside like a group of vampires, and just like vampires, if I let them inside, they'd turn my world upside down. Much like these results were about to do to mine.

I stopped at a convenience store for a bottle of water and aspirin. Plus Junior wanted a bag of chips and a drink. He'd already eaten with his dad. The older he got, the bottomless his stomach got. I desperately needed the pounding in my head to stop before I made it to the girls. Their jibber jabber would only make it worse. Sadly there wasn't anything that could rid me of the agony which loomed in my heart. It radiated throughout my body. Dare I say my soul?

It appeared I arrived at Lorraine's house at the same time as Brooklyn and Tammy. They were going on about it as if this was the most exciting thing they'd done in years. Meanwhile I was to the point of hyperventilating. Those results were guaranteed to change the trajectory of my life. The question was, would it be a positive or negative outcome?

Am I ready for change?

This gave a new meaning of, if it isn't broken, don't fix it. I have a pretty good life. I own a divine home. My son's happy, healthy, and bringing home A's and B's. I have money in the bank and an amazing career. Not much going on in the love department, but you take the good with the bad. It will come when it comes.

The six-week wait for the results felt more like a year. Then Lorraine added a few more days to that year by having us meet on Sunday. Meanwhile our results came on Thursday. I spent the next three days talking myself out of deleting the email altogether to wash my hands of it once and for all.

Poor Brooklyn stayed on the phone with me around the clock. Much the same as someone on suicide watch. But she gave me a listening ear to explain why going through with this may be a bad idea for the both of us, and how we should walk away while we still had our sanity.

But dear old Brooklyn annihilated my theory that I couldn't miss people I never knew with one sentence, "*I already missed them before I knew them.*"

As an adopted kid, Brooklyn had years to figure out if she wanted to know her family. It's a different set of circumstances. I wasn't adopted. Our extended family decided not to be in our lives. It's only been me, my mom, and my dad.

The moment we walked inside Lorraine's house, she

hurried us to the dining room. Everyone ate, drank, and laughed about their day. I couldn't eat and my voice box stopped working. However I kept calm and went with the flow, moving food around my plate in hopes of them not noticing while they bombard me with fairytale outcomes. That's the thing about my friends. For some strange reason, they thought of themselves being on the same level as a licensed therapist as if they had the tools to fix any problem that arose. But their constant yapping only told me they didn't know a thing about this particular situation. They weren't even observant enough to see I'd gone on a food strike.

Some therapists they were.

"Before I forget," Tammy said, turning to Brooklyn. "I know you're a silent partner now. But we really could use your help updating our business plan. Do you think you could set aside some time next week to help us out with it?" She pressed her hands together in a prayer stance.

"Sure, I'll swing by the office and knock it out."

Lorraine walked over behind Tammy's chair. "Miss Prissy went to a wedding Friday. Tell them what you did."

More small talk.

"You're like a bratty little sister who can't keep a secret to save her life." Tammy rolled her eyes.

"Deflecting is as ugly on you as the color yellow."

"Hey," Tammy shrieked, running her hands down her yellow blouse. "I look good in any color. You should put on a yellow shirt and test your theory. With that red hair, you'd look like Ronald McDonald's little sister."

"I just bought a beautiful yellow dress. It looks good on me. Even the sales lady agreed."

"Duh, she's trying to make a sale. She'd say a potato sack looked good on you."

"No way, you don't know this lady. She's brutally honest.

She once told a lady she hopes she has thick skin because she'd need it if she wore that dress."

"I probably would've cried in the dressing room," Brooklyn confessed. "We need to focus. Tell us about this wedding. Did you try the laxative thing again?"

"I only took laxatives to help with bloating and I haven't done that in years," Tammy blurted out. "But thank you for bringing it up in front of Iris. She's the only one who didn't know about the most embarrassing moment in my life. Now I'll bet she wants the story behind it."

The girls fell silent for a moment with all eyes on me. I was too deep in thought to tell her I already knew about it. So I laughed it off and made a mental note to give Tammy hell about it another time. You'd think she'd know by now Brooklyn tells me everything.

"First of all, I don't know why she invited me to the wedding. We aren't friends. We're associates. Why do people do that? Do you think it's to get a gift?" Tammy asked.

"Could be," I said. "Or maybe she wanted to rub her coming nuptials in your single face."

"Yeah, she's the type to pull that kind of stunt. She's such a bitch you could smell it on her in passing."

"Stop stalling and get to the good part," Lorraine urged.

"Be patient, I need to set the scene," Tammy explained. "When I arrived at the wedding, I realized I went on a date with the groom three days before the wedding on Wednesday. Then there we were on Friday. The world is smaller than you know."

"Oh my God, did you tell your friend?" Brooklyn gasped.

"Once again, she's not my friend. We're associates," Tammy replied. "I didn't say anything to her."

"What? We're women," Brooklyn shrieked, looking around

the table. "We should stick together. She should've been warned about the type of *man* she's marrying."

Lorraine rolled her eyes. "Tammy should've stood up the moment they opened the floor for anyone to object to their sham of a marriage."

"It wasn't my place. Yeah, the guy is a two-timing jerk. But who the heck am I to blow up her day?"

"Well, what did you do?"

"I gave him and his new bride my best wishes at the reception, ate a small salad, and got the hell out of dodge."

"You should've told her." Lorraine guzzled her glass of wine, wagging her finger.

"It was the woman's wedding day for goodness sake," Tammy shrieked. "She had a ton of family there. As the odd woman out, I made an executive decision to not be chased down and pulverized. Girl code was the last thing on my mind."

"That poor woman is about to have a lifetime of tears," Brooklyn sighed.

"I would've busted the jerk. Some men need to be put on the spot for the stupid shit they do." I blotted my forehead with a napkin. Maybe my nerves were working overdrive. But my body boiled from the inside out.

"So none of you would be afraid of being tackled by a group of people?" Tammy asked.

"Oh I would've taken my heels off, screamed my truth, and ran out of there keys in hand," Brooklyn admitted.

I laughed for the first time in days at the visual of Brooklyn running barefoot out of a church, leaving it in shambles. I'd pay to see that.

After an hour, the time had come. We took out our laptops and decided to go one by one and read our results. Lorraine went first; she didn't learn anything new aside from elder relatives. Tammy didn't discover a rich uncle. Then it was Brooklyn's turn. She could hardly speak through her sobbing. She matched with a possible maternal grandmother and an aunt in Marseau. She always wanted to find family on her mother's side to get to know more about her. Her emotional reaction affected me so much my finger hovered over the button to delete my results. I'd rather not feel anything than to feel emotions I couldn't work through.

Brooklyn sighed, rubbing her eyes, "I'd given up all hope of ever knowing my family. But now I have names."

Lorraine walked over and pointed at the screen. "If you click here you'll have the option to send a message. You should do it."

"Wait a second," Brooklyn yelped. "This is too much too fast. I'm not ready to reach out to them," she cried.

"Your birth dad has been in your life for over seven years now. He never talked about them?"

"No, back in their days it wasn't easy to make international calls on a consistent basis. When my mom moved here, she only came with a few worldly possessions and a dream. Britt said she'd call her family from the diner where she worked because the owner was family centered and wanted her to have contact with her family at least once a month."

"What if they're good people ready to welcome you into the fold with open arms?" Tammy asked.

Brooklyn slammed her laptop shut. "It's too many what ifs. I can't go any further than reading the results tonight. Give me time to get myself together." She pointed to me. "Let's see your results."

"I don't know if I can do this."

"Before you two get pushy, don't." Brooklyn gave Tammy and Lorraine the evil eye. "If you aren't ready, don't look at it.

Give it some time. Build up the nerve and maybe then, read the results. Take it from me. It's a lot." She rubbed my hand.

"Oh please, Iris needs a push," Tammy fussed. "If not, she'll never see it through. We've already talked about this. You need answers. This is it. Open the email."

I looked at Brooklyn. She rubbed my hand and gave me a nod.

"Screw it." I opened my laptop to read the results. A long list of names of my paternal and maternal family members appeared. Things got real and hit me like a ton of bricks. I had family out there. I wasn't alone. But why didn't I know them? They've missed every milestone in my life and vice versa.

The ladies hovered over me as I scrolled through the list. I had family members spread over different cities. I had so many questions, but sadly my parents couldn't give me any answers. Not that I'd expect much from them anyhow. They were never any help.

"Wow, look at this. You have a bigger list than Brooklyn." Lorraine said with her hands clasped to her chest.

"It's insane you don't know any of them?"

Brooklyn thrust her fist in the air and yelled, "It doesn't matter, Tammy. Give her a chance to think."

"Calm down," Tammy walked back to her seat on the other side of the table. "I'm excited for her. Lorraine and I know you're her number one. We don't need a reminder."

"Don't put me in this," Lorraine piped up.

Brooklyn walked over to Tammy with her arms stretched out. Tammy begrudgingly accepted her embrace. "I apologize; I got caught up in the moment because I know my sister. I can tell she's overwhelmed and trying to make sense of it."

I shut my laptop down and slid it inside my bag. "I need a drink."

Lorraine hopped up, waving her arms in an attempt to

bring the tension down. "I'll get the wine. Anything specific you have in mind?"

"The kind with alcohol," I said, rubbing my temples. "I can't understand any of this. I'm sure my parents had their reasons, but it's the secrecy that hurts."

Lorraine returned with a bottle of Chateau Petrus and four glasses. I couldn't wait for her to open the bottle. She always fiddled with it for too long. I gulped an entire glass before the others could take their first sip.

"I want to know more. I'm going to contact them," I blurted out.

"Yes." Tammy pumped her fist in the air. "That's my girl. Let's make a trip out of this so you and Brooklyn can meet your family. You guys could go with me to La Isleta Sanguinea for five days. After that, we could go meet Brooklyn's family in Marseau, and then we could go with you to meet your family. I won't take no for an answer."

"That's like a two or three week trip," Lorraine said with wide eyes. "Are you forgetting about the business?"

"Business this, business that." Tammy rubbed the back of her neck. "You need time away from work more than any of us. You're so tightly wound up you're about to explode."

"I actually think it's a great idea. We haven't gone on a girl's trip in a while. Meeting our family would be the cherry on top," Brooklyn agreed, swirling her finger in her wine.

"International girl's trip," Tammy squealed, expanding like a flower. "I've got some shopping to do."

"Wait, what do we do about the business?" Lorraine asked.

"We've hired capable people who know it inside out. We could conduct virtual meetings as often as you see fit. Every-thing will be fine. Take a deep breath. This'll be good." She gave Lorraine's shoulder a gentle caress. I could see her anxiety dissipate.

"Fine, I'll go." Lorraine gave in.

None of us ever stood a chance against Tammy. That's why she was the one who made the connections with vendors. It's her gift of gab that keeps their business in the black.

"I'll reserve one of their best villas tonight. That way you guys can't back out of it. No excuses. I mean it." She pointed at each of us as if she were chastising a group of children.

I wasn't in the mood to argue. I needed them with me in case things took a turn for the worst.

Brooklyn asked, "do you guys know how long it's been since we took a trip together?"

"It's been about six years, right?" I asked, eyeing the three of them.

"Yes, we went to Summerton Beach."

Lorraine fell over in laughter. "Oh yeah, that's when Iris tried to compete against a twenty-year-old model for a man who was way too young for her."

"Please don't bring that up," I begged Lorraine.

"Once your heel tipped to the side, down goes Frazier. But you didn't just fall. You took two people down with you. We had to drag you out of there."

"That girl dropped her tube of lipstick on purpose after she spread it over her fish lips."

"But why did you spread your entire body out like a starfish? I thought that old man broke his hip when you pulled him down with you." Without realizing it, Lorraine spit a glob of saliva.

"I did whatever I could to break my fall. He was a casualty of war."

"Oh that's cold," Tammy replied out of breath from laughing. "You could've given that old man a heart attack. But there's something else I need to know."

"What now?" I asked.

"Did you pee on yourself when you fell down?"

"I would never," I screamed with my hand over my chest. I almost forgot the kids were upstairs. I didn't want to pique their curiosity to listen in on our conversation. "That old man spilled his drink when he fell. That's what you call karma."

"You think," Tammy laughed. "All this time I've been secretly judging you."

"Wow, you're such a great friend," I said.

"Hey, at least I kept my judgment to myself," Tammy laughed so much she went into a coughing frenzy from almost choking on her wine.

"That's what you get," I teased.

"See, this is what I look forward to when we're together. I love how we can laugh and have a good time. I adore you ladies." Brooklyn swam in the deep end of her emotional pool.

"Uh-oh, Brooklyn's about to get all sappy on us." Tammy walked over to hug her.

"I just want you all to know how much I love and adore you. I'm so happy to have you in my life. But I can't wait to go on this trip and meet all of our family."

"Oh no, don't change the subject. Tammy just annihilated me. But I'm not the only one in this sisterhood with issues. Lorraine's so buttoned up she can't enjoy life. Tammy enjoys life way too much that she lacks self-control, and Brooklyn you've gone from not enjoying life to getting married to not making time for anyone outside of your perfect home." I pointed to each of them.

"Oh yeah, and what about you?" Tammy asked, crossing her legs.

"I'll admit, I'm a mess," I sighed. "Since we're doing this, I'll take Junior to his favorite restaurant to explain why I'll be away for three weeks."

Junior's the most understanding kid on the planet. My girls

were there for me. But he topped them all. My son was wise beyond his years. He challenges me to be a better person, woman, and mother even when he doesn't realize what he's doing. Perhaps I embodied a bit of the same issues I pointed out in my friends. Truth is, we were all a work in progress. But, what were we going to do about it?

4

ISLAND TINGS

After a four hour flight, we safely arrived on La Isleta Sanguínea for five glorious days in paradise. The island smelled of freedom and coconuts. June weather wasn't so bad on the island and Monday sure felt like the weekend. The weather reminded me of Fall. This time back home, you'd melt like pudding after a few minutes outside.

I could get used to this.

It's baffling how I never realized how much I needed a break until I took one. I don't know when my life changed, but it'd become lackluster. I guess it slowly happened over time. A polar opposite from my old self before adulting. People knew me as a spontaneous live in the moment kind of girl. It'd be nice if I got a warning to let me know when I reached the brink of losing myself. Instead, I woke up one day a shell of the person I once knew.

The girls and I decided to make Pinemoor our last stop to give me time to mentally and emotionally prepare myself. So, on the island, my only goals are to breathe and relax. No stress, responsibilities, or worries—if it's at all possible.

To make sure I stayed in line with my goals, I bought a cute little journal to commemorate the time me and my girlfriends took off to travel the world. It'd be cool to read it to my grandchildren one day. I could see it now, I'd be sporting a cute short gray haircut with red lips in a fashion forward outfit, because I'm going to look good no matter what age.

The beauty of the island traveled through my eyes straight to my soul. The tall coconut palm trees, sandy white beach, and adults leaving their stress in the ocean. I could feel my own stress slowly dissipate. "So, it takes a beautiful tropical island to get you all to finally admit when you're wrong. Tough crowd," Tammy laughed, tipping the driver.

We followed her inside the grand hotel. It had a unique design. There were palm trees, waterfalls, and living walls with leaves covering the ceilings. Jovial employees greeted us with a quirky song and dance. True to form, we broke out in dance. They ended their show with a complimentary tropical drink. Now they were speaking our language. We loved a good drink.

Tammy reserved each of us separate rooms for the night until she got the call for us to move into our villa tomorrow. After we got our key cards, we split up and retreated to our prospective rooms for a couple of hours to get some rest before our night out on the island.

Floral aromas filled the air of my spacious suite. The color scheme of my room invoked the ocean, palm trees, sand, and rocks. I dropped my bags, peeled out of my dress, and sunk into the queen sized bed. In a matter of seconds, I fell into a full on slumber. Though it wasn't the kind of sleep I got back home. It was like time fast forwarded. I woke feeling refreshed, showered, pulled my hair up into a bun, got dressed, and made it to Tammy's room in record time. I wanted to avoid her fussing at all costs. She hated it when we made jokes about her age. But she made it easy when she became the mama bear of the group.

"You look great," Lorraine said, taking my hand. "Turn around. I want to get a good look at your outfit. I love it."

"Thank you." I smoothed my updo. "Where are we going to dinner?"

Tammy clasped her hands together with a smile. "We'll be doing some fine dining at the Lotus. It's a cute restaurant right off the ocean and later we're going dancing at a live music club, and hopefully meet some new people," Tammy said. "Oh, and if your shoes are already hurting, change them now. I don't want to hear any whining about it later."

Lorraine bumped shoulders with Brooklyn. "I don't know why you're looking around. She's talking to you."

"Don't worry your pretty little heads. I'll be fine." Brooklyn pulled out a pair of black foldable flats from her clutch. "Worry about yourselves." She pointed at me and Tammy. "You'll be lucky if your feet aren't hurting in less than an hour after chasing men, and Iris will more than likely be crying about her feet before any of us in those heels."

"Don't do that." Tammy placed her hand over her chest with a gasp. "I come here to unpack my stress, not add to it. Men are nice. But they aren't my priority when I'm here. Just wait, you'll see."

"And I don't know what you're talking about," I chimed in. "I have shoe gummies. They make my heels feel like I'm walking on clouds." I strutted across the room to prove my point. I came prepared to look good and feel good. Contrary to what people think, fashion doesn't always equal pain.

"Yeah, we'll see," Brooklyn huffed.

"You're becoming too much like judgmental Lorraine over there. If I want to chase men, I'll chase men. We should be worried about Iris's sexless life. I don't know how she functions," Tammy babbled in the most contemptuous tone ever.

"Thank you for your concern, but I function just fine," I

said matter-of-factly. "Let's be real. Most of the time, penis only brings trouble."

Tammy ran across the room to answer the ringing phone. "We'll be right down," she sang. "Alright ladies, our driver is downstairs. Time to make moves."

We each had our own style. Tammy wore a short super flowy white dress. She loved to show off her breasts and long legs. I can't say I blame her. Any woman would kill for a body like hers. Lorraine wore a tan and black two piece skirt outfit. She had a little love handle action going on, but it didn't take away how breathtaking she looked in her outfit. She's all about body positivity. You can't say anything negative about her and think it'll stick. Brooklyn showed off her thin figure in a tight mini skirt with a side split. We were fashion killers. We turned heads just walking through the lobby. Even got a few whistles.

A man dressed in black slacks and a white shirt held the door open to a black Lincoln Aviator.

"Is he our driver?" Lorraine asked.

"Yes, he's our driver for the night. We're going to drink and dance until the sun comes up. So let loose and live it up."

"Nice, I finally get to see how the other side lives." I slid inside the black SUV next to Brooklyn. She gave me a high-five.

The warm leather seats paired perfectly with the cool air conditioning. After the driver made sure we were safely inside, we were on our way. By the looks of it, the island came to life at night. Bicycle juice bars strolled through the streets. Vendors pushed exotic foods and trinkets. Groups of friends and couples walked hand in hand, filling the air with laughter. This is what I'd call living. I missed it.

Patrons were elbow to elbow at the restaurant. Tammy didn't embellish this time. It's definitely a hotspot. An older couple danced to the music while they waited for a table. The ambiance encouraged me to loosen up.

"Are you sure we'll be able to get a table? I'm so hungry I don't think I could wait thirty minutes." The smell of the spices made the glands in my mouth work overtime.

"Really Iris," Tammy said, scrunching her eyebrows. "Have a little faith in me. I made reservations. I'm no rookie. I know how things work here."

"Hello, do you have reservations?" A middle-aged woman got right to the point.

"Yes, my name is Iris Reid. I have a reservation for four."

She pulled her glasses down to examine the tablet, and then she said, "I'm sorry, I don't have a reservation with that name."

"Yes you do," Iris stopped to regain her composure. "I made the reservation a month ago. There must be a mistake."

"We don't make mistakes." The woman glared.

"Well, there's a first for everything." Iris slammed the side of her hand on the hostess stand. "I demand to speak to the manager."

"Very well." She coolly walked away, careful to not bring anymore attention to the already fiery situation.

"I knew we wouldn't be able to get a table in here tonight. Look at this place," I whispered to Brooklyn.

"I heard that, Iris. You're going to eat those words," Tammy said.

"Good, at least I'll have something to eat."

A jovial middle-aged man with a pompadour haircut and a black suit came around the corner with his hands out. "Iris Reid, what a sight for sore eyes. Is it already that time of year?"

"Tad." They kissed each other on the cheek. "You know this is how I like to start my vacation. What's going on with my reservation?"

"Nothing is going on. The new girl made a mistake. I have you at the best table in the house. Follow me."

Tad led us through the patrons to a table smack dab in the middle of the restaurant. He must've alerted the staff of the mix-up because they waited on us hand and foot. Even gave us a bottle of their finest wine on the house. I mean, I appreciated the peace offering, but with our group, one bottle was hardly enough. He would've impressed me with two.

"Okay lovely ladies," Tammy held her glass in the air. "Here's to friendship and making new memories on the island. I love you girls."

"We love you too," we sang in unison, toasting to the occasion.

"I hate to admit it, but you were right, Tammy," Lorraine admitted. "I needed a vacation. I don't know if any of you've noticed, but I'm a bit of a stick in the mud."

We looked at each other and exploded in laughter. "Nooo, we didn't notice at all."

"Hear me out. The business and Violet have become my life. I never do anything for myself. I mean, look at my hair." She tugged on her long red curls, showing more than a few gray hairs. It didn't suit her. "I need to make more of an effort when it comes to pampering myself."

"I can relate," Brooklyn chimed in. "I spent the better part of my life living in fear of dying from Huntington's. Even with Iris encouraging me not to focus on it. But when I met Kai, and became a mother, it wore me down after a while. I put all my focus and energy into them. Totally forgot about my wants and needs." She held up her glass. "Let's make a vow right here to make more time for ourselves."

"Yes, self-care is self-love," Lorraine held her glass up.

Tammy quickly followed suit, snapping her fingers with a wide smile.

"Well, Iris, aren't you going to get in on this?" Brooklyn asked.

"I never make promises I can't keep. My career siphons my time. People need me. Besides, my son is almost a full-fledged teenager. Seems like he requires more of my time now that he's older with all his activities," I explained.

"Your son has an active father. Surely you could commit to one day out of the week to doing something for yourself. You're no good to Junior if you're run down and stressed out."

"You're right," I raised my glass. "Self-care is self-love."

"There you go," Tammy said. "Explain to me again why you and Rodney aren't together?"

"Time hasn't been aligning for us since we broke up, and he also thinks I'll always hold what he did against him. He doesn't want to be with me if I can't fully trust him. But hey, as long as we're good co-parents, that's all I need. He supports everything I do, and he's always there for me when I need him."

"I could learn a thing or two from you on that one. I'm done with Michael." Lorraine dug into her dinner.

"You say that every other month. I'll believe it when I see it," Tammy said, pushing her half-eaten plate away.

"I'm serious this time. Michael has worn out his welcome in my life. It's time for me to accept my loss and move on from his toxicity. I don't want my daughter thinking he's the type of man she needs when she becomes a woman."

"Just in case she means it this time, let's toast to that," Tammy said.

Another toast, another bottle of wine. We drank like we had no liver and ate like calories didn't exist. It's what I considered the makings of an amazing girl's trip.

"It's time to dance. Where's this club you've been telling us about?" I busted a move in my seat.

"It's on the other side of the island. You're going to love it."

Tammy left a hefty tip and we danced out of the restaurant hand-in-hand to the car.

I'm sure the driver had grown tired of us acting like teenage girls away from their parents for the first time. We rolled the windows down and sang at the top of our lungs as we rolled through the dark streets.

The nightclubs were bursting at the seams with partygoers. Thanks to Tammy and her connections, we were able to skip the long line. We pushed our way onto the dance floor and vibrated on a higher level. We practically defied gravity.

"My throat is on fire. I need a drink," Lorraine screamed over the thumping music.

"I'm with you on that," I said, following her to the bar.

I guzzled my drink in 0.5 seconds. That's how quick it took Lorraine to show us she meant every word she said about moving on from Michael when she made out with a guy she'd been dancing with since we made it to the club. I waved the girls over. We watched them like sick voyeurs until they came up for air.

Lorraine finally pulled away with a deep sigh.

"Yeah, we've been watching you for all of twenty minutes." Tammy glanced at her watch. "What the hell are you doing?"

"This is what moving on looks like," she giggled, motioning for the bartender.

"No, that is what reckless looks like," Brooklyn corrected her.

"Hello, we're her straggler friends, and you are?" Tammy asked the mysterious man.

"My name is..."

"You don't need to answer that," Lorraine quickly interjected. "Thanks for the good time." She winked, turning her back to the man.

He laughed and walked away with his hands stuck in his pockets.

"Wow, I kind of like this side of you." I gave her a high-five. I can't remember a time when Lorraine allowed herself to be free without worrying about the worst that could happen. The kiss alone made her look at least five years younger, and I loved that for her.

"Do not give her props for letting some strange man stick his tongue down her throat," Tammy chastised.

Boy, how the tables have turned. Lorraine's the wild child and Tammy's the mother hen. Never thought I'd see the day.

"You don't know where his tongue has been." Brooklyn scrunched her face in detest.

"It's funny how all of you are ganging up on me for a kiss, but whenever I say anything to you, it's the end of the world. Save it. We're on vacation, and you told me to get out of my shell. This is what you get," Lorraine said, dancing with her hands in the air. "I'm going to enjoy *my* vacation however I choose to enjoy it. Ooh, that's my song. Let's dance." She never stopped talking long enough for us to continue placing our judgements on her. Instead, she downed another drink and ran off to the dance floor.

"Is that the same man?" Brooklyn asked.

"Yup," Tammy answered. "That's the tongue bandit."

We laughed and joined Lorraine on the dance floor. She couldn't be trusted to be left alone for too long. Who knows what she'd get into next.

"Tammy, how in the world are you going to top tonight for the rest of the trip?" I asked.

"Just you wait. I have a few more tricks up my sleeve." She winked, dipping low to the floor, twisting around right into the arms of an admirer who took the opportunity to dance with her for the rest of the night.

I held Brooklyn's hands as we swayed side to side, singing along to the song.

If this isn't love, tell me what it is. 'Cause I could be dreaming or just plain crazy. If this isn't love. Tell me what it is. 'Cause I never felt like this, baby. If this isn't love. L-O-V-E, what it means to me. L-O-V-E, oh, if this isn't love. L-O-V-E, what it means to me. L-O-V-E, oh, if this isn't love.

It's an oldie but a goodie. College memories flooded my mind of me and Brooklyn driving to the beach. We'd play that song on repeat to the maximum volume of my jeep. Our past had a special soundtrack. Every once in a while, we'd hear a song, and it has the power to take us back to a time before life became complicated.

The island men loved us. We didn't stop dancing until the DJ made the last call for alcohol. A few people hung around besides us. At our age, we closed the club.

I shivered at the thought of how our over-the-hill butts would feel in the morning. But it didn't make a difference to me. We were young again. Funny, how I usually found comfort in curling up in bed to work on a case after making sure Junior was asleep. On the island with the girls, sleep was the last thing on my mind. The old Iris was back and in rare form.

Hey girl, hey.

5

THESE MAGICAL WATERS

W aking up the next morning wasn't so bad. I didn't have a pounding headache. I could move with ease, and I wasn't face down in porcelain heaven. The bright light didn't sting my eyes. I actually felt refreshed. Blowing off steam did my body good.

Tammy got the call at breakfast for us to move into our villa for the rest of our time on the island. Though we enjoyed the beautiful hotel, we wanted to experience the island in our own private space. So we abandoned breakfast, packed our stuff, and raced out of there.

After a twenty minute drive, we arrived at the perfect location right off the ocean. The villa came equipped with an infinity pool, five bedrooms, walk-out deck to beach, indoor and outdoor dining, maid service, and a cook.

An island after my heart.

The cook had breakfast waiting for us. Perhaps I did suffer a side effect from the drinking because I consider myself a foodie, but the bacon, eggs, bagels, waffles, and fruit did nothing for me. My eyes zeroed in on the hot pot of coffee. I wanted the entire thing to myself. But I knew better. It would come with a fist fight—me vs them.

I searched the cabinets for the biggest mug I could find and poured a cup, and then made my way to the daybed outside by the pool. The sun-dappled water stood still. I could tell the owners took great care of the property. The cushions on the outdoor furniture were fluffy and bright with a fresh laundry scent free of stains and debris.

I instantly felt a sense of peace, staring out to the ocean. A giant dolphin jumped out of the water to say hello. Pure heaven. But I made sure to stay under the patio out of the sun. No one wants to deal with sunburns on vacation.

Tammy eased outside onto the patio. She sat Indian style in the egg chair across from me, releasing a long sigh before taking a sip of her coffee.

"What's on your mind?" I asked before she began to put on an entire show in order to get my attention.

"Oh, nothing, just living in the moment," she replied with a half-smile. "I usually come here alone. So it's nice to have the people I love here with me to make new memories."

"I see why you come here. It's beautiful."

"Yes it is." Tammy sipped her coffee, tapping her fingers on the warm mug.

For the first time I recognized a sense of peace over Tammy that I'd never seen before in all my years of knowing her. This was her safe place. It brought her peace. But it made me wonder, where was my peace on earth?

"All we ever do is work and every now and again we'll hang out for a few hours. Then work some more. This," she paused. "This is life, and we should press pause on the monotony of our everyday lives to just breathe."

"You're right," I replied. "I really admire you. Some people, mainly Brooklyn, describe me as fearless. But you're the fearless one. You have your own business, but you don't allow it to consume every aspect of your life. You make time to enjoy the fruits of your labor. I haven't quite figured out how to separate my career from my personal life. But when I factor my kid into it, I can't find the time for myself. I desperately want to get back to me, but I don't know how to do that."

"Well," Tammy huffed, shifting in her seat. "For starters, while we're here you should forget about your job and take in the beauty of this place." She stretched her arms. "Enjoy it. Revel in it. I saw you dancing last night. Your entire body smiled from the crown of your head to the tip of your toes. Didn't you feel it?"

"Oh my goodness it felt amazing."

"Hold on to that feeling going forward—even when we're back home. Do more things that give you that feeling. I don't care if it's just an hour to get a massage or get those chewed up nails done."

I bawled my hands into a fist and smashed them into my stomach.

"Yeah, I saw it when we were at the airport. You need a medi and pedi while we're here," she chastised. "But seriously, that's why I vacation alone. If I waited on my lovely friends," she said, pointing with a cunning smile. "I'd never go anywhere. We all have our own lives and responsibilities. So, I understand. But I'd rather go alone to explore the world than miss the opportunity all together while I'm still sexy and full of energy. What makes you happy?" She leaned her head to the side, sizing me up. Tammy had the gift of gab. But, she also had a gift at reading people's emotions. If she sensed anything off, she'd certainly call me out on it.

"Outside of my son, I haven't the slightest idea anymore."

"Well, my gorgeous friend, that's something you should focus on while we're on this journey."

"How am I supposed to figure that out?"

"Damn girl, I'm not Gandhi. I'm a woman with a hangover, praying this cup of coffee and a nap will cure it. I don't have all the answers."

Lorraine strutted outside and sat beside me in the egg chair. "What are you two yapping about?" She asked, popping a grape in her mouth.

"That nasty kiss you shared with a stranger at the bar last night. What were you thinking?" Tammy asked.

Brooklyn raced over and hopped in Tammy's lap.

"Oh my goodness, don't jump on me. You're not as light as you think," she laughed, dodging Brooklyn's playful swat.

Lorraine stood, waving her hands. "I wasn't thinking. I kissed him because I wanted to be spontaneous for the first time in a long time. I knew I was safe because you guys were there. So, I threw caution to the wind and planted a big juicy one on him. It was exciting and hot as hell." She flipped her red hair over her shoulder. "He was an amazing kisser. Easily one of my top three. His tongue did tricks."

"You can throw caution to the wind without having an unfamiliar tongue down your throat," Brooklyn giggled.

Lorraine is the friend who'd call the cops on you for stealing because it's wrong. So, for her to do something so far out of character baffled us. Then again, wasn't that the purpose of the trip? Finding ourselves? Doing things we've never done before. Letting our hair down. All the cliches.

"It was more fun to have his tongue down my throat, thank you very much," Lorraine giggled. "But seriously, my life has been a snooze fest. You have no idea how monotonous my days have become. I go out of my way to keep up appearances. But really, who gives a damn what people think? It's time for me to color outside the lines. Life is too short."

"Sign me up for the Ted Talk with Lorraine," I yelled, filled with pride. She may as well have been standing on a soap box because she had my full attention. I learned a long time ago to live in my truth. The opinions of others would leave me bored, unfulfilled, and downright depressed. Frankly, it was never worth it.

"Is that why you give me a hard time about my dating life? You're jealous?" Tammy asked.

"Maybe I'm a tad bit green," she said, pinching her fingers together.

"I remember when I had two dates in one day and you gave me one of your speeches."

"Touché," Lorraine said with a wink.

"Serious question for you girls," Tammy stood. "I've been married before. Wasn't my cup of tea. I didn't find the benefit of it for me as a woman. My husband was the one who benefited from that sad situation. I cooked for him. I did the laundry. I cleaned the house. He was an average provider, but I've done better for myself by myself. That's why I decided to end the marriage. I say this to explain to you all why I'm not so quick to attach myself to a man. Your partner should give as much as you in every aspect of the relationship. So when you go into these things, think about what it adds to your life or does it take too much from you as a woman."

"You're right," I replied, fully invested in the conversation. "If you wear yourself thin by giving your all to your partner and they aren't reciprocating your efforts, you may as well be a hamster on a spinning wheel going nowhere."

"A big one for me is emotional transparency," Brooklyn chimed in. "I never knew men like my husband existed until I met Kai. I never had to guess how he felt about anything. He was an open book. It's a rare trait and I love that about him."

"I agree," Lorraine interjected. "You all know how many years I've poured into Michael, and where did it get me? He never shared his feelings. The more I tried to pull it out of him, the more he resisted." She turned to Brooklyn. "Envy is a horrible emotion to feel. But I feel it when it comes to your marriage. You found your person. It's because of you and Kai that I refuse to give up on love. So thank you for that."

Brooklyn held her hand to her chest and blew Lorraine a kiss. Lorraine blew her a kiss back in return.

The doorbell interrupted our bonding moment. Tammy hurried to greet the uninvited guest. Moments later she returned wearing a devious smile. "Lorraine, it's for you."

We were all hot on her heels. We had no clue what she'd do next. We were captivated by this new Lorraine. First a kiss in a bar. Now an unexpected guest. The girl was morphing into Tammy's twin right in front of our eyes.

"Hi, I hope this doesn't seem creepy," the tongue bandit from the bar explained. "I'm staying in the villa next door and I saw you guys move in this morning. Would it be presumptuous of me to invite you on a guided tourist hike in the Majestic Roxsonee Forest?"

"You want us to go into the woods... alone... with you?" Lorraine asked, looking back at us with questioning eyes.

There's the old Lorraine. *Good to see you, ole girl.*

"No, it's a guided hike, which means we'll be with a group of people and a tour guide. It's a hike through the forest to a waterfall. It's said to have magical powers." He wiggled his fingers. "They say if you swim in the waters it'll bring you success and happiness in all you do."

"Say less, I'm in," Brooklyn blurted before Lorraine could give the man an answer.

"Count me in," Tammy seconded Brooklyn. "I've been there before. It's not a myth. How do you think I live so lavishly?"

"If you already knew about it, why in the hell weren't you going to take us?" I asked.

"I didn't think you'd want to go hiking. The most we've roughed it is walking in the heat across a long parking lot to a boujee store, and even then, one of you will complain," Tammy explained.

"Okay, okay," Lorraine stopped us from going off on a tangent in mixed company. "It looks like we're all in."

"Great, meet me at my villa at two. I have a friend picking me up. You ladies can ride with us. I'll see you then." He smiled.

"Hey wait," Tammy stopped him before he turned to walk away. "What's your name?"

"She knows it." He gave Lorraine a wink. "We didn't only kiss last night. We had a great conversation."

"Oh, well color me impressed." Tammy closed the door and locked it. "Good job Lorraine. He's handsome and seems well-mannered. But aren't most serial killers described the same way?"

"Ted Bundy comes to mind," I replied.

"You're freaking me out. Are you guys sure we should go hiking with him?" Brooklyn asked.

"As long as we're in a group I don't see it being a problem. But just for the record, what's his name?"

"It's Keith Dixon. He's a single father on vacation. His daughter is with her mother for six months. They share custody."

"How in the world did you get all that information in a loud bar?" Tammy asked.

"I may be coloring outside the lines, but I am who I am." She strutted away. "We've only got two hours before it's time to meet up with him. Be ready or you will be left behind."

"She impresses me more and more by the minute," Tammy said with a smile. "I adore vacation Lorraine."

I hurried upstairs to take a nap for an hour. Lorraine was so focused on her vacation bae she'd more than likely spend two hours trying to find the perfect outfit. I've never been a fan of hiking. The dirt and bugs alone were enough to turn me off from it. But when you factor in sweating under the hot sun, yuck. I'd rather go on a shopping excursion. In my book, a girl could never have too many pretty things. Then again, magical waters do sound interesting. Plus it's something I've never done.

YOLO.

Sleep became a fleeting thought after Tammy and Brooklyn barged inside my room to talk about Lorraine.

"We want to get your opinion on something," Tammy explained. "I think Lorraine's going through something major that she's not telling us about. I love this new evolved woman she's showing us, but..."

Brooklyn interrupted, "Is it genuine? This isn't her."

"You guys are thinking way too much. Hasn't she always been transparent with you two, even when it's embarrassing?" I asked. "Lorraine's a smart woman. She's blowing off steam. She gives so much of herself to Michael and he constantly lets her down. She's finally reached her limit of allowing him to hurt her. What are the famous words of Albert Einstein about insanity?"

"Insanity is doing the same thing over and over expecting different results," Tammy recited.

"Bingo, the girl has been insane for far too long when it comes to her love life. Let her have her island romance."

"I guess you're right. But I'm not leaving her alone with this Keith guy. Who knows if that story he gave her about being a single dad is even true," Tammy said, standing with her hands on her hips. "This is Lorraine we're talking about—fragile Lorraine. He could be a luntic, and now he knows where we're staying."

"Now look at who's being uptight," I pointed out. "Both of you get out of here. I want to take a nap before we go hiking." I pushed them out and climbed under the covers. But just my luck, the phone rang. I guess sleep wasn't an option. "Hello?"

"How's the trip going?" Rodney asked.

"I can tell by the tone of your voice this call is not about our trip. Quit stalling and tell me what you need. Is Junior okay?"

"Did you know our son has a girlfriend?"

"I knew two months ago."

"Why didn't you tell me?"

"Junior is thirteen-years-old. You should have known it was coming, and you also shouldn't be dressing him like he's your twin," I fussed. "Usually mothers are the ones who hold on longer than we should and have to be convinced to let the bird fly out the nest. But you've taken holding on to a whole new level."

"Junior's birthday is in five months. Do you remember our pact?"

"I remember, but we were plastered when we made it."

"You weren't too drunk if you remember the details. Have you changed your mind?" He asked.

"Why do you want to keep having children with me but not marry me?"

"Here we go," he huffed.

"Yes, here we go, and I'm going to keep going. I don't want to have another child out of wedlock. If you want more kids, I suggest you find someone else to be your incubator. I'm not interested. I'm a woman with feelings and needs that you don't seem to want to meet."

"I didn't call you to piss you off. I miss the days when

Junior needed me. Now he's getting older and becoming more independent."

"He'll always need you," I assured him. "You're his father."

"Just so you know, you're too good for me. I screwed up anything we could've had long ago. I cheated and I know you'll never trust me again. So, making you my wife is out of the question. You'll never be happy."

"You can't speak for me."

"You'd make me pay for what I did for the rest of my life. Go have fun with your girls. I'll call you in a few days."

I tossed the phone on the other side of the bed. Rodney and the feelings that come with him clung to me like a cheap suit for the rest of the day. The least I could do is look cute. So I dressed in a pair of blue jean shorts with a floral crop top tied at the bust with a yellow bikini underneath it. I wasn't leaving that waterfall without swimming in these so-called magical waters. I needed a little luck on my side before we went to Pinemoor.

"Let's go," Lorraine screamed.

"We're coming, we're coming," I said, following the girls downstairs.

Tammy made sure the villa was locked and secure, and we headed next door to Keith's villa. As promised, he and his friend were waiting outside. We piled inside the dusty jeep to start on our journey to this magical place.

The warm breeze blew around us with a powerful force, releasing an earthy smell. The usual streets lined with villas and bungalows turned into tall trees with coconuts hanging from the branches. A monkey scurried up a tree and snatched a coconut. We made eye contact for a second, and then he flashed a huge smile. I could hardly contain my laughter.

Thankfully it was a bigger group than we expected. There were at least twelve people not counting us. We introduced ourselves and ten minutes later, we were off on our excursion. My feet sank into the bed of green leaves that covered the ground. The palm trees were rough to the touch. But one thing I hated I hadn't planned on—mosquitoes. Those annoying things wouldn't let up. Little red dots appeared over my skin. I always knew I was sweet. But, not this sweet.

The hike wasn't kind. We had to climb, slide, and crawl through the forest, but the waterfall made it worthwhile. A frothy cascade of water fell into nature's pool. We didn't waste a second. We peeled out of our clothes down to our swimsuits, and climbed over the outcroppings of slippery rocks to dive into the waters.

Our voices echoed in the cave behind the waterfall as each of us blurted out our wishes to whatever magical force was behind the myth. Knobby pebbles pressed into the soles of my feet, but not even they could take me from this moment. I walked away from everyone to become one with the mystical waters.

Thoughts of my long lost family were front and center in my mind. What were the untold truths? If this water had any special powers at all, I needed it more than ever.

"Are you okay?" Brooklyn panted.

"I'm better than okay." I splashed her with a handful of water.

It quickly turned into a domino effect amongst the group, and soon we were all at war.

6

ADVENTURES IN THE NUDE

My legs felt like flimsy overcooked noodles hours after we made it back to the villa from our hike. Over the years I constantly brag about being fit. But after that hike, I decided to take a vow of silence on that particular topic.

The second we arrived back at the villa, I retired from the hike to a warm bath. I rested in it for an hour. I loved my bathroom. It had a huge window directly across from the bathtub so I could relax and appreciate the beautiful sunset with a glass of wine.

After I managed to drag myself out of the bath, I slathered a handful of bengay over my legs and took a nap to rest up for the five-course dinner Tammy reserved for us on a yacht. Once again on the island, sleep came easily. If only I could bottle up this peace and take it home with me.

* * *

They'd decorated the yacht beautifully with romantic soft lights and a mix of pink and white hyacinth centerpieces.

Thankfully the yacht had a maximum of twenty people, so it wouldn't be too crowded. The round tables sat four people per table along the deck. Thankfully our table wouldn't include any strangers.

"Good evening ladies," a distinguished man moved his chair to our table. "My name is Max." He stuck his hand out.

"Well aren't you handsome, my name is Tammy." She'd staked her claim that fast which meant Max is off limits to the rest of us. I didn't care as long as he didn't end up in our villa at the end of the night.

Tammy still lived life with a free love mindset. I don't know how she did it. I'd be exhausted after giving myself away so often. But that's my opinion without judgment. She lived in her truth, and she does it unapologetically. For that, I respect her.

"Are you ladies from the island?"

"No, we're from..."

"Don't tell him where we're from," Lorraine interrupted. "We don't know him."

"Let me get this right," Tammy huffed. "You'll let a stranger put his tongue down your throat. But you draw the line at me having a harmless conversation?"

"Now, ladies, we're in mixed company. Let's at least pretend we get along?" Brooklyn chastised. "This is why I became a silent partner. I had to get away from the constant bickering."

"Oh stop it," Tammy said. "You became a silent partner to follow your dreams. Nothing's wrong with your decision. But it wasn't because of us."

"Yeah, what she said," Lorraine said.

"So you're all entrepreneurs?" Max asked. "What type of business do you own?"

"We own Three Angels Event Planning. Have you heard of us?"

"No, I'm not familiar. But congratulations on your entrepreneurship." He placed his hands together in prayer mode with a nod.

Max was well put together with a sexy accent. Definitely a star in his own movie. But he could stand to lose the dangling earring in his left ear. I could tell he was an athlete in his former days. He had the frame of a basketball player and he carried it well–tall and solid. Tammy better consider herself lucky she's my friend or there would be a repeat from the bar. Watch out, old men. If I go down, you're coming with me.

"Thank you, it's been a crazy ride. But I wouldn't change it for the world. What do you do?" Tammy asked.

"I'm a designer. This suit is actually one of mine." He ran his hands down his black snake skin stitched jacket.

"Wow, I'm impressed. It looks amazing on you." Tammy ran her fingers down the collar of his jacket.

"Thank you, I appreciate the compliment." He proudly smiled. "I'll leave you all to enjoy your dinner." He backed away as the waiters made their way around the deck to serve goat cheese stuffed mushroom hors d'oeuvres.

"Give it up for the master," I teased, playfully hitting Tammy's leg under the table before devouring one of the mushrooms. Every bite soothed my famished soul.

"Slow down, Iris. You're going to scare my new man away," Tammy laughed, blowing a kiss to Max.

"Max is the least of my worries. I'm thinking about what may happen once we get to Pinemoor. So, I'm eating to calm my nerves."

"You're doing yourself a disservice. Remember what we talked about. The island is for relaxing and rediscovering yourself. Not for stress."

"It's your family." Lorraine rested her hand on mine. "That should mean something to them."

"Yeah," Brooklyn chimed in. "We'll all be right by your side. Everything will be okay."

"We don't know why or who severed the connection in my family. I could be walking into a hornet's nest."

"You don't live near those people. If they're holding on to old grudges that have nothing to do with you, keep your distance from them and move on as a better woman with all your questions answered," Tammy explained.

Brooklyn leaned over to give me a hug. "I have a good feeling about it. Just you wait and see. Now relax and enjoy the night."

"You're meeting your family in a couple days. Aren't you nervous?"

"No, I'm excited. They're the closest thing I have to my mother. I'll finally get to hear stories about her, see more pictures, and I hope they have videos too."

"What if you don't feel any connection to them?"

"You can't walk into a situation being that pessimistic and expect it to turn out in your favor." Brooklyn munched on her food.

"She's right," Tammy said, covering her mouth as she ate another mushroom. "You could manifest a negative outcome. Think positive." She gave me a wink.

"I mean, when she's right, she's right," Lorraine wiggled in her chair. "All the missing pieces are finally going to come together."

The waiter cleared our table and replaced the empty platter with the appetizers—seared scallops with cauliflower mash and walnut butter. They melted in my mouth. I closed my eyes to savor their flavor. "I could die and go to heaven right now."

Lorraine gasped, "Don't say that while we're in the ocean at night, genius."

"You're such a baby. We'll be fine." I assured her.

"You don't know that."

"And you don't know if it'll turn into the Titanic," Tammy argued. "You do this every time. You project your fears onto us when all we want to do is enjoy the moment."

"No I don't," she replied. "Do I?"

"Yeah, you kind of do," Brooklyn replied.

"You think so too, Iris?"

"Sometimes." I sipped my wine, gazing out to the dark ocean.

"Wow, I didn't know you guys thought of me as a killjoy."

"It's not your fault. You're just a worry wart." Tammy helped the waiter clear her house salad.

The chef prepared burrata with North Atlantic Lobster as the main course. I appreciated how thoughtfully they planned the menu. We wouldn't leave feeling heavy, but nourished. The best part about traveling was trying new dishes. Back home its chicken and fish—all baked and sometimes burnt.

The engine growled as it glided over the rolling waters as the yacht turned to head back towards the island. I hadn't realized how far we'd drifted from shore. We were far enough to need binoculars to see the island. Right then, I understood Lorraine's fear. But I wouldn't dare tell her that.

"Thank you for letting us crash your vacation Tammy," Brooklyn said. "I have truly enjoyed myself. Probably way too much," she explained. "Don't get me wrong, I miss my family. But I needed some Me Time."

"I get it," Lorraine said. "I love my Violet, but this has refreshed my soul. We should do this annually."

We raised our glasses to the promise of taking more time out for ourselves to be more present in our friendship. Outside of motherhood, nothing compared to the joy each of my girls gave me. Taking a break from the dead helped me remember I was a part of the living.

I didn't earn the name firecracker for no reason. In college I didn't have a care in the world. Life was easy. I was confident, fearless, and happy. Then, my parents died, and all of that changed. I learned a big lesson about life. It's good until it's not.

"As much as I adore the island, it's been a blast being able to experience it with you three." Tammy pointed with a goofy smile.

Before the yacht docked, Max made his way back to our table. "I was invited to a party tonight. Would you ladies like the info? It may be fun," he explained. "I could meet you there."

"Sure," Tammy replied with a wide smile without asking us if we wanted to attend. "We'll see you there." She accepted Max's business card with a seductive smile.

"I look forward to it." He kissed her hand.

"Wow, that is one beautiful man." Tammy went on about her new beau.

"He has no idea," Lorraine giggled.

"What is that supposed to mean?" Tammy asked.

"You're going to eat that man alive."

"You make it sound like I'm a hot mess."

"You are a hot mess," Lorraine teased.

"Says the woman who made out with an unknown tongue bandit at a bar in the wee hours of the night," Tammy joked.

"Wait," Brooklyn interjected. "Repeat what you were saying on the boat about your bickering not being the reason I'm a silent partner now."

"It's not," Tammy said, dancing off the boat and waving Max's business card in the air.

"You know what?" Lorraine slid her arm around Tammy's waist. "I love you."

Tammy and Lorraine were as dysfunctional as they come. If you didn't know them, you'd think they were sisters who grew up fighting, so it's all they know. Personally, I believe they were enemies in a past life and sometimes their duels seep into the present time.

"That's the spirit." Tammy kissed Lorraine's forehead. "I already know what I'm wearing to the party."

"What time does it start?"

"It starts at ten. So we have more than enough time to get dressed and out the door."

"Don't you know how old we are?"

"Old enough to go out after ten. Live a little." She continued dancing to the car.

* * *

After we arrived back at the villa, we disbursed in search of the perfect outfits for the party. We took turns modeling at least three outfits. The majority vote won. Of course we had wine. You'd think at our age we'd pass out and forget about the party. But with a group of middle-aged women who'd forgotten how it felt to be young again, the more wine the better.

Tammy modeled a silver cross neck sequined jumpsuit, a short teal ruched dress, and a brown cut out backless halter dress. She looked stunning in everything she wore. That's the thing about Tammy. She's so confident she made the clothes, the clothes didn't make her. The silver jumpsuit won.

Lorraine modeled a form fitting blue sequined dress that stopped at her calves, a mini white bodycon dress, and a mini tan satin backless dress. Her beautiful big red curly hair brought the outfits together. She had a way of pairing her clothes with her hair in a way it all meshed together. The mini tan dress won. Such a gorgeous being.

Brooklyn brought out the big guns. She modeled a bodycon snakeskin printed dress that hugged every curve of her body. Her other two outfits were a pink asymmetrical one shoulder dress and a floral spaghetti strap mesh dress. The snakeskin dress won. I taught her well.

My three outfits were a red split sling spaghetti strap bodycon dress, a blue crisscross cut out bodycon dress, and a black bandage corset mini dress. The red dress won the majority vote.

By the time we arrived at the glass house by the ocean, the party was already in full swing. It was all white—white walls, white carpet, and white decorations. There were more glass walls than anything. It reminded me of Brooklyn's old condo. Ceiling to floor windows all around. I could really take in the view of the island and the ocean. It was breathtaking.

But we should've turned around and headed back to the car the moment we walked inside. Though none of us uttered a word. Instead, we let our curiosity lead the way and we carried on. The thick air of marijuana would surely have given us a high in less than five minutes. Though, the marijuana wasn't our biggest problem. We were at a nude party. Somehow Max forgot to share that small detail, yet he was nowhere in sight. Certainly, we didn't give him any indication we were these types of people.

We saw things we'd never wish upon anyone's eyes—some boobs bounced around while others hung low. Funny, that rang true for the male lower region too. Some were smooth-shaven while others resembled cave men who didn't know about the existence of razors. We'd crossed over into the Twilight Zone.

Where were Rod Serling and Jordan Peele when you needed them?

The naked congregation danced without a care in the

world. Even free love Tammy was taken aback, and it's hard to rattle her.

"I better not see Max strutting around this house in his birthday suit," Tammy said. "This is just..."

"Sodom and Gomorrah," Lorraine went straight to the Bible.

"I don't know what it is, but it's interesting." Brooklyn kept moving forward, forcing the rest of us to follow her. That's the thing about our group. We come together, we stay together, and we leave together. "Never tell Kai about this."

"You don't have to worry," I said. "I won't ever speak of this again. Well, maybe later. But then I'm done."

"Swear it. All of you," Brooklyn ordered.

"Okay, okay, we swear," Lorraine replied. "Calm down."

"What in the heck is going on with her over there?" Tammy asked.

"Who?" We asked simultaneously.

"The lady with the short green hair."

"Oh my goodness," Lorraine gasped. "I would never show my ass if it looked like that."

"Yeah, it's like a couple of flat chicken breasts mashed together to form an ass, or at least some resemblance of one," I described through winced eyes.

"Stop staring before she comes over here," Tammy fussed.

"Oh my goodness," Brooklyn gasped. "That man looks like he's wearing a vest." She described his black chest and back hairs perfectly. I instantly began scratching at the sight of him.

"Eww, disgusting," Lorraine shrieked loud enough to turn a few heads.

"You see," Tammy said. "You're going to get us kicked out before we get to see more." She could hardly get it out without laughing. Our curiosity had taken full control over reasoning.

"It's like a bad car accident you can't turn away from." Alas,

I'd found the words to describe what we saw. There was no rhyme or reason to the madness we witnessed.

A wheelchair bound man popped wheelies in the nude and almost ran over Lorraine's toes. I don't think I know anyone who could say they've gone to a nude party and almost been run over by a nudist in a wheelchair. That's something to check off a bucket list. It's the kind of stuff that makes memories. When we're in our golden years, we'll look back on this night and laugh until our dentures fall out. Only then will I talk about it again.

"So, it's true," Lorraine whispered.

"What?" We asked.

"The older men get their balls shrivel up like prunes and hang low."

"That's it," Brooklyn said, grabbing me and Lorraine's hands. "It's time to go. I can't believe Max invited us to this kink show in the first place."

"Hey, don't blame me. I'm as surprised as you. I didn't know it was this kind of party," Max walked up behind us looking confused with his hands up wearing a green suit with an embellished design on the right shoulder and bottom of the left sleeve. It was unique and eye-catching. "I should punch the guy who invited me."

"He was probably putting the moves on you. See, that's the thing about you men. You act like you don't understand when you're being hit on unless the conversation is sexual."

"Well, whatever the case, I'm not staying long enough to run into him. I've seen *Eyes Wide Shut*. This isn't my type of party."

"I never thought about that," Tammy said. "We should go before they start chanting and carrying out cult activities."

Max safely chauffeured us through the house to make a quick exit. "How long have you all been here?"

Tammy looked at her watch, and then us. "About twenty to thirty minutes."

"What?" He asked with wide eyes. "Why didn't you leave?"

Tammy shrugged with a smirk. "We were kind of stuck. We've never seen anything like this before."

"I could've gone the rest of my life never seeing some of the things I saw in there," Max explained. "There was a woman with so much hair under her arms she could braid it."

"I think I saw her," Lorraine said excitedly. "Did she have long curly black hair?"

"Yeah that's her," Max exhaled. "I wish we would've had more time to talk." He glanced at his diamond watch. "But it's late, and you ladies should be getting home. Who knows what kind of crazy these people will conjure during the wee hours." He helped us inside our SUV. "Make sure you lock up tight. Freaks come out at night."

"Well aren't you the gentleman," Brooklyn said, nudging Tammy.

"Here's the address to our villa. Come over for lunch tomorrow if you aren't busy."

"Consider me there." He closed the door and gave the truck a pat before waving goodbye.

"He's nice. That's the kind of man you need," Lorraine pointed out.

"Please stop pushing relationships on us. We're strong accomplished women. We don't need men to enrich our lives. We do that on our own. I've told you a million times, I'm not interested. I've been married. I've been in monogamous relationships. I don't want it again unless it is extraordinary and that doesn't exist."

Lorraine turned to Tammy with her hand resting on her

chest. "Why are you biting my head off? I only said he was nice. Big deal."

"Oh no, you're not sorry," I said. "Tammy isn't wrong. You do this all the time. You're like a pushy parent trying to marry off their not so attractive daughter to any man who'll have her. I stand with Tammy. We're strong, beautiful, accomplished women. We don't need a man, especially if he cannot compliment our lives."

"Say something, Brooklyn," Lorraine urged. "Don't let them gang up on me."

"I didn't say anything because I agree with them. You've got to stop thinking a man is the only thing that brings happiness. You give your heart away so easily, and when it's shattered into a million little pieces, you're left to put it back together by yourself. But what you don't realize is, you'll never be quite the same. They are taking away pieces of you with every heartbreak."

"Where is Lorraine who kissed a stranger in the bar and walked away from him without dreaming of a relationship?"

"I had a lapse. Don't hold it against me."

We rode back to the villa in silence. Lorraine's a lost cause. A hopeless romantic. It didn't matter how many times a man stepped on her heart; she'd choose love every single time. Then force it on us.

"Can I just say one thing?" Lorraine asked as we filed out of the truck.

"What?" Tammy rolled her eyes.

"How in the heck were those naked people sitting on wicker chairs?"

"I was thinking the same thing," I shrieked.

We erupted in laughter at the mere thought. It certainly cut the thick air and allowed us to have an amazing night outside by the pool instead of going our separate ways. We did what we do best, girl talk with snacks. No wine this time. Then a few hours later, we called it a night.

I rested in bed for a while, staring out the window. The sound of the swooshing and crashing waves against the shore became a sweet lullaby. A few more days and nights like this and they'd have to drag me off the island, kicking and screaming. Or hold Junior's picture up to bait me onto the plane.

My time on La Isleta Sanguínea Island recharged my battery to reconnect with myself. I came alive doing nothing but breathing. Sometimes a simple disconnect from our day-to-day lives is all we need to reset our mind, body, and feel mentally good again. You can't put a price on that.

7
GUESS WHO'S COMING TO LUNCH

The next morning Tammy woke up before sunrise and ran through the villa to make sure everything was presentable for her dear old Max. He'd be stopping by to have lunch with us. I'd never seen her act this way over a man. Dare I say, she appeared nervous?

Somehow she thought of us as the help the way she bossed us around. Personally, I wasn't going for it, so I snuck out to explore the market while they cleaned. Time alone is better than meditation. Besides, I needed to do something in order to get through lunch with Tammy fawning over her new boy toy. Keeping my food down would be a big enough task. Tammy doesn't shy away from PDA.

The island had an amazing market. There's a huge variety of fresh homegrown fruits, veggies, teas, produce, and flowers. All their scents attacked me at one time. The sellers showcased their best under colorful tents. Not even my wildest dreams could hold a match to it. I bought a dozen yellow fully bloomed tulips–Brooklyn's favorite, and red roses which are my favorite, for the villa.

"Max is here. Max is here. Nobody move. I'll get the door," Tammy yelled.

I screamed through the cracked door from my bedroom, "Don't wait for me. I'll be down in a bit." I turned my attention back to my phone. "Sorry about that. Tammy met some guy when we had dinner on the yacht. You know the rest."

"Who's the guy?" Rodney asked. "Do you think it's safe to have a stranger in your villa?"

"I think we'll be fine," I assured him. "What do you and Junior have planned today?"

"Are you changing the subject to keep me from asking questions about Tammy's so-called male companion? Is he bringing any friends?"

"Are you jealous?" I asked.

"I just want to make sure you're all safe."

"Is that the only reason you want to know if he's bringing friends?" I pushed a little more.

"Yes," Rodney replied without saying a lot. I knew him well and could hear concern in his response. But I knew better than to push. We didn't do that to each other. "You asked about Junior. We're going to my parents for dinner."

"You know you should really learn how to cook. Junior's used to having a home cooked meal."

Rodney laughed, "We've been eating takeout and he hasn't complained yet. I think he's okay."

"Oh my God, takeout," I shrieked. "I told you not to give him junk food. But as always, you do what you want to do. Then you expect me to trust you. This has been an ongoing issue between us since hello."

"I haven't given him any junk food," Rodney confirmed. "I order meals that consist of baked chicken, broccoli, and all those good things. I listen to you because I respect your parenting style as his mother. But you don't respect me as his father enough to trust me. That shit hurts my feelings," he sniffed.

Could he be crying?

"Damn you Rodney, now I owe you an apology. It's not easy for me to be away from Junior this long. I take pride in being his mother. He's the most important person in my life. But so are you. I respect your role as his father and I trust you. I'm sorry for hurting you."

"Thank you for acknowledging my feelings. You're not raising Junior alone. I'm here and willing to do whatever it takes as a father. Give me a chance to be more hands on with our son, emphases on *our*. It's been thirteen years now," Rodney went on. "I try not to push back because I don't want to piss you off. But he's my kid too, and time is moving way too fast. I'm missing out on everything. All I get is a weekend here and there. Sometimes I feel like I'm being punished."

"Why do you think that?"

"I don't know," he replied. "I made a huge mistake that I wish I could take back every day. But it's like I'm constantly being punished for it."

"Say it," I pressed. "What huge mistake did you make?"

"I cheated okay," he said. "I made a mistake and you're still punishing me for it."

"I'm not punishing you. I have control issues. Junior's my only child. I have to raise this kid to go out into the world and be able to stand on his own two feet while having values that serve him and whoever is in his life. But you're right, Junior has two parents. So, when I get home, we'll sit down and figure out a way for us both to spend an equal amount of time with him."

"You should go on more vacations," Rodney laughed. "When you're well rested, you're more inclined to work with me and not against me. Junior's a teenager. We'll be fighting for his time against sports and his friends. We should be working together."

"I hate it when you're right." I rubbed my aching heart at the mere thought of Junior growing up and not needing me as much. Then who would I be?

"I'll call you later to check on you since you all are expecting a weirdo for lunch."

"Talk to you soon." I peeked out to see if Rodney was right about Max. Surely he wouldn't bring friends without an extended invitation to do so. I couldn't hear anyone other than my girls. But that didn't mean anything. Their natural volume is level ten. So, I eased downstairs.

"Finally," Tammy said. "We've been waiting for you to get down here."

"I told you not to wait. I was talking to Rodney."

"Oh good, how are they making it without you?" Brooklyn asked.

"Oh they're peachy keen." I pouted. "Doing so well Rodney wants us to work something out so he will have more time with Junior, but I don't know how I feel about it. We already have a schedule that runs well for all of us."

"Not if he's asking for more time," Lorraine mumbled.

"What was that? Seems like you guys think differently." I gave the table a once over.

Max took that as his cue to butt into the conversation. "Is he the biological father?"

"Yes, why?" I asked.

"Why wouldn't you want the father of your child to spend more time with his son? Is he irresponsible?"

"No," Lorraine interrupted. "He's a wonderful father. Actually, he's a wonderful person all around."

"So what's the problem?" He asked.

"Who are you to question me about my co-parenting?" I slammed my glass on the table.

Max raised his hands in a surrendering stance to back out of the verbal battle. "No need to bite off my head. I only wanted to join in the conversation."

"That wasn't cool, Iris." Tammy helped Lorraine set the table. "He's a guest. Naturally he'll weigh in on the conversations. I'm sure he's not judging you." She stared at Max with questioning eyes. "Are you?"

"No, I'm not judging. I understand the difficulties of co-parenting. I meant no harm."

Food was our love language. So I wasn't surprised to see such a large spread to welcome Max into our inner circle. And right at the center of the table were the dozen of red roses I bought at the market. Roses helped lower my anxiety. To me, they signify beauty, elegance, and command attention. All the characteristics I aim to embody as a woman.

"You know what, I apologize," I said. "I miss my son. I've never been away from him this long. I don't know if it's good or bad to have such an attachment. But now that I've had this moment of separation, I understand what Rodney is feeling."

"I have a daughter, and I hate being away from her for too long myself," he explained. "That's the only reason I asked if he was a good father."

"You have a daughter," Tammy said with wide eyes. The grandmother of the group who detests the idea of motherhood now that her children are grown and on their own.

"Yes," Max replied, whipping out his phone. "Her name is Maxine. She's twelve-years-old."

"Twelve," Tammy's voice raised and so did her eyebrows. We knew this wouldn't go any further than lunch.

Max looked around the table. "I take it you don't like kids?" He put his phone away.

"No, it's not that. I have two children of my own. Well, they're adults now, and my son has a daughter."

"Really, you have a granddaughter." This time Max raised his voice an octave.

"Don't say it like that," Tammy squealed, covering her face with a linen napkin.

Poor Max wore confusion as badly as Lorraine wore yellow. So I figured I'd help him out. "Tammy prefers to be called Gigi."

"That's cool," Max said. "Does it bother you that I have a twelve-year-old?"

"Not at all," she reassured him, touching his hand.

"Good, because I like you."

"I like you too." She gulped her mimosa.

"How long will you ladies be on the island? Tomorrow's my last day."

"We're leaving the day after you. Then we're off to Marseau." Tammy did a little wiggle and dance in her seat.

"Marseau is nice. Are you traveling around the world or something?"

"You could say that," Tammy replied. "We took ancestry tests, so Iris and Brooklyn are meeting their extended family members for the first time. But me and Lorraine knew everyone from our results so we opted to spend our time here," Tammy explained. "This is my favorite place, and I wanted to experience it with them."

"Oh, so you come here often?" Max asked.

"Every year."

"Does that mean I'll see you again if I come back at the same time next year?"

Tammy nodded with a smile. "Is that your way of asking me to meet you here next year?"

"What do you think about that?"

"I'd love to see you again. But if you play your cards right, you could come visit me in Woodcrest for more than just a few days and certainly before next year."

She surprised us all with that invitation. I for one thought he had no chance in hell since revealing he had a twelve-year-old child.

"Really? I'd love that." Max smiled, grabbing a shrimp and pineapple kabob.

"What are we even doing here?" Lorraine piled food onto her plate. "I'm going out to the patio. These two obviously need some alone time."

"Sounds like a plan to me." Brooklyn filled her plate and raced behind Lorraine. I gave Tammy and Max a nod and got out of dodge before Tammy turned her flirting up a notch. My stomach wasn't strong enough to see it.

"I wonder how many island flings Tammy's had on the island." Brooklyn chuckled.

"You never know with her," Lorraine ate a forkful of rice. "Maybe I should take a page out of her book and have one of my own."

"Are you talking about the tongue bandit?" I asked. "I knew you wanted to do more than kiss that guy."

"Of course I wanted to do more. I'm a woman. He's attractive and intelligent." She shrugged.

"Why aren't you inside with Lover Boy?" Brooklyn asked.

"He's relieving himself. I'll see him out once he's done," Tammy explained. "You better be careful and know your rights if you get pregnant. The laws aren't on our side anymore when it comes to our reproductive system."

"Isn't that terrible," I butted in. "It reminds me of an old case. Nothing to do with the law. But, this young woman suffered from an existing health issue. She was advised to terminate her pregnancy to save her life. She decided against it and lost her life. My point is, abortions aren't just for women who don't want to have a child. Some pregnancies should be terminated to save lives, and a bunch of men shouldn't have the right to tell a woman what to do with her body."

"I agree," Brooklyn said. "This will open the door for a lot of anarchy with men against women and women harming themselves to terminate."

"Bingo," Tammy said. "I fear the state of womanhood."

"Well, if I did have sex, I'd be careful. If I happened to get pregnant, I'd have my child. I don't believe in abortions."

"Here we go," Tammy huffed.

"What?" Lorraine asked.

"You're about to get judgy."

"My stance on abortions is not to judge. It's about me and what I want and don't want. Why are you being so defensive? Have you had an abortion before?"

"Actually I have," Tammy admitted. "I got pregnant the summer after high school graduation. I had to make a decision to follow my dreams or become a mother with no resources to raise a child. I didn't want to be a burden on my parents. So, my friend took me to have the procedure done and I went on with my life. If I didn't have that option, I don't know which way my life would've gone. This is terrible." She hurried back inside to see Max off.

"I give you a hard time. But I admire your free spirit and how you take control of your life." Lorraine touched Tammy's face. "That's what life should be about. Learning more about ourselves, living outside of the norm. Making each day different."

"Living outside the norm doesn't mean giving yourself away to strangers because they're attractive. Everything that looks good on the outside isn't always good on the inside,"

Brooklyn preached. "I love Tammy, but I don't understand her free love lifestyle."

"I don't think Tammy's all about sex," I offered my two cents. "Tammy has total control of her life. She doesn't allow anyone to tell her what to do. She does what makes her happy without feeling ashamed about it. Sometimes that's sex. Sometimes it's her taking a trip to clear her mind from everyday nuances. Remember when she bought her Lamborghini? We thought she was having a midlife crisis. She does what makes her happy. What's so wrong with that?" I asked.

"So this is how you talk about me when I'm not around," Tammy announced. "I live my life not to have any regrets. I do what makes me happy. But I do it safely. And just so you know, I don't have flings when I vacation. I know what you all think of me because I date a lot of men. But I don't sleep with all of them. I enjoy meeting new people and having great conversations."

"I enjoy life too without sleeping with strangers," Brooklyn said, carrying on the conversation.

"But it took you a long time to get there until your luggage spilled out in the airport and a stranger twirled your panties on his finger."

"I didn't sleep with him." She put her hands over her face. "But, I did want to slap him into next week."

"Aren't you happy you didn't? Kai is one in a million," I said.

"Yeah he is, but it seems like you've turned into the old me. You haven't been the feisty firecracker we've known. What's up with that?" Brooklyn nudged my shoulder. "Conversations only work when two or more people engage each other."

"I've spent my life being the cheerleader for everyone else that I've lost myself. But I didn't realize it until we were here. You're married so you don't need me as much. Rodney wants

Junior to spend more time with him. Where the hell does that leave me?"

"Well my dear, this is why we're here. You need to find your fire again." Brooklyn winked.

I never realized how much friendships are a necessity until I found my forever friends. My girls uplift me even when I'm unaware that I need upliftment. After my parents died, I thought I only needed Brooklyn's friendship. Being on my own wasn't so bad. I'd spent my entire life before college being a popular girl. People can be energy suckers if you let them.

In high school, my friends and I were what you'd consider the "popular" group. Most wanted to be us and many wanted to be with us. I naively thought we'd be friends forever. Especially my best friend, Bianca. We spent the most time together. Hung out in my bedroom every Saturday morning. We promised to always be friends. But it didn't turn out that way. After graduation, she went away to college, fell in love, had children, and went sight unseen.

I guess that's life.

Standing alone gave me a false sense of strength. When in fact, strength comes from having people in your life who accept you and allow you to be vulnerable. That is where you learn the most about yourself. There is power in being a loner.

"Here's the deal. I love my parents with all my heart. But they're gone and I don't know how I'll process my emotions without their input. I don't want to have any ill feelings towards them for keeping secrets. But they've kept a lot of things from me. I don't know what I'll be walking into when I meet these people."

"Someone will have those answers for you. Have a little faith." Lorraine draped her arm over my shoulder.

"I agree," Brooklyn chimed in. "Think more positively.

You'll have more people in your life to love and protect you and Junior."

I gazed out into the seemingly endless body of water. It sparkled under the sun every time it moved. Though as beautiful as it was, it's equally dangerous. This journey of meeting my family could be the same as that beautiful ocean —dangerous.

"It's too quiet. What are Tammy and Max doing in there?"

"I don't want to know," I laughed, wiping my tears away.

"Go check if you're so curious." Brooklyn urged Lorraine.

"Heck no, I don't want to witness Tammy executing any of her kinky tricks. That would scar me for the rest of my life."

"Right," Brooklyn yelped. "I'd probably leave my family to become a nun."

"They won't have you," I explained.

"Why not?" She asked.

"You've had sex, children, and you've been married. You're rotten fruit."

She looked at Lorraine with questioning eyes. "Is she for real?"

"Yup, rotten to the core."

The three of us toppled over in laughter.

Tammy sauntered outside. "What's so funny?"

"You," Lorraine blurted out.

"We thought you took Max upstairs and tied him up or something."

"Is that what you think of me?" She rested her hand over her chest.

We smiled at each other and said, "Yes."

Tammy laughed, "Fair enough. I'm proud of who I am. But no, I didn't even kiss Max goodbye."

"What?" Lorraine asked with a concerned stare.

"This is like the movie, Freaky Friday. Tammy has become

Lorraine, and Lorraine has become Tammy." Brooklyn stood.
"You know she's thinking about sleeping with the tongue
bandit."

Tammy gasped with her hand over her chest and wide eyes.
"Is this true? Little Miss Goody Two Shoes wants to have a
vacation fling."

"No, I'm only weighing out my options." Lorraine paced
around the patio. "I've lived my entire life doing what I believe
is morally right. Don't speak too crass, you're a woman. Don't
sleep around, you're a woman. Don't speak too loud, you're a
woman," She huffed. "I give Tammy a hard time about how she
expresses her sexuality..."

Tammy interrupted, "Preach on, sister."

"I've walked a straight and narrow line all my life. Still no
ring." She wiggled her finger. "Who am I doing this for? Surely
not for myself because I'm so unhappy."

"There you have it." Tammy pointed. "The worst thing you
could do is deny your body what it naturally desires. All you
need to do is be smart about it and protect yourself. Guys are
nuts, so be selective."

"You must have never heard about soul ties?" Brooklyn
asked.

"Oh, I know all about soul ties. But I also know how to
break them. You acknowledge it, do something about it, forgive
yourself, and boom, your soul tie is broken."

"How do you know?"

"We're friends, but I don't share every part of myself unless
the moment calls for it. I have spiritual beliefs that I practice to
keep myself protected and grounded. I take healing baths to
cleanse my body and my soul. I use the sun to neutralize negative energy. I love to come here because I can connect with my
primal senses with nature."

"You do all that?" I asked.

"Tammy, you never cease to amaze me," Brooklyn chirped, kicking her feet in the pool.

"Why don't you share more of these things with us?" Lorraine asked.

"There's some stuff I prefer to keep to myself because it's personal," she explained with a wink. "All I'm saying is, live your life the way you see fit without worrying about people judging you. But make sure you find ways to protect yourself."

"Whew, that's deep. I needed to hear this. Thanks Tammy," I said.

"So basically you're saying I can call our neighbor, AKA, The Tongue Bandit, and do the do. Then I could take a healing bath to get him out of my system?"

"Lorraine, have sex with the man if you want to have sex with him. You're a grown woman. You don't need our approval."

Our laughter went on for hours, and honestly, I wished we could live in this moment forever. One thing I appreciate about my girls is how much I can learn from them. Though never in a million years would I have imagined Tammy as a spiritual person. She's in touch with herself more than any of us. We could learn a thing or two from her.

8

GOODBYE ISLAND, HELLO
FASHION CAPITAL

The next morning I woke with bittersweet feelings. We'd reached our last day on the island of daily perfect weather. We met interesting people. We had amazing adventures. We stepped outside of my comfort zone. If the rest of our trip is as life-changing as our time in La Isleta Sanguínea, I was all in for our next destination.

I used to be known as the unpredictable one. For goodness sakes, my friends nicknamed me Firecracker in college. We put soap in a water fountain at a hotel and danced in it. Crashed a BBQ of an unknown family and pretended we were long lost family members, and they bought it. But after having Junior, I became a creature of habit with no excitement.

I pushed Brooklyn to live without fear—have faith that whatever she wants she can have. Now she's married with kids and she's doing what she loves career-wise. But somewhere along the way I became the stagnant one.

There's one thing I didn't lose—my love for shopping. So naturally the girls and I made a unanimous decision to spend our last day on the island shopping for our next stop on the trip to Marseau. It's known for fashion, and we didn't want to stick out like a bunch of weeds. I dress for myself. But I also welcome compliments.

Tammy took us to all the great boutiques on the island. But she saved the best for last—Petals and Pastels Boutique. According to her, the boutique was known for their high-end pieces. I actually prefer shopping at boutiques rather than big box stores. It's easier to find unique pieces. I take pride in my individuality. From the time my mother relinquished her role as my stylist, I never played it safe. If you want to make a statement, you have to mix the black polka dots with yellow stripes. That's how you turn heads.

My mouth dropped when we arrived at Petals and Pastels. The external structure of the boutique was designed in the likeness of an oversized armoire. The tall doors even opened the same as an armoire. There were glass doors and a lobby in between the tall wooden doors for customers to enter the boutique to keep bugs and moisture away from the clothes. Brilliant.

They took the name literally with walls of artificial flowers and grass floors throughout the boutique. The scent of rosemary filled the air. It was all nice and inviting.

A white silk floor length dress caught my eye the moment we entered the boutique. The slanted deep V met a long slit on the left side. It showed just enough with leaving the rest to the imagination. It's perfect for an elegant event. Even if we weren't going to one on the trip, that dress was coming with me, and if it came in other colors, I would've bought them too.

"Oh, you're lucky I didn't see that dress before you. You would've had a fight on your hands," Brooklyn said, holding the dress up to admire it on her body.

"Don't even think about it." I snatched it away. "You do this every time we shop. Now you're going to miss out on this one too." I held an off the shoulder navy blue dress with an ombré of white flowers. The most interesting part of the dress were the sleeves. A gold button held the top and bottom of the sleeves together that stopped just above the elbow.

"Okay that's it. I need to get the heck away from you and keep my eyes on the prize."

Brooklyn never stood a chance shopping with me. You see, her problem is she wants to see what I get and it distracts her enough for me to find more. The girl has an undiagnosed case of ADHD when it comes to shopping, if you ask me.

"You better stop talking and look because now you've missed out on this one too." I showed her a chiffon spaghetti strap romper with a yellow and green leaf print.

"Okay, I need that one more than you. I only have one short romper. Please let me have it."

I pulled it to my chest with all my other finds and turned away from her. "Nope, it's all mine. Oh, what's this?" I pulled a pair of royal blue flowy high waisted shorts with a matching belt that ties and hangs long.

Brooklyn covered her eyes with a squeal and ran to the other side of the store. Tough love is the only way to push her to find her own style.

"Are you finding everything okay?" A tall woman with full curly black hair asked. I could tell she shopped here. She wore a wrap dress with a multi-patchwork print of black and white stripes, leopard, and snake skin.

"No, but I need that dress. Is it here?" I looked around the racks of clothes.

"Yes, but unfortunately I never buy three of the same thing. The other two sold within an hour of me putting them out."

"Very smart." I wagged my finger. "People will come often so they won't miss out on new pieces. Are you the manager?"

"I'm the owner," she replied with a proud smile, rightfully so.

"How did you come up with the design of the store? I love it. I've never seen anything like it."

"When I was a little girl, my mother had a beautiful armoire in her bedroom. All I've ever wanted was my own boutique because I love fashion. I lost my parents when I was eighteen. So, I built my store in the likeness of my mom's armoire from an old picture my grandmother had."

"I lost my parents too. I was twenty-two at the time. They were involved in a fatal car accident."

"I'm sorry to hear that. It's been the most difficult part of my life," she took a deep breath to maintain her strong demeanor. "My parents died in a house fire. I snuck out that night to go boating with my friends. So, there's a tiny voice in my head that makes me question if I could've saved them if I were home."

"I'm a medical examiner. Once a person or persons inhale lungfuls of smoke from a fire, it certainly causes uncomfort, but they would have perished in less than a minute of heavy coughing. Giving the fact it occurred while they were sleeping, they may not have even felt that much discomfort. If you would've been there, you would've experienced the same. There would be no way you would've helped them. The flames had to engulf the home in a major way to cause death by smoke inhalation."

An expression of peace came over her the moment I finished my spill. "Thank you for saying that. For so many years, I've tortured myself with these thoughts."

"I'm happy I could give you some consolation," I replied. "How has losing your parents at such a young age affected your life?"

"My grandmother found an amazing counselor for me not even a month after we lost my parents. I had to go every week until I was nineteen. I don't know where or who I'd be if it wasn't for her loving me enough to make sure I got the help I needed."

"You're extremely lucky to have had her. I was away at college when my parents died. I never got counseling. I leaned on my friends instead. But looking back and knowing how much I struggled, I shouldn't have entrusted my mental health to my friends."

We shared a good laugh. I've learned over the years, laughter has a way of washing sadness from the soul. The same as a good cry.

"It's never too late. It's a necessity in order to live a fulfilling life free of guilt and depression," she explained. "I see you got the plunging high slit dress. I also have it in black. You have an amazing body. It'll look great on you."

"I should take you home with me. Hearing those compliments on a daily basis could do me some good." We shared another good laugh. I never hit it off well with a stranger. Perhaps us being in the club of orphaned kids—*yes I'm an orphan*—gave me comfort in sharing with her. "By the way, my name is Iris Reid." I stuck out my hand.

"Silly me, I've told you my whole life story without ever telling you my name," she chuckled. "I'm Victoria Beaudet, nice to meet you."

"Oh good, you've met Victoria," Tammy interjected herself into our conversation. "Isn't she a sweetheart?"

"Yes she is, and she has amazing taste in fashion. Now I see why you do annual vacations here. This boutique alone is worth the trip."

"Oh wow, thank you. But I can't take all the credit. I get my fashion sense from my mom. She was as stylish as they come," she sighed. "Could I get anyone a glass of champagne?"

"Sure we'll take a glass," Tammy answered for everyone.

"Okay, I'll be right back. You ladies have fun shopping." Victoria sauntered away.

We sat down to enjoy Brooklyn's impromptu fashion show. She'd been quiet for way too long as she perused the clothes. She's a competitive shopper. There's no way she'd let me outdo her.

"You have to buy that dress. It's made for you," Tammy declared as Brooklyn strutted around in the short gold lace scalloped cocktail dress.

"You think so?" Brooklyn inquired, taking a spin around in the mirror.

"Keep that one. Now go try on another one," Lorraine urged, sipping her champagne.

"I wish I had girlfriends like you," Victoria stood next to Lorraine. "I'm the only one of my friends who stayed on the island after graduation."

"That sucks," Lorraine frowned. "Consider us your long distance girlfriends."

"I'd like that," Victoria replied with a smile.

Brooklyn emerged in a blush draped corset midi dress. My mouth hung open. I balled my fist in anticipation of a fight that I knew I would never win. "That dress would look great on me. I need it," I exclaimed.

"Unh, unh, unh, this one's mine." Brooklyn wiggled with a sly smile.

"Come on Brooklyn," I pleaded. "I'll trade the romper for it."

"Yeah right, that romper could never compete with this masterpiece." She twirled. Her boobs, butt, and legs looked perfect. I don't blame her. I wouldn't give that dress up either.

After we paid for our clothes and exchanged phone numbers with Victoria, we walked down the street, passing a variety of galleries, shops, and restaurants to the Celestial

Jewelry Store. The shopping district faced the ocean. A buff security guard stood outside the store. He'd make you rethink a well-thought out heist if you had one.

The smell of Windex on the glass display cases attacked us as we walked inside the quaint store. I zoned in on a diamond and pearl drop necklace and earring set. It'd go perfect with my new dress.

"Ah, you have excellent taste. Care to try it on?" An older woman with silver hair unlocked the case to give me a better look at the set.

"Yes, thank you." I pulled my hair up while she clasped the necklace. It was dainty enough to bring out the femininity of any woman. "Sold."

"Great, I'll pack it up for you." The sales woman didn't waste any time. She's definitely what you'd call a closer when it came to business.

Brooklyn pointed to four white gold rings with open loop bands where diamonds were in the shape of a red rose as the star piece. "I'm buying one for all of us. They'll commemorate our trip around the world."

"Thank you, they're beautiful. I'll never take it off," I said.

"So what's next on the agenda?" Lorraine asked with all of us turning towards Tammy for answers since she knew the island so well.

"I'm glad you asked," Tammy replied. "I scheduled a photography shoot for us. The plan is to go back to the villa and change our clothes, and then we'll meet up with the photographer by the ocean." She glanced at her watch. "The shoot is at sunset. So, we need to pay and get out of here like now."

"Wow," Brooklyn said. "That's perfect."

By the time we left, the sales woman had a smile from ear to ear. I'm sure she made a nice commission from our visit.

We settled on wearing sea green and white for our photo shoot. The smooth-talking photographer mastered candid shots. We wanted to look like a group of girls laughing, talking, and having fun with our toes in the sand, and he made it happen at sunset.

I tip my hat to models. The heat coupled with constant movement took a lot out of us, so we stopped at the Moon Hawk Whiskey Bar for a drink to cool down before calling it a night at the villa. It had a tropical botanical garden ambience loaded with live greenery throughout. There was even a wall of lava that resembled the island's volcano–Mount Woe.

"Let's raise our glasses to Tammy." Lorraine said. "You've been a phenomenal hostess. I think we should make this our annual girlfriend's trip, if you'll have us."

"Are you freaking kidding me? I'd love that."

"Here's to friendship," Lorraine declared.

We toasted and squealed, *friendship.*

A woman sitting with her group of friends yelled, "Why do tourists always come to the island to make a show as if we want to hear and see everything they do?"

"Yeah," her friend stood from the barstool. "And not to mention they come here to sleep with our men."

"Tramps," another friend stood with her hands on her hips with laser eyes focused on us–the tramps.

"What is your problem?" I stood, moving closer to the women.

"Forget them." Brooklyn pulled me back. "This is our last day. Don't feed into their nonsense."

The last one of the women in their group stood. "Shut up before I give you a going away black-eye."

I'd reached my limit. No one threatens my sister and gets

away with it. I reached back as far as I could and punched the ring leader to the floor. Then chaos erupted. Bar stools were thrown over, glasses were broken, shoes were thrown, and hair was pulled.

"STOP!" Brooklyn stood on top of the bar screaming at the top of her lungs.

"We're all grown women. This is ridiculous and embarrassing."

The police raced inside the bar. "You." One of the officers pointed. "Get down from there right now. All of you get down on the floor."

"But I wasn't fighting. I tried to stop them," Brooklyn pled.

"I don't care what you were doing. Get down on the floor with the rest of them."

"I'm not getting on that floor. I did nothing wrong."

"Don't make me pull you down from there."

"You better not lay a finger on me. You'll hear from my lawyer."

"Brooklyn, get your ass down now," I screamed.

"Listen to your friend," the officer said.

"Fine, but those women started it. We were trying to enjoy our last day here."

The cuffs were tight and cold around my wrists. Two more seconds and I'd have a panic attack. Thankfully the owner pulled the police to the side and moments later they let us go. Well, except for the nasty women. Apparently they were known for starting trouble with tourists.

To thank the owner, we sat down to have a few more drinks.

"Okay, okay," Lorraine said. "I have a game."

"Oh Lorraine, I don't want to play a game right now." Tammy rubbed her wrists.

"Come on, indulge me," she said. "Never have I ever gotten into a bar fight and been arrested on a tropical island."

We threw our shots back in a fit of laughter.

"This one goes down in history," I said. "Brooklyn, what were you thinking about when you started arguing with the police officers?"

"I don't know about you guys, but I didn't come here to see the inside of a jail cell," she laughed.

"Me either," Lorraine agreed. "I've never been arrested and those handcuffs hurt. I don't see how reoffenders do it."

We thanked the owner again and walked out of the bar with a standing ovation from the other patrons. "Good job ladies. I didn't think you had it in you."

"Looks can be deceiving," Tammy proclaimed with a wink.

Perhaps the other patrons were regulars who'd grown tired of those ladies' antics. But in light of the events, we spent the rest of the night in our villa safe and sound. The cook made a feast fit for our last night. We ate in delight with laughter and great conversation—just the four of us, no men allowed.

"Iris, what were you thinking when you went up against that woman? They were clearly out of their minds with nothing to lose."

"Either they were going to throw the first punch or us. I had to let them know we may be cute, but we could get as dirty as them. I think we were worthy opponents."

"Yeah we were, but I don't ever want to do that again. I'm way too cute for fighting." Lorraine adjusted the collar on her silk pajama top.

"Oh hey, the photographer emailed our pictures." Tammy waved us over.

We sat side by side on the floor, admiring our beautiful pictures. The perfect ending to our crazy day.

"I have to say," Lorraine spoke. "I've been against taking

time away from work for years now. I've ignorantly thought of vacations as squandering time. In three days, I'm already replenished with energy and good feels, you know?"

"I get it," I replied. "I'm in the same boat as you. I let my job run my life. I haven't taken Junior on a family trip in God knows when. It's sad because it's not like I don't have the means to do it. Going forward, I'm making it my priority to take time away from the daily hustle to smell the roses and relax my mind."

"Here, here," Brooklyn squealed, racing into the living room with two bottles of wine. "To new beginnings."

We laughed at Brooklyn wiggling with her pooched lips. I never expected to feel the weight of the world lift from my shoulders on the island. Neglecting my well-being has done a great disservice to me and my son. How could I call myself a good mother when I'm not being good to myself?

Tammy turned on the radio and summoned us to join her in a dance break. We twisted, turned, and jumped all over the place. We owned the night, and took full advantage of it.

After breaking into a full-on sweat I strolled over to the window. It brought a tear to my eye to feel such freedom. Truth is, my career sometimes weighs heavy on me mentally. All those lives lost—some in horrible unimaginable ways. To carry out my type of job without a break is enough to drive a person mad.

I looked over at my girlfriends, Brooklyn fighting Huntington's, Lorraine chasing the next big account, and then there's Tammy who had it right all along, living her life in a way it serves her.

A change was long overdue.

9

NOT SO LOST ANYMORE

We arrived in Marseau early Saturday morning around nine o'clock. Somehow we stepped off the plane and onto a movie set—perfect weather, blue skies, and chirping birds. Marseau was that breathtakingly beautiful. It had all the makings of the perfect day until we learned Tammy's luggage was lost or delayed. She'd find out which one tomorrow. I silently prayed for a delay because if her luggages were lost this trip would be over before it starts. She'd complain and whine nonstop. Not that she wasn't already doing both. But at least it'd only last a day instead of the entire time in Marseau. Personally I'd be sick to my stomach after buying all those new outfits from the boutique on the island. Thank goodness her jewelry was safe and sound in her carry on bag.

We gathered in the living room of Brooklyn's room at the hotel. She had the best room at the Cape Grace Hotel–a corner suite with a fireplace. We sat around the living room, eating yogurt and fresh fruit with a glass of green tea on the side. She also had the most beautiful view of the canal. We marveled at Marseau's beauty under the rising sun that reflected off the glowing waters. We could even see the rainbow-colored houses beyond the view of historical downtown architecture. Their structures are extremely different from our country. Marseau maintained the integrity while Woodcrest demolished anything they considered old. Then they tore down beautiful old buildings and replaced them with cheap run-of-the-mill cookie cutouts.

A profound sense of mindfulness took over me. The scenery. The food. The language. I wanted to dive deep into the culture and immerse myself in it—become it.

The monotony of life back home slowly ran through my veins until one day I woke up and was hardly able to recognize myself. This trip has allowed me to simply breathe and exist. Oftentimes, being a Forensic Pathologist didn't allow me those simple things. I'm constantly reminded of death so much that I forget to live. The world as wonderful as it is should be appreciated and ventured.

"What the hell am I supposed to wear to meet Brooklyn's family for dinner?" Tammy scooped up the last of her yogurt and shoved it in her mouth. "And why can't we find a piece of bacon around here? This isn't going to hold me. I'm not a tiny girl. I need something sustainable."

"You'll be okay. We're all so used to eating unhealthy portions. This could give us a better outlook on how much and what we consume. I for one want to practice better eating habits going forward." Lorraine popped an oat in her mouth.

"Blah, blah, blah." Tammy rolled her eyes. "I would've ordered myself two sandwiches if I were in charge of breakfast. Thanks Iris."

"You were too busy crying about your luggage to care about food. Cut it out." Lorraine replied, rolling her eyes.

"Speaking of my lost luggage, who's going to let me wear

one of their new outfits? Keep in mind, if it wasn't for me you never would've been on the island to buy it. You owe me."

No one spoke. We gave each other looks and disbursed. I walked over to the window to admire the beauty of the city.

"Oh don't all speak at once," Tammy said. "If it were anyone of you, I'd give you the clothes off my back."

"Fine," I finally spoke up. "You can wear one of my outfits but not my new clothes. No way you're wearing it before I do."

"Whatever, you're just scared I'd wear it better than you. Show me what you've got."

"Does it matter?" I asked. "Beggars can't be choosers. Just know I have style." I winked.

"You're lucky you remind me of myself. You're so damn cocky."

"Wait," Brooklyn said. "Tammy can't possibly fit your clothes. You're... well... screw it. You're tiny and she's..."

"She's what," Tammy interrupted with her hands on her hips.

"Curvy," she replied. "I was going to say curvy. Calm down."

We all laughed, except Tammy. Her weight often fluctuated. One month her curves weren't as pronounced. Other months, they're very noticeable.

"I beg your pardon. Iris and I are the same size."

"If you are, it's only for the month," Brooklyn curtly replied.

"My curves may be more defined but we're the same size."

"I only mentioned it because you may want to borrow something from Lorraine instead."

"Great." Lorraine slapped her leg. "Now you're calling me fat."

"Fat," Tammy shrieked. "Is that what you all think of me?"

"No one is fat, okay. We all look great in our own unique

way. Tammy has a tiny waist with beautiful hips, Lorraine has breasts to die for with long legs, and Iris, you've mastered your gains and your thighs are gorgeous. Then there's me." Brooklyn ran her hands around her body. "I'm what you'd call perfection."

"Someone's in denial." Tammy threw a grape at Brooklyn. "First of all, you got that move from me." Tammy mimicked Brooklyn. "You've gotten a big head since you started working with a trainer. I mean, I get it. You look amazing. I guess the days of having the shape of a teenage boy are in your rearview mirror."

"I never looked like a teenage boy. You're a hater."

"You've gotten sassy." Tammy wagged her finger. "I've got my eye on you."

"She certainly has gotten sassy over the years." I said with a proud smile. It was high-time Brooklyn put her fears behind her. She's more like the girl I met before she knew she had Huntington's disease, and I loved every second of it. I felt like a proud mom. Kind of like the first day I took Junior to school and he didn't cry.

"Great, talk about me like I'm not sitting here hearing it all." Brooklyn grabbed a grape and popped it in her mouth. "How is it possible that everything tastes so much better here? Grapes have never tasted so sweet and fresh."

"That's because all their stuff is home grown and doesn't have to be shipped into the country. So it's fresh. The majority of our food is processed junk. I've been telling you all that for years. Heck, I've even tried to get you to start growing your own vegetables and fruits," Lorraine paused. "Wait, did you just change the subject?"

Brooklyn winked and popped another grape in her mouth. An evil genius.

"May I remind you ladies Brooklyn's aunt will be here in

an hour. Surely we don't want to meet her for the first time, covered in airplane funk, barely combed hair, and wrinkled clothes." Tammy pointed at each of us as if she looked like she'd stepped off a runway.

We dispersed to our designated rooms. It gave me enough time to check on Rodney and Junior.

"Where are you now?" Rodney asked.

"Marseau and it's beautiful. I wish you guys could see it."

"You always wanted to go there. I'm happy you took some time off. It's doing you loads of good."

"How's our boy doing?"

"He's at Frank's house playing video games with his cousins."

"I'll fight the urge to call him while he's having fun," I replied. "I'll wait until tomorrow. I love you guys."

"I love you too."

"Ah, you love me. Why are you fighting this? We're so back and forth. One minute I'm in and you're out. Then I'm out and you're in. What gives?" I asked, rolling onto my back, sinking into the soft mattress. It was like an oversized pillow. Dare I say like resting on clouds.

"I'm always in, but then I hear that voice in the back of my mind," he huffed. "Go be with your friends. A relationship is out of the question for us right now."

"No, I want to expand on this. Why is a relationship out of the question? You don't love me anymore?"

Rodney sighed, "I have a pile of work in front of me that I need to finish before Junior comes home. So, I'll say this and leave it at that. I messed up and you broke up with me rightfully so. But with that mess up I broke your trust. You've been dead set against us being together and I haven't pushed the subject."

"Fine, I'll think about everything you said. But just so you know, yes, my trust was broken. But I love you the same." I pushed the button to end the call so hard I almost sprained my finger. Perhaps I'd push to explore it more at a later time. Right now, it's all about Brooklyn and exploring this beautiful side of the world with my girlfriends.

* * *

We were waiting in Brooklyn's suite when her aunt NoeMi Pichette arrived, standing in the open door with a huge smile, full of excitement. Their family must have strong genes because she looked exactly like Brooklyn's mother, and Brooklyn looked exactly like them both. There was no need to imagine the rest of the women. I already knew what to expect.

NoeMi could teach a class on femininity. She moved with grace. She had a calming tone—even and full of excitement. I wanted to rip off her jumpsuit and claim it as my own. I'll bet her perfume matched her lavish lifestyle.

"I don't need to ask which one of you is Brooklyn." NoeMi held her arms out to embrace Brooklyn. "You look just like us."

Just as I thought. I knew their feminine bloodline was quintessential.

"Us," Brooklyn repeated.

"You'll see," NoeMi chuckled, extending her warm embrace to me and the girls.

Seeing NoeMi so joyful made me hopeful about my own family. Hopeful they'd be excited. Hopeful they'd be warm. Hopeful we could relate to one another. Though I wasn't naive to the fact that having hopes could birth expectations and those pesky things could destroy a person.

We spoke for a moment about the beauty of the city and the food. She laughed at Lorraine and Tammy bickering. They didn't care about NoeMi being there. They fought like two old lesbians who'd been in a relationship for too many decades. We all knew that kind of couple. They stayed together long enough to hate each other. But they're too comfortable to leave the relationship. That's Tammy and Lorraine in a nutshell.

NoeMi's presence commanded attention. You could tell she's a woman in charge. She had a head full of bouncy curls. She didn't wear much makeup, and she didn't need it. Her cheeks had a natural blush, rosebuds lips, and beautiful freckles sprinkled over her nose. A complete knockout.

"I must say, you all look amazing. You're giving me a run for my money." NoeMi went down the line inspecting us. Reminds me of a documentary of how they used to measure the showgirls waistlines. "No one will look at you and think you're tourists." She smiled. "Are you all ready to go to my mother's house?"

Brooklyn slowly inhaled and exhaled. "I'm ready." She gripped my hand until we were inside NoeMi's car.

NoeMi talked the entire drive over to Brooklyn's grand-mother's house. We learned she's been married for twenty years. She has a career in the fashion industry. She has three children, which I'm sure were as perfect as her. She traveled the world doing what she loves on movie sets and fashion shows. The woman's a true rock star in every sense of the word.

After arriving at the massive estate, the driver punched in a code to open the gate. Then we rolled down a long driveway to a hillside stone farmhouse. Though farmhouse wasn't the best description of this massive estate.

"Is that a garden?" Lorraine's eyes just about popped out of their sockets.

"Yes, my mother's most prized possession. She has every-thing you can think of growing out there," NoeMi laughed. "It's a running joke with the family that she probably grows marijuana in between the lettuce and the cabbage because she's always so happy."

"Sounds like my kind of woman," Tammy joked with a soft hand clap.

We walked through the tall double doors that poured into a grand circle entryway. Laughter echoed throughout the house. The smell of whatever was cooking put an instant smile on my face. Reminds me of my mother. She loved to cook grand dinners.

"Brooklyn," NoeMi softly rested her hand on the back of her shoulder. "I want you to meet..."

"I'm your grandmother, Sylvie Boileau," a short petite woman interrupted NoeMi as she shuffled across the room with open arms. She rocked her gray hair in a short stylish pixie cut and she was the older version of NoeMi. Go figure. "You're finally home. Oh my goodness, you're finally home," she cried, pulling Brooklyn into a bear hug.

They cried together. Time actually stopped. I held my breath because I knew how much this moment meant to Brooklyn. We'd stayed up until the wee hours talking about how she'd feel meeting her family. Little did I know I should have shared the same sentiments.

Neither of them spoke. They communicated through sobs. I warned Brooklyn about her mascara. For goodness sakes, she's meeting her family for the first time. She's a softy by nature. Now black lines covered her face.

"It's something about our family. We're replicas of my great-great grandmother Fuana."

"Mother, these are Brooklyn's closest friends, Iris, Tammy, and Lorraine," NoeMi introduced us.

"It's nice to meet you lovely ladies."

We smiled and nodded. Then got out of the way. This wasn't about us.

"You're my grandmother," Brooklyn managed to speak. "I don't know what to say."

Sylvie rested her hand on the side of Brooklyn's face, staring into her eyes. "I sure am kiddo. I'm so happy to finally meet you and I'll never let you go." She led us inside a massive living room. It had a mirror version of the furniture on the other side of the room. It's fitting with their family being full of doppelgangers. "These are your cousins, Camille and Amelie. They're twins," she explained. "This is your cousin Pepper and your cousin Delmar. Your aunt Dorothee is running late. But she's excited to meet you. She'll be bringing your other cousin Henri. Just keep in mind he'll have to grow on you."

"I know what that means," Tammy said. "He's a handful."

"A handful is an understatement," Sylvie emphasized. "Come, come, have a seat everyone. Help yourself to the hors d'oeuvres."

"Is this my mom?" Brooklyn fixated on a picture inside a silver frame.

"Yes, she was nineteen there. We took that picture a few days before she moved away."

"Wow, she's so beautiful. I want to know everything about her."

Camille and Amelie sat on either side of Brooklyn. "You said you were married, right?"

"Yes," Brooklyn replied.

"How old were you when you got married?" Camille played with one of Brooklyn's curls.

"In my 30's."

"That's old." Camille frowned.

"Oh hush, that isn't old." Sylvie swatted Camille's leg.

"How did you meet your husband?" Amelie asked.

"We met at an airport."

I cleared my throat. "Tell them what he did when your things spilled out of your luggage."

The girls looked at Brooklyn with waiting eyes.

"I dropped my bag and everything spilled out. When I looked up he was laughing, dangling a pair of my underwear."

"Eww, I would've decked him." Camille said.

"Trust me, I almost did. But you have to know him to appreciate his crass sense of humor."

The girls and I excused ourselves while Brooklyn bonded with her grandmother. Lorraine couldn't take it anymore. She led us right outside to the garden. There were watermelons, green beans, zucchini squash, peppers, tomatoes, dill, lavender, chives, and the list goes on. It's no wonder whatever was cooking smelled so amazing.

"Now see, this is what I'm talking about. I wish I had this much land to grow my own food."

"I have to admit, this is extremely impressive." I ran my hand across the leaves as we walked. "So what do you guys think of Brooklyn's family so far?"

"They seem nice. I'm happy for her. This is huge," Tammy raved.

"Do you think this will change Brooklyn?" I asked.

Tammy and Lorraine looked at each other, and then came to my side. "You're afraid of what's to come when you meet your family."

"Yeah, you're afraid of how it will change you." Lorraine chimed in. "Talk to us."

"Okay, I got another email last night. A woman says she's one of my four aunts. I also have three uncles and a ton of cousins."

"Wow, that's good, right?" Lorraine pressed her hand against her chest.

"Why would my parents keep this secret from me? I don't understand any of this."

"I didn't want to say anything, but something huge must've happened. People don't cut ties with their family and move away without ever speaking to them again."

Lorraine pulled me further into the garden where no one could see me at my most vulnerable state. "I don't care what they say. You need to get all the answers to move forward with your life. I'm a firm believer in positive thoughts. None of you know this about me, but I'm a foster kid."

Tammy gasped, "What?"

"Yes, I was placed in a foster home at eleven-years-old. My father killed my mother and I was the one who found her. He's still in prison today. She wiped the streak of tears running down her face. "You guys would've loved my mother. She was always singing and dancing. I got my red hair and hazel eyes from her. I wished I'd gotten her freckles, but here we are. Fortunately I was placed with an amazing family. I was an only child to my birth mother and father. So it took some time for me to adjust to having four siblings. I was officially adopted when I turned thirteen." She smiled until her eyes lit up like a Christmas tree. "So, you see, I've experienced the worst of the worst. But I never speak of it because I refuse to let the darkest moment of my life define me. I'm telling you this because I don't want you to live in the darkness. Whatever you learn from your family, accept it for what it is and deal with it. Don't store it away. Talk to someone. Lean on us. As long as you're surrounded in love with shoulders to cry on and people to listen to you unload, you'll be okay. And that's us." She smiled with her hand on my shoulder.

By the time Lorraine finished telling her story, Tammy had me in a bear hug, crying like a baby. It also made me respect her even more because when something like that happens most people are jaded and don't believe in love. "Our broken families must be the reason we gravitate to each other. We all have a story."

"Does Brooklyn know?" I asked. "When she went through all of her revelations with us and Kai as an audience she could've used this."

"Brooklyn is a vault. I shared my story with her long ago. Now I'm sharing it with you." She touched my face. "That's what friends are for."

I rested my hands on Lorraine's shoulders and stared into her eyes. "You're a phenomenal woman. A phenomenal woman you are, and I love you with all my heart. I love you more than you'll ever know. I'm going to take your words and walk into the next phase of my life without fear." I smiled. "Now how about we stop being horrible guests and get back inside with Brooklyn."

"Yeah, I don't want to miss dinner." Tammy inhaled.

"All you ever think about is food. But I'll tell you this," I said, wagging my finger. "You better not get a spot of sauce on my drvce ur it'c your avv."

Lorraine spanked Tammy's butt and walked away giggling. I owed Brooklyn so much, but I owed her even more for bringing Tammy and Lorraine into my life. They're the best girlfriends I never knew I needed. I couldn't imagine life without them.

10

SHE'S A BOSS

The next morning couldn't have come any faster. Brooklyn's Aunt NoeMi had an exciting day planned for us. First on the agenda was lunch at the Fort du Champibeuge Castle with her colleagues and friends. Spending the day at a castle on a beautiful sunny Sunday afternoon sounded way too unreal to play it safe with fashion. So, I wore my new emerald green v-neck silk dress and jewelry set I bought on the island. Best of all, Tammy's luggage had arrived, so she wouldn't need to beg, borrow, or steal an outfit from any of us.

NoeMi and her driver picked us up in a black VIP Audi limousine. Yesterday we were stuffed in the car. She did better this time. We walked out of the hotel like royalty ready to take on the city. People stopped and stared. They were more than likely trying to figure out who the hell we were or thought we were. Didn't matter much to me. The limousine was spacious with two tv screens, a bar, heated leather tan seats, and cooling cup holders. We were royalty in our own right.

We were dressed to the nines, sporting our red rose rings Brooklyn gifted us. I don't know if it was hysteria or if the rubies were sparkling brighter under the Marseau sunny skies, but they were shining.

Confusion struck me when we arrived at a boat dock until I realized we had to take a short boat ride from land to the castle as it stood on a rocky islet on an island of its own with the gulf surrounding it. I appreciated her thoughtfulness of ensuring we were in an enclosed boat so our makeup and hair would withstand the ride.

Magnificent.

The castle superseded my expectations in every way. It was elaborate and true to form, constructed of varying stone sizes and shapes melted into a solid square-shaped fortress with four tall stoned towers.

A hostess showed us to the dining room upon entrance. It was named the Peacock room. The name came from the painted ceiling of a peacock's tail bursting of purple, blue, yellow, orange, and gold colors.

My eyes darted from the people, to the decor, and the food. After a few minutes I became dizzy from excitement. We were on a once in a lifetime venture. The focaccia barese appetizers alone sent my taste buds into overload.

The waiters wore tuxedos and smiles that set the mood for dinner. Whenever one of our glasses were more than half-empty, they'd refill them without being asked. The conversations consisted of fashion industry business affairs. NoeMi impressed me with her wealth of knowledge. She pretty much led the conversations. Some of it I understood. Some were spoken in Italian. Probably trade secrets they didn't want us to know.

NoeMi styled herself in a classic Audrey Hepburn look for the evening—a simple black dress, hair pulled up, and pearls. But she steered clear of the ballet shoe. Instead she wore a pair of black leather Giuseppe high heels. NoeMi intrigued me to no end. It'd take years to peel away her layers, and still there'd be more to uncover. A person with such depth is a person to study. I hoped my family embodied the same class and intelligence as her.

Brooklyn watched NoeMi with proud eyes. I nudged her and whispered, "How are you feeling? I'm sure your brain and heart are in overload."

"I'm overwhelmed. They're all so refined and successful. I feel out of place, sort of like a black sheep," she whispered in a shaky voice that I'd grown familiar with over the years which kicked me into protective mode.

"Hold on," I touched her arm. "You're no slouch. You were raised by intelligent parents who taught you values. You're well-educated and accomplished in business. Yes, they're classy. But so are you. Don't look down on yourself. You fit in just fine. Furthermore, if you were a black sheep, you'd be the most beautiful one of them all."

She smiled. "This is why I love you."

"I love you too. Now have fun. We're in a castle for God's sake."

"You're right, you're right," she said, downing a glass of wine. The waiters topped her off as soon as she sat her glass down. "You'll understand where I'm coming from in due time."

Her words echoed in my head. *You'll understand in due time.* The thought left me shaking like a leaf on a tree in springtime. Kudos to Brooklyn for having the courage to be here with no control over the situation.

My imagination ran amuck. I hoped at least one of my aunts resembled my mother. I missed her terribly. I know it wouldn't be her but a chance to see some likeness of her in the flesh would be priceless. Life cheated me when I lost them at such a young age.

I had a child without my parents ever meeting him. I had

no help to understand how to take care of him outside of Brooklyn's parents. But they were globetrotters at that time. My dad will never walk me down the aisle, assuming marriage is in the cards for me. I'll never get to sit down with my dad as a professional to discuss our cases. Their deaths have never sat well with me, and I don't believe it ever will.

"What if my family is the opposite of yours?"

"What do you mean?" Brooklyn asked.

"What if my family is full of drama?" I asked almost to the point of trembling in fear of what I was walking into.

"So, what if they are full of drama? All they need to do is embrace you." She spoke in a soft enough tone for us to have a private conversation while everyone else carried on. No matter the environment, when me and Brooklyn needed to connect, we would always make a way. Our relationship was like magic.

"But I hope we'll share some commonalities."

"You're blood. That's all the commonality you need."

I sat in silence for a moment to do some inner work. It's hard to look in the mirror and be brutally honest with myself. It's even harder to dissect my negative thoughts. But in order to change, I have to acknowledge it, explore it, and accept it.

"Your names are Brooklyn, Tammy, Lorraine, and Iris, right?" A woman asked with a heavy accent. She wore a ton of makeup with hair as red as Lorraine's hair.

"Yes," I replied with a nod.

"And you are NoeMi's family from another country?"

"I am," Brooklyn answered. "These are my best friends. Well they're more like my sisters." She wiggled her arm inside mine and rested her head on my shoulder for a moment.

"Ah okay, what do you all do? Are you in fashion?" The woman asked the best she could in our language.

"No, I'm in marketing," Brooklyn proudly replied. "Tammy

and Lorraine have their own business in event planning, and Iris is a Forensic Pathologist."

"Ooh, a Forensic Pathologist," a man at the end of the table repeated with his fingers wiggling.

"That sounds interesting. Would you mind going more in depth about what it entails?" The woman asked.

"Yes, what exactly does a Forensic Pathologist do?" The man reiterated.

"I'm responsible for examining post mortem bodies to determine the cause and manner of death. I'm actually the Chief Forensic Pathologist in my county."

"Impressive," the man replied. "How long have you been a Forensic Pathologist?"

"Actually, thanks to Brooklyn I went back to school five years ago. I used to be a Forensic Examiner. So I obtained the needed education to take the next step in my career." I touched Brooklyn's hand. I didn't need to speak. We were beyond words. She knew exactly what that touch meant.

"What a lovely friendship. Not everyone has that." The woman sipped her wine with contention plastered over her face. One would assume she's had a friendship like ours in her lifetime and lost it or never had it at all.

The thought saddened me. Having Brooklyn as my friend all these years has been beyond extraordinary. I couldn't imagine a life never having found that one person I enjoy doing life with. It's funny, people often consider soulmates a romantic partner and you only get one. When in truth it could be a relative or a friend, and in many cases some have more than one soulmate. Brooklyn is my soulmate.

In college, the next semester after Brooklyn and I met, we became roommates. We looked out for each other. She taught me how to apply makeup. I ignited her passion for fashion. Brooklyn wasn't the type to sit in a corner at a party. She was the party. But after her diagnosis of Huntington's disease, she changed. It took years for her to find that confidence again, and it's so fragile. So whenever she feels down on herself, I jump in action to remind her she's a badass.

"I'd love to hear about one of your most profound cases. Could you share it with us," the curious man asked with his hand under his chin.

"Have you ever lost a loved one?"

"Yes." His smile deflated.

"How would you feel if you found out the Forensic Pathologist who conducted your loved one's autopsy used it as dinner conversation?"

"I understand what you're saying." He waved me away.

But I was on a roll. "I treat every case with kindness and respect. They are someone's mother, father, sister, brother, child, uncle, aunt, friend, etc. They deserve respect, even in death."

"My apologies, I overstepped. I overstepped," he repeated.

"I took an oath and I take it seriously. I'm a true believer in bad karma."

"I agree that it could bring you bad karma," NoeMi interjected. "You're feisty. I like that. No one has ever made Efrain apologize."

"This is one for the books," the woman with a ton of makeup laughed.

"Let it go already," Efrain said, turning as red as the woman's hair.

"Will you ladies be attending the fashion show tonight?" The woman asked.

"Yes, they'll be my guests." NoeMi glanced at her Rolex. "Speaking of, we need to get back to the car." She whipped out her phone to make sure the driver was ready to roll.

"How have you all been enjoying your time in Marseau so

far?" Another woman wearing a pair of black diamond eyeglasses with tassels asked.

I hardly ever felt envious, but being surrounded by a group of people who unapologetically embraced their own unique style and chased their dreams made me rethink my choices in life.

I love my career. It gives me a sense of fulfillment. But I chose my career path to follow in the footsteps of my father. I can't remember a time when he wasn't influencing me to become a Forensic Pathologist. Going back to school to honor his wishes for me was still my way of seeking his approval.

One evening back in high school, me and my friend Kelsey were hanging out in my bedroom doing things preteen girls do —painting our nails, playing with our hair, talking about boys, and what we were going to do once we graduated college. I told her I wanted to become an architect. I had a weird obsession with buildings. I'd even drawn blueprints. Plus, I'd make loads of money, if I'd pursued it. Somewhere along the way with my dad constantly bombarding me about following in his footsteps, I lost my way.

"Okay ladies, I hope you enjoyed dinner. Are we ready to head over to the fashion show? I know it's early, but it's my job to make sure everything goes smoothly as the director."

"I sure am ready." Lorraine rubbed her hands together.

"Will we have the opportunity to go backstage or will we need to sit in designated seats to wait for the show to start," I inquired with the hopes of seeing some behind the scene madness.

"I think I may be able to sneak you ladies backstage as long as you promise to stay out of the way and be invisible for the most part. Things can get pretty hectic back there." NoeMi sighed, more than likely in anticipation of a long night of being a superwoman. "There's our boat." She pointed.

The girls talked about the dinner on the way back. I sat in silence to take in what we'd experienced. We actually had dinner in a castle on its own island. Now we're on our way to a fashion show. A week ago, I was in a cold lab. Now I'm boating to castles and going to fashion shows. This trip has tapped into my adventurous side post motherhood. It would be good for me to give Rodney more time with Junior, so I will in turn have more time to further explore the world and have more adventures.

We hurried off the boat and into the car. NoeMi must've told the driver of her time constraint because he zipped across the city in record speed. People were already lining up outside. But just like the important people we were, we entered through the back.

"Stay close to me at all times. But not too close if you know what I mean," NoeMi explained.

We gave her a nod and followed her lead.

"Richard." NoeMi embraced a frazzled man with a kiss on both cheeks. "Dinner was lovely as always. Thank you for hosting me and my family."

"Oh darling, it's a pleasure to be in the company of beautiful inspiring women. I hope we will see you all again soon. Especially you, Brooklyn. I haven't seen such a twinkle in NoeMi's eyes in years."

"I'll make it my business to get back here regularly," Brooklyn replied. The man pulled her into a bear hug. I could tell she was on top of the world.

I held Brooklyn's hand and she squeezed mine. It's our way of letting each other know we were there but giving the other the space she needed.

Everyone ran in different directions with concerned expressions. Busy was an understatement. People were building, decorating, setting up lighting, and putting the chairs in place. But it didn't faze NoeMi. She pushed through the crowd like a boss. As the Fashion Show Director, NoeMi gave detailed instructions on everything to make the show a success from the clothes to the lights to the music. Every aspect of it running smoothly rested upon her shoulders.

"This is my aunt," Brooklyn whispered. "Can you believe it?"

"Right," I replied, wiggling in excitement. "She's a boss. I love her."

"Me too."

"She could rule the world," Tammy said.

NoeMi called a young man over. "Eliot, these ladies are my family. There are four seats marked with my name. Please take them to their seats." She turned to us. "The show will start soon. I never sit with the audience. I have to stay back to make sure things go as planned and if they don't, I need to think quickly. So you all go out there and enjoy. Meet me back here when it's over." She grabbed Eliot's arm. "Make sure you bring them back after the show."

"Ce l'hai fatta," Eliot replied with a smile.

People poured inside dressed in fashions that rivaled the designer's pieces. They had their notepads out ready to buy. No more than a few seconds later every seat was filled, and then the lights dimmed. The designer walked out onto the stage to introduce his new collection.

He didn't disappoint. Heck, I wanted to get my hands on a few of those pieces.

Lorraine hugged Brooklyn. "Thank you for bringing us with you. I'll never forget this."

"Me either," Tammy chimed in. "Thank you."

We found NoeMi backstage celebrating with champagne. "There they are," she screamed. "Did you enjoy the show?"

"How could we not?" I said. "It was incredible."

"You put all this together?" Brooklyn asked.

The designer crept up beside her. "She sure did. There's no way I could've pulled this off without her." He put his hands together in a prayer stance. "You're a gem." He kissed her cheek.

"Oh you smooth talker. Thank you." They embraced. "Congratulations on everything. I know you'll do well. Now go have some fun and live it up. We did it."

"We did it," he squealed. "Nice to meet you. But, especially you," he pointed at Tammy. "You're wearing my dress."

"This was a once in a lifetime opportunity for me to wear a designer piece in the presence of the designer. I had to wear it." Tammy stood tall and proud in the black sheer tiered ruffle gown. Nothing would be able to wipe her smile away.

"You look amazing." He kissed both her cheeks.

Tammy almost passed out in excitement. It set the tone for the rest of the night, and we certainly did more shopping because NoeMi had access to designer pieces not available for regular shoppers. I tried my best to break my bank account. Tomorrow will be our last day in Marseau. Who knew if we'd ever have this opportunity again? I wasn't leaving any chance behind.

Yolo.

"Excuse me." A short bald man stood in front of me. "My name is Art."

"Nice to meet you, Art."

"Are you by chance a model?"

"Actually I'm a Forensic Pathologist."

"Humm, that's impressive, but not my type. I prefer beauty, without the brains." He quickly walked away.

"What in the hell was that?" I asked.

"A lot of men cruise for models in this area. He's a superficial rich guy who more than likely uses his money to control not so bright beautiful women," NoeMi explained. "He'd never date you because you have your own mind and money. You wouldn't put up with his crap. Take it as a compliment."

If you want my heart, just say it.

We ended the day at Brooklyn's grandmother's house for another family dinner. This time everyone was in attendance. They told stories about her grandfather and uncle. They both succumbed to Huntington's the same as her mother. I thought it would bring her down. But she was a trooper. Perhaps being surrounded by family made her stronger—even more so than when she was with us.

Maybe there's something to this family thing after all.

11

TIME IS WINDING DOWN

Three days came and went in the blink of an eye. Sure, the island was beautiful. But, Marseau had been out of this world. The beauty of the city felt like a dream come true, especially with NoeMi as our tour guide. Her connections got us into places we never would've experienced without her. It pained me to leave. But, it was our last night and my turn was next.

I've never been a fan of stepping into uncontrollable situations. The thought made me want to break out in hives. My life could change, and the scary part of it all was, I didn't know if it would be a positive or negative one.

My heart did kicks and flips. But, I had to actively push those thoughts to the back of my mind and be present for our last night with Brooklyn's family. I gave her my word I'd be there for her and she gave me her word she'd be there for me. Being mentally present is just as important as being physically present. That is the only way sisterhood works.

Brooklyn's family were the perfect hosts. They took us in as their extended family without reluctancy. So naturally we agreed to spend our last hours with them which turned out to be the best decision because Brooklyn became terribly ill. Although, it did give me a chance to see how well-versed Brooklyn's family was at taking care of her. Huntington's disease is extremely tricky. I learned over time how to take care of her, but her grandmother made me look like a complete amateur.

I walked around their maze-like estate for over ten minutes in search of the guest room where Brooklyn rested. I almost woke her up when I found her because I was excited to finally escape my Stanley Kubrick, Shining nightmare.

"You could never move in silence." Brooklyn sat up, resting against the oversized brown leather headboard that practically covered half the wall. Her grandmother had her change into a pink blush silk pajama set with feather trim. "I ruined everyone's day, huh?" She looked refreshed and that calmed my fears of her health.

"Of course not." I climbed onto the bed beside her. Laying next to my sister calmed my soul. She had been the cure to all my issues. But most of all, my happiness. "Your family knows what to do. You're in good hands."

"Yeah, it got me thinking," she paused. "I don't know how much time I have left in my right mind with all my physical abilities. I need more time with my family in this way. So, I was thinking about moving here." She took my silence as her cue to keep talking. "You think I'm crazy for wanting to uproot my family and move to an unknown country around a bunch of strangers, don't you?"

"Yeah, actually I think it's insane. We're your family; and that includes your mom and dad—you do remember the people who raised you. Or have you forgotten about them now that you've met your mother's family?"

"I could never forget about my parents. In fact, I want to bring them with me."

"You're serious, aren't you?" I stood from my comfy spot on the bed and backed away. "What about Kai? Shouldn't you talk to him before making a huge decision?"

"Of course I'll talk to him." Brooklyn scrunched her eyebrows. "Why are you reacting this way? I thought you of all people would understand. We've been waiting all our lives to know more about our family. Now that I've met them, I want to know more and time is not on my side. I don't have the luxury of putting things off."

"This is the dumbest idea you've ever had."

"What dumb idea?" Tammy and Lorraine asked, prancing inside the bedroom.

"Close the door," I urged. "Go ahead and tell them what you told me. Go on, tell them."

"What the hell is your problem?" Brooklyn screeched.

"Wait," Tammy stretched out her arms. "Usually it's me and Lorraine at each other's throat. What's up with you two?"

"Yeah, this is weird," Lorraine said, darting her eyes between Brooklyn and me.

"Tell them," I said. "Well, go on."

"I was telling my best friend that I was thinking it would be a great idea to move here so I could get to know my family while I still have all my wits before my disease takes its course."

"It makes sense to me." Lorraine shrugged. "But, without question, I'll miss you."

"Miss her," I replied. "She's not going anywhere. She's just caught up in her feelings."

"I'm almost forty. That's a lot of time for never knowing my family. My son should know them. He'd have a big family to lean on once I'm no longer capable or alive to be there for him. How is it a dumb idea?" Brooklyn asked, staring straight into my soul.

"It's a dumb idea because you don't know these people. I

TASHA HUTCHISON

mean really, they've been nice for three days. They could be total wack jobs for all you know."

Tammy put her arm around me. "I love you Iris, but you're bugging."

I pulled away from her. "It is stupid for her to uproot her family and move to a place where she doesn't know anyone or even the language for that matter. It makes no sense."

"My boys are super intelligent. They'll adapt. Besides, it'll be beneficial for the boys to speak two languages in the long run." She sat on the side of the bed. "It's pretty shitty of you to make me feel bad for wanting to be closer to have a relationship with my family. You know how long I've wanted this. I know you want the same too."

"Don't throw my family issues into this. I'm not the one moving across the world after one visit," I argued. My head felt like it was about to pop. "Ask her about her parents."

"What about your parents?" Tammy and Lorraine's heads snapped to Brooklyn like they were watching a tennis match, and what a match it was.

"I'll tell you about her parents." I didn't give Brooklyn a chance to repeat her stupid decision. "She wants to move them here too. Hasn't asked them a damn thing about what they want. She's living in a fairytale."

"My parents stopped traveling the world to be full-time grandparents. They'll happily relocate to wherever I go. They're travelers at heart."

"So because you want something everyone has to change their lives to appease you. I guess their happiness doesn't matter." I paced, massaging my temples.

"I get both of your points of view. Brooklyn wants to know more about her family. But your decision to relocate does seem rash," Lorraine reasoned.

122

"I must be a man named Paul," Brooklyn said with her hand over her chest.

"What does that even mean?" Tammy asked.

"Are you okay?" Lorraine laid her hand over Brooklyn's forehead.

"Stop it, she's saying she's appalled," I explained.

"Yeah, that's exactly what I'm saying and it sounds like you all bought a lot of it and failed to tell me it was on sale."

"Now you're being a drama queen," Tammy giggled. "Iris, what is this really about? You're being passive aggressive. It's time to reel it in."

"Fine," I yelped, jerking my hand away from Tammy. "I don't want to lose my sister. We've never lived more than twenty minutes away from each other. Now she wants to move clear across the other side of the world because I'm not enough for her anymore. What the hell am I supposed to do without you?"

"Live life," Brooklyn replied. "I love you with my whole heart. No one could ever take your place. You are enough," she sighed. "It's not like we'll be moving anytime soon. I'm smarter than you think."

"That's the problem. I know you're smart, and you're strong as hell. You've got this life thing down. If you want it, you'll have it."

"Thanks, but there are some obstacles that even I can't overcome. However, I'm willing to commit to at least visiting more now that I know them," she explained. "If I moved, would you girls at least agree to visit every now and again?"

"Do we have a choice?" I sighed. People change their minds every day. Brooklyn is no different. By the time we make it home, she'll be singing a different tune. If it's in her heart to move, she'll be on the first plane smoking. Meanwhile, I'll be finding the nearest psychiatric hospital to admit myself.

"So this is where the party is," Brooklyn's cousin Pepper, danced inside the room. "Oh wow, why does everyone look so serious? Should I go?"

"No, no, it's okay. We're just keeping Brooklyn company until she feels like getting out of bed."

"I'm better now. I don't know what concoction grandma gave me, but it helped."

"She used to give grandpa the same thing. He'd be feeling sick one minute, and the next they'd be dancing. She should've been a nurse."

"I'd take being a housewife any day with a kind husband and a beautiful family inside a beautiful castle." Lorraine looked around.

"It's not quite a castle," Pepper giggled.

"It's her castle. That's all that matters." Tammy helped Brooklyn onto her feet.

"The chef is just about done with dinner and Grandma set up the family table in the garden. Do you want to follow me out?"

"Give me a second to change my clothes and I'll be ready."

"Wait, we're eating in the garden?" Lorraine asked.

Pepper smiled. "Have you seen grandma's garden?"

"Yes, it blew me away. She's my idol."

"Well on the west side of the garden is where Grandma had a family dinner table built. When we all get together and the weather is nice we usually eat in the garden. She decorates it according to the season with candles and garden lights. You're going to love it."

"Wow, that sounds lovely." Tammy put her hand on my shoulder and whispered, "You better start preparing yourself for Brooklyn's move because I don't even want to leave this place and they're her family."

"Oh shut it." I freed myself from her.

They were having a ball, dancing and singing to music we couldn't understand. They were a real family. One I've never seen outside of movies. A little too perfect if you asked me. I wanted to see the cracks.

Brooklyn grew up an only child. She'd have a ton of cousins, aunts, an uncle, and a grandparent here. The fact that they love her already is a cherry on top. I can't say that I blame her.

I loved life with my parents. But there were many mind-numbing days with it only being the three of us and no other family. I had an abundance of friends. Though, cousins would've been nice. We'd have a family connection. We could gossip about family drama, laugh at each other, and bond over old memories.

It's in my son's best interest for me to make this right. He has his family on his father's side. But I want him to know my family too.

"Hey Brooklyn, we were just talking about you." Her uncle Bert danced with her.

I felt an overwhelming sense of guilt. How could I be so selfish to keep my best friend from fully experiencing this? The joy in her eyes is undeniable. This only comes once in a lifetime.

The music stopped with Brooklyn's grandmother inviting everyone outside to the garden. The lighted path directed our steps to a long wooden table. She decorated it with flowers, candles, and framed pictures of departed family members. Brooklyn's mother included. It was a thoughtful addition that solidified things for me. They were genuinely good people.

A small menu sat in the center of the table. For appetizers we'd have olives, nuts, and cheese. A charcuterie platter of salami, mortadella, prosciutto with cheeses and bread. The main course; lasagna with a house salad. Then finally for dessert, we'd have zeppoles.

It reminded me of the Sunday dinners we used to have before everyone got too busy to keep them going. They weren't as fancy. But, we'd pile into the dining room of the house for whoever was hosting, eat great food, and have good-hearted conversation.

Brooklyn's uncle Alfio tapped his glass with a butter knife. "I'd like to take this time to say how much we've enjoyed you all the past few days. We hope you won't make this your last visit to Marseau."

"Hey, maybe we could visit her in the states?" Pepper blurted out with excitement in her eyes.

"Oh I'd love that," Brooklyn joyfully replied.

"If nobody else wants to go, I'll go on my own," Pepper reiterated.

"Hey, don't leave me here," Amelie blurted.

"The more the merrier," Brooklyn said with a wide smile. She had a new sparkle in her eyes. Even though I'd fight her tooth and nail about moving. It warmed my heart to see her so happy.

"You say that now until you see how high maintenance the girls are with all their shopping, hair, and nails. They drain my pockets."

"Oh Dad, we're not that bad."

He pulled his empty pockets out. "I rest my case. But seriously, will we see you all again? I don't want this to be the one and only time you visit us."

My heart couldn't take it anymore. I ran away from the table and into the darkest part of the massive garden. It was about a mile long, so it wasn't hard to seek privacy after the sunset. Tears streamed down my face. My breathing came fast. I was losing my sister to this freaky Hallmark family. Things were going to change whether I liked it or not. I never considered all the possibilities of taking this trip. Never in a million years did I think Brooklyn would consider relocating.

Brooklyn called out in a soft whisper, "Iris, where are you?"

"Are you alone?" I asked.

"Yes, where are you? It's too dark."

I walked out from the darkness and said, "I'm sorry."

"Please talk to me."

"About what?"

"Let's start with why you ran away from the table into the pit of darkness."

"Why is it so easy for you to leave me? I thought you were my sister."

"Listen to me." Brooklyn walked closer, gently holding my face. She smelled of a rose reinvented. "The thought of living so far away from you is downright scary. You can't get rid of me that easily. If I move here, I want you and Junior to visit us often and we'll do the same."

"Yeah, that's what you say until life gets in the way."

"Iris, I love you, and a friendship like ours is rare. I'll only be a flight away."

"If I can't drive to you, it's too far. What about our Sunday dinners? Dropping by each other's house out the blue to sit and talk while the kids play. They're practically siblings and you want to break them up. Junior will be all alone."

"You're breaking my heart." Brooklyn pouted.

"It's not my intention," I replied. "Honestly, I can see why you want to move here. You'll have a big family. What about Britt? Are you leaving him behind too?"

Brooklyn's shoulders dropped with her head hung low. "I've spent the majority of my life worrying about everyone else while slowly dying inside. It's time for me to put myself first. None of us are promised tomorrow. I want to know these people. I can see the beauty of their hearts. There's no awkwardness—only love," she thoughtfully explained. "I will leave an open invitation for him to come with us. It's up to him. I can only extend the olive branch."

Yes, I see it, and I'm happy for you. Call me selfish." I hunched my shoulders. "I don't want to lose my sister."

"You're not selfish for feeling." She kissed my cheek. "But neither am I. We'll talk about this later. Right now, I want to get some food before Tammy polishes off everything. You know that girl can eat."

"Oh my goodness, tell me about it. The first time I went out to dinner with her I thought she ordered for the both of us. But then she looked at me and asked, *"Well, aren't you going to order something?""*

We slapped hands and wiggled our fingers. "The dynamic duo forever." We returned to the family table.

"Well that wasn't awkward at all," Alfio joked. But no one laughed. "I'm sorry, I shouldn't have said that. I'm an ass. That's my thing. Are you okay?"

"Yes, I'm fine. I should explain," I said. "Brooklyn and I met in college more than a decade ago. We've been glued at the hip for that long. Now she has all of you in her life and I felt threatened. I'm not ashamed to admit it. She's my person and I hold her in high regards."

"I'm happy she has you. But don't think of us as taking her away from you. We want all of you to be a part of our lives as well. Since Brooklyn considers you her sisters, you're our family," Delfina explained.

"Oh really Aunt Delfina," Casaid. "You never welcomed Gisela into the family."

"That girl was a pot smoking freak and a bad influence on you."

"You've had countless boyfriends since you've gotten

divorced. No one is rude to them when you bring them around."

"That's enough," Sylvie said. "Do you want to scare them away?"

Just the cracks I needed to see. I laughed and poured myself a glass of wine.

"As I was saying before I was rudely interrupted." Delfina cut her eyes at Pepper. "We'd never want to come in between your relationship. Is it okay if we share Brooklyn with you?"

"I would love that," I replied with a nod. My heart fluttered with joy. My biggest fear is losing Brooklyn to Huntington's and now to her newly found family. So, to be included and considered was euphoria.

They didn't hold my outburst against me. I realized at that moment I needed to face my defeat.

"I hope this doesn't come out the wrong way, but why didn't you all ever look for Brooklyn?" I regretted asking the question the moment I said it in fear of ruining dinner.

"After her mother died we lost all contact. We never heard from her father again. We tried a million times in a million ways. Now we know why we couldn't find her. She didn't have the same last name anymore." Her grandmother walked over to kiss her forehead. "I'm sorry if you felt abandoned by us. It's quite the opposite. I wish Britt would've called us if he felt he couldn't handle being your father. We would have welcomed you here with open arms. You never should've been away from us this long."

"I don't know why he didn't send me here. That's something you'd have to ask him. But my mom and dad are amazing people. They gave me everything I needed emotionally and financially." She pulled her phone out. "I'd like to FaceTime them to introduce you? I'd hate to leave without you speaking with them." She made a call before anyone could attest.

"Sweetheart, it's Brooklyn," her mother called out to her father. "How are you doing? We miss you."

"I'm great. Hey dad," she said. "I wanted to introduce you to the family."

Sheila never stopped smiling the entire call. They told them stories about Brooklyn growing up and all her accomplishments. Before the call was over they'd made plans to meet in person.

Brooklyn made her next call to Britt. He almost fainted when he learned we were in Marseau with her mother's family. He apologized relentlessly. He was embarrassed about his inability to be a father. But no apologies were needed according to Brooklyn's grandmother. All that mattered was they were together now. Brooklyn was all cotton candy and sweet nothings.

The pieces to Brooklyn's puzzle had come together. In spite of her plans to turn our lives upside down with this possible move, it was great to see her excited about life. It's something she's desired since her diagnosis. Now she wouldn't have any regrets. Not many people in her position could say the same.

Tomorrow my life will be on full display. My family made plans to drive to my hometown in Pinemoor. It's a six-hour drive from where they live. I'd be the wicked witch of the west if I called it off now.

Once again, unbeknownst to Brooklyn, she inspired me. If your friends don't educate and inspire you, it's time to re-evaluate the friendship.

12

RUN-INS AND HELLOS

We arrived in Pinemoor at noon the next day. My disposition changed the moment I stepped off the plane. It was necessary to protect my mental state. No one and nothing could shake me. That's the name of the game. I didn't want to give them one tear because I wasn't sure they deserved it.

Even busy. I was only hanging out with my friends. It was the hardest lesson I'd ever learned thus far in the most horrendous way.

After Tammy paid the check, I found it hard to breathe. Time was running out. I had to face these strangers soon and I couldn't control the outcome. If I could back out of it all, I would in a heartbeat.

"Hey, hey, calm down. You're not alone." Brooklyn rubbed my arm to help me slow my breathing before I had a full on panic attack.

"Yeah, we'll be right by your side to see this through," Lorraine reminded me.

"Some things are uncomfortable when you're growing and

learning about yourself. But you have to allow yourself to feel those things in order to get to the other side," Tammy preached.

"Iris Reid, is that you?" A voice came from the other side of the restaurant. A voice I didn't expect.

"Derek Carter," I screamed. "Qué diablos estás haciendo aquí?"

"I was about to ask you the same thing. I haven't seen you in years." He grabbed my hands. "You're still a hottie. Wow."

I couldn't control myself. I ran my hand over his chest. His muscle mass had doubled over the years. He'd grown a beard. By now he's thirty-nine, but he looked twenty-five. I could tell life has been good to him. "You're not too shabby yourself."

"I'm in town on business. I'm a private investigator now."

"You would be a P.I.," I teased. When we were in high school, Derek was quite the investigator. Without fail, he wanted to get to the bottom of everything–breakups, thefts–you name it.

"What are you doing these days?"

"I'm the Chief Forensic Pathologist in Fallbrush County," I proudly replied.

"Wow, good for you. I'm not surprised. You're the smartest person I know. Are you married? Do you have children?"

"I have a son, but no, I'm not married. What about you?"

"I have two daughters and am currently going through a divorce." He hung his head.

"Aww, I'm sorry to hear that." I put my hand under his chin to bring his head up. "Don't feel defeated. Sometimes relationships run their course."

"You're right, it was for the best. We weren't good for each other. So we certainly weren't good for our girls," he sighed. "How long are you in town?"

"Three days," I quickly replied.

Tammy cleared her throat.

"Oh," I yelped. "Where are my manners? These are my best friends and sisters, Tammy, Lorraine, and Brooklyn."

They quickly excused themselves after shaking Derek's hand. "We'll go get the rental car and wait for you when you're ready."

"No rush." Lorraine winked.

"I hope this isn't too forward, and I know I'm assuming you aren't busy. But would you like to go out to lunch tomorrow?" Derek asked.

I pondered for a moment. Then thought, what could it hurt? "Sure, I'd like that." I passed him my business card. "I better get out there before the girls get too antsy. It was great to see you again."

Derek didn't want to let me go from his bear hug and I wished he wouldn't either. Then I wouldn't have to go to the house and face these unknown people. But there was no more putting it off. The time had come to finally make sense of my family dynamics.

The girls were chatting away once I joined them in the car. Brooklyn took off at lightning speed. The house was only twenty minutes from the airport. But, with her driving, it'd only be fifteen minutes at the most. Jumping out of the racing car wasn't an option with Brooklyn behind the wheel. No way I'd survive a tuck and roll. For some reason the girl loved to drive on two wheels these days after giving me grief about my driving all these years.

The house looked different. Perhaps the lack of life dwelling within it made it appear dilapidated. I put the key in the gold lock and took a deep breath before opening the door. Every memory I'd created came rushing back all at once. It reminded me of near death experience stories.

Brooklyn had covered all the furniture after the funeral when we were in college. A ton of dust covered those sheets. Cobwebs were everywhere. I hated to think of it as a tomb, but that's exactly what it had become.

The girls jumped into cleaning, starting with removing the sheets from the furniture while I stood without moving a muscle. Small things were left in place from my parents—my mother's brush on the accent table next to a coffee mug. She had the most long beautiful thick black hair. She'd sit in the living room with her coffee, watch tv, and brush her hair. My father's reading glasses sat on top of the newspaper. They were going about their usual morning routine before they left home that day. The fact that Brooklyn left everything in place made me want to kiss her.

Yet and still, it saddened me to know they had no idea their lives were going to end that day. How one distracted driver would crash into them head-on. Life is so uncertain. It only takes one second for everything to change or be taken away from you. It's devastating.

I walked inside my parent's bedroom to remove the bedding so I could put them in the wash. My mother's long white silk gown rested on top of the bed. I held it to my nose, hoping to smell her scent. But it was long gone. So, I sprayed her perfume on the gown and inhaled. I ran my hand over my dad's bathrobe.

I climbed onto the bed, pulled my legs to my chest, and buried my face into my knees. I couldn't handle the flooding of my emotions. I wanted my parents to walk in there and tell me it was all a horrible nightmare. But that didn't happen. The reminder of their death was absolute, and it hit me hard.

Tammy softly tapped on the door. "How are you doing here all by yourself?"

"I wasn't expecting the house to be in this state. It's like they're making a quick run to the store and coming back home."

She sat next to me and put her hand on my shoulder. "Sweetheart, I can't say I understand how you feel, but we're here with you and for you. Take as long as you need. In the meantime, if you need us, we'll be here dusting and cleaning."

"You guys are too good to me. Thank you." I kissed her hand.

In return, she kissed my forehead, and then left me to my thoughts. I eased down the hallway to my bedroom. My parents never changed it when I moved away to college. My posters of 90's heartthrobs covered the walls. Some of my old clothes I'd left behind were still hanging in the closet and folded inside the dresser. Talk about a time capsule.

"Hey," Lorraine peaked inside the bedroom. "There's a lady at the front door asking who we are. You should talk to her."

I raced to greet the unexpected visitor and her familiar face put an instant smile on mine. "Mrs. Fields, how are you doing?"

"Oh, wow, Iris, it's been so long." She hugged me. "How are you doing sweetheart? Are you moving back home?"

"No, I'm only here for a few days."

"We haven't seen you since, well, you know," she said, shying away from my gaze.

"Yeah, coming here would force me to face my reality and I could never bring myself to it." I ushered her over to the green iron bistro table on the porch. Mom would cook a romantic dinner for her and dad on Saturday nights when I'd go out with my friends. She would burn long stemmed candles and break out her best china. Nothing was too good when it came to setting the mood. Before I'd announce I'm leaving I'd watch them for a few moments, but not long enough to be considered a voyeur. They'd hold hands and gaze into each other's eyes.

Then giggle and smile without ever saying a word while soft music played in the background. The love they shared was everything. It's no wonder they left this earth together. They were meant to be.

"How have you been?" Mrs. Fields asked.

"I've been well. When I graduated college, I moved to Woodcrest. My best friend's parents opened their home to me and picked up right where my parents left off. I was blessed to have them in my life."

"That's so wonderful. They sound like wonderful people. What do you do there?"

"Well, first I'm a mom to an intelligent and handsome thir-teen-year-old, and I'm the Chief Forensic Pathologist." I showed her a picture of Junior.

"Oh he's your twin. You're doing so well for yourself. I'm proud of you. Are you married?"

"Well that's the one area of my life I have yet to figure out."

"It's not your fault. Men are fickle as hell," she giggled.

"I can't argue that."

"Would you like for me to call Bianca and tell her you're here for a few days? She doesn't live in town anymore, but I'm sure she'll be happy to hear your voice."

"That'd be great."

She quickly FaceTimed Bianca. "Wow, you look exactly the same. What fountain of youth have you been drinking from? I need the deets."

Bianca covered her beautiful smile with her hand. "Stop it, you're making me blush. Tell me everything about you. What do you do? Are you the life of the parties? Do you have all the men eating out the palm of your hands?"

We spent almost an hour catching up. I learned Bianca had three children. She's been divorced for two years and she's still finding her footing as a single mother. I only had one child. I couldn't imagine having to raise three on my own. Bless her heart. But one thing I noticed was her smile. She's still the same happy Bianca who'd always worn a smile no matter what, and I admired her.

It also made me appreciate Rodney that much more. Sure, we had a failed relationship, but we never deviated from co-parenting our son. We are both very present in his life and hands on. I couldn't imagine not having him as my partner. I would always love him for going above and beyond doing his part.

Mrs. Fields stood with her arms stretched out. "I hope I'll see more of you from time to time."

"I'll do my best to come home more often. It was good to see you and Bianca."

"You as well." I walked Mrs. Fields across the street. The girls had pretty much taken over cleaning the house.

I hung outside for a while to watch the sunset. It set the sky on fire, and in Pinemoor, it could actually happen. I held my head back to allow myself to feel the warm breeze graze over my skin with a deep breath. I could smell the scent of fresh cut grass throughout the neighborhood. It reminded me of summers when my friends and I would meet up to spend the entire day out and about.

Tammy ran outside with my ringing phone in hand. "How are my guys doing?" I answered.

"Everything's good here. Are you in Pinemoor?" Junior asked.

"Yes, how is school going?"

"School's good, mom. Don't worry about me. Dad always takes good care of me."

"I know he does," I replied. "How are things going with Audria?"

"This week I've been calling her Ms. Richmond. She's been

laser focused on her science project," he explained. "She wants to go on a date, but dad's acting weird about it."

"Your dear old dad is having a hard time accepting the fact that you're growing up because then he'd have to admit he's getting older," I laughed. "I'll have a talk with him."

"Thanks mom," he replied with a deep sigh. My poor son sounded as stressed out as me. "I miss you a lot."

"I miss you too honey. I'll be home sooner than you know."

"Oh, I have to go. My friend is here to play Madden with me."

"Okay, I love you. Give your dad the phone so I can have that talk with him."

"Iris, honey, how are you?" Rodney answered.

"I'm well, but I hear you're not," I got straight to business. I can't have him stressing our son out with his issues. "Junior told me you're being weird about him taking his girlfriend on a date. I thought we talked about this. He's growing up. You have to come to terms with that."

"He's too young, isn't he? Don't you think so?"

"No, he'll be fourteen in a few months. Dinner and a movie is okay. This will also give you the opportunity to teach him how to be a gentleman—pull her chair out, open her door, allow her to order first. You know, teach him how to treat a young lady. These are crucial years for him. He needs to learn the values of how to grow into an upstanding man."

"I guess you're right. Have you met any of your family?" He quickly changed the conversation.

"They'll be here in a few hours. The girls are cleaning, and as soon as we hang up, I'll order food to be a gracious hostess and pray this all doesn't blow up in my face."

"Are you staying at your parent's house?"

"Yes, thankfully I listened to you and Brooklyn and paused the utilities every six months instead of totally canceling them. All I had to do was call and resume them while we're in town."

"Good deal, that saved you a lot of time and money. Call me later if you need to talk."

"Thank you for being here for me," I said. "Not many co-parents have this type of relationship. I appreciate you and your friendship."

"What can I say? I love you kiddo."

"Oh you love me?" I reiterated.

"Don't start, Iris You know how I feel about you. But I've screwed it up from my mistakes."

"Let's be clear," I said. "Cheating isn't a mistake. It's a well thought out process. You met up with her, didn't change your mind. You more than likely had a little foreplay, didn't change your mind. You took your clothes off, didn't change your mind. You put the condom on, didn't change your mind. You penetrated her, definitely didn't change your mind."

"You're right. I won't debate you on that."

I ended the conversation before we veered too far off track. This wasn't the night for it. My nerves wouldn't allow it. Love is a complicated thing. At least I had it. My parents shared a great love, but I've never experienced it myself. Rodney was the closest I'd come to experiencing that. With the loss of my parents and the heartbreak I suffered from my failed relationship with Rodney, it's no wonder I had so many issues of not allowing people to get too close.

I could smell a strong scent of Pine-Sol and bleach when I walked inside the house. The girls cleaned it so well we could eat off the floor. Lorraine vacuumed with her earbuds on. I'm sure she was streaming conspiracy videos on Youtube. Tammy went from room to room with a duster. Now Brooklyn, well, she was stretched out on the sofa playing on her phone. Cinderella finally made the stepsisters do the housework.

"Hey, I was about to order dinner. Your family should be here in a few hours. What did you have in mind?" Brooklyn sat up.

"Here I was thinking you were slacking off," I giggled. "I don't have the slightest idea what they like."

"I'll figure it out. Go get yourself together. You don't want to meet your family for the first time looking like that." She wagged her finger up and down from my head to my feet.

I fanned myself. "Yeah, you're probably right." I'd forgotten how much my hair hated the humidity here. A few minutes outside and I was a puffy mess. But I knew the remedy—a slick high bun. I'd already picked out the perfect outfit for the night. One of Marseau's finest. Fashion people hadn't seen our side of the world.

After a long shower, I sat down at my mother's vanity and stared at my reflection. Even I could see the terror in my eyes. But after all the preaching I'd done to Brooklyn over the years when it came to her having Huntington's, if I didn't lead by example in this moment my words would never mean anything to her. I couldn't live with that.

Qué es la vida?

The sound of the doorbell snapped me back into reality. I took a deep breath and stood with my head held high. "It's time."

I eased around the corner. My heart raced. I thought it would leap right out of my chest. My fingers and lips went numb. My legs wobbled. My stomach turned. It was time.

I could see them through the glass door. There were two middle-aged women, two younger women, and two distinguished gentlemen. Their terrified faces mirrored what I felt inside. The time had come to finally meet.

"Hello everyone," I opened the door. "Please come inside."

"Are you Iris? I'm Alisa Moreno," one of the young girls stuck her hand out.

"Hi, I'm Jova Moreno, this is Yoana Cruz, Taiana Moreno, and finally our twins, Mateo and Matias Cabello—your uncles." She took a deep breath. "We're all so excited to meet you."

They bombarded me with hugs and kisses. Usually I didn't go for that kind of affection. But in a strange way they felt familiar. Perhaps this wouldn't be as bad as I thought.

"These ladies are my best friends. This is Brooklyn Rahimi, Tammy Avalos, and Lorraine Collins."

"Nice to meet you all," Tammy greeted everyone with a smile.

"It sure does smell good in here," Mateo followed the scent to the kitchen.

"I must admit, I was afraid to meet all of you. I didn't know if the lack of your presence in my life was intentional or not."

"Not on our end," Jova explained. "But I'm not here to play the blame game. My love hasn't changed one ounce for my sister and brother-in-law. Where are they?" She looked around.

I froze. Why didn't I think this through? Of course they wouldn't know mom and dad died if they hadn't had contact with them for years.

"Oh gosh," Brooklyn shrieked. "You guys should sit down."

Jova gasped with wide eyes as if she already knew it wasn't good news.

The rest of them followed her lead to take a seat except for Mateo who was busy exploring the food.

"I'll go get Mateo." Lorraine raced away. "Hold one second, everyone."

"What's with the sad faces?" Mateo walked inside the living room still chewing whatever he'd picked at.

"I don't know how to say this, so I'm just going to say it," I sighed. "Mom and dad died in a car accident over fifteen years ago."

The howls and cries that came from her siblings opened old wounds. It catapulted me back to my dorm room when the police came to give me the bad news. All I remember was screaming. Then I went into zombie mode.

"I can't believe my sister's gone. We'll never have the chance to make things right," Yoana cried. "Mateo and Matias sat on either side of her. They cried together. It showed me the benefit of family.

Having people who share the same love and sense of loss to hold each other up. My friend's love for me was unequivocal and intentional. But my mother's siblings grew up with her. They had their own bonds. They had memories. To lose someone and not know you've lost them is on another level of heartbreak. Only they would know how to hold each other up and mend their hearts.

Jova walked to the other side of the room to be alone.

"Maybe we should regroup and get together tomorrow night," I offered an alternative to allow everyone a chance to soak in this revelation.

"No," Jova snapped out of her daze. "We lost the chance to make things right with our sister. That's even more a reason to spend this time getting to know you and pour love into each other. We need one another more than ever right now at this moment."

"Good, because I have questions," I quickly retorted. "If you stay, do you think you'll be able to give me those answers?"

"Yes, to the best of my ability." Jova wiped her tears away.

"I want to know where the family has been all this time."

"Oh, so you want to jump right into it. Are you sure you're ready to hear it? I can't lie to you."

"I prefer the truth," I insisted.

"Then the truth is what you'll get. But only after we sit down for dinner. Then we'll talk about everything. Deal?"

"Deal," I replied with a smile although I wanted to scream for her to spill it right in that second. But you catch more bees with honey and patience is of virtue. Not to mention, I just broke their hearts with the news of my mom's death. But, time was winding down, and I'd have to return to life as I knew it. I just want to return to that life with more knowledge of self.

"Oh no, my sweet sister," Jova cried, while staring at one of our family portraits. "I'm so sorry we lost touch. I'm sorry I wasn't there." She kissed her hand and placed it on the portrait. "I don't think I have the stomach to eat. But if you have wine, I'd love some."

"Now see, you guys do have something in common. Iris is a wine connoisseur. She has a wine cellar in her house," Brooklyn explained.

"You got that from your grandmother, Elenor Cabello," Jova said with a crooked smile. "She turned one of her bedrooms into a conversation room with a wall of wine."

Tammy, Brooklyn, and Lorraine made Parole Rojo Brooklyn could cook a top chef under the table, so of course she took the lead. Tammy made fresh guacamole and mexican rice. Lorraine made roasted zucchini in olive oil and chopped onions.

I wanted to rush everyone through dinner. Hear the family secret and finally know the big thing that divided us. But I'd probably scare them if I went into Firecracker Iris mode.

The girls knocked dinner out of the park. Despite my nervousness I enjoyed every bite. However, the small talk fell on deaf ears when I had a much more pressing conversation in mind.

Instead of joining in, I opted to study each of my family members. Jova was the eldest of the siblings. She appeared to take her role seriously. She wasn't pushy, but she took charge. I knew if I wanted answers, I'd more than likely have to go through her. Therefore I'd need to remain on her good side.

Yoana was next to the oldest. She was a true entrepreneur in every sense of the word. Her phone never left her hand. How she ate her food and typed on that thing took a special talent. A trait I definitely didn't inherit.

Taiana was an undiscovered comedian, or so she'd like to think. She made a joke out of everything. I mean really, read the room. I'd need the patience of Job if she made a joke while we're discussing their absence in my life. Alisa was a typical Gen Z, watching TikTok videos during dinner. The twins didn't talk much. They ate their food in silence aside from crying every two seconds. I hated having to be the bearer of bad news. But those are the chances you take when you go no contact with the people you love. No matter whose decision it was to cut contact, it happened, and death also happened during that time.

13
THE WORLD AS I KNEW IT

The moment of truth had finally come. Dinner was over and I was about to get the answers I'd wanted to know for thirty-seven years. Jova and I sat in the emerald green suede wingback chairs by the bay window inside my parent's bedroom. My mother called it her conversation nook. Anytime I had a problem or if we just wanted to talk, we'd sit there and go on for hours.

Alisa and Taiana made TikTok videos outside. Hopefully they were getting paid for all the time they spent on that silly app. Otherwise it made no sense. They're in their twenties. They should be laser focused on their careers. Then again, I used to be like them when I was in college. But my assignments came so easy for me that I was able to have more fun than anything.

Mom and Jova were considerably different. Yet, they shared many similarities. For instance, they both had the same button nose, gray eyes, and long legs. I found myself staring at her just to get a glimpse of what my mother would have looked like had she aged. But the soul inside Jova was much different

145

than that of my mom. I could see light and love in my mother's eyes every time she looked at me. Jova had hardened inquisitive eyes. Perhaps it's me who shares that similarity with Jova since so many people say I have a wall up. Then again, we were getting to know each other. So, that observation could change.

Jova took a deep breath and crossed her legs. "You want to know why the family is disconnected, right?"

"Yes, please tell me." I moved to the edge of my chair.

"Okay, there are six of us siblings. Although one of us is missing today. Her name is Daphne. She was afraid to face you."

"Yes, I saw her name on my ancestry. Why is she afraid to face me?" I asked.

"Daphne is the youngest of the bunch. She was a senior in high school when she conceived you. The rest of us had already moved out and onto the next phase of our lives. My parents didn't want to raise another child. So, they made the decision for Daphne."

"What do you mean?" I asked her totally confused beyond the ability to make sense of all this. "What was the decision?"

"Daphne's hands were tied. My parents demanded she give you to Brenda or she'd be sent away."

"Wait. What?" I shrieked. "What are you saying? My parents aren't my biological parents?" I stood from the chair. A thick layer of sweat covered my forehead. My heart made its way to my throat. For a moment, I thought I'd throw it up right there on the floor at Jova's feet. "I don't believe you. That's a damn lie." I had one hand on my forehead and the other over my stomach. I feared if I pulled them away, I would fall into pieces.

I instinctively walked over to the dresser next to a framed picture of my mother and father. I took the picture when we were on summer vacation. Dad rented a beach house for an entire month in New Bay. After the first two weeks, it felt like we'd moved there permanently, and I enjoyed every second of it.

We spent our days on the beach and went to nice restaurants for dinner. Sometimes we'd stay in and cook together while watching movies. My camera was practically glued to my hand during that time. I took that picture on our first day in the house. Mom and dad were dressed in matching beach short sets.

"Please, calm down Iris."

"Calm down? You're sitting here in my parent's house telling lies. You've got to be one sick individual to pull this kind of stunt."

"I'm not lying. Hold one moment." She typed on her phone.

I could feel myself about to pass out because I couldn't slow down my racing heart. The room spun out of control the same as my life. Everything unraveled in a matter of seconds. Who were these people?

"I don't know you. But I do know my parents. They wouldn't keep something this important from me. They loved me."

"I have no doubt they loved you. But they were your aunt and uncle who accepted responsibility for you. What would I gain from lying about this?"

"Don't ask me. I'm not mentally sick enough to understand your motives. If this is true, and that's a big if," I said. "Why drive all the way here to turn my life upside down?"

"You wanted the truth. This is it. I want to make things right."

"This wasn't the way. You dropped a bomb in my lap and didn't bat an eye." I couldn't wipe my tears away fast enough. "I wish my parents were here."

"For what it's worth, I'm sorry you had to find out this way. But you needed to know. You still have a chance to have a parental relationship with your biological parents when you all are ready."

"I don't believe you're sorry at all."

"I know you're upset, and I obviously have no idea of timing," she sighed. "Could you tell me more about my sister? What did she do for a living? What did she do for fun? Was she happy?"

"You have some nerve."

"I'm begging, please," she said with a stream of tears raining down her red cheeks.

"Fine," I sighed, "Mom told me she gave up her career as a dancer when I was born. But she figured out a way to keep dance in her life by becoming an instructor. She even had her own studio downtown." It was a punch in the gut to share that information with Jova since she more than likely could've put an end to our exile from the family. She held a lot of power. I understand she's just learned of my mother's death. So, if I want answers, I have to play my cards right.

"Wow, I'm so proud of her." She tried her best to chase her tears. But they came too fast. "I missed my sister terribly. Out of all my siblings, she and I shared the deepest connection. We were together all the time," she laughed through the pain. "Your mom and I would stay up late looking through fashion magazines. We dreamed about moving into a glamorous apartment together and hosting dinner parties and going on dates with rich hot guys."

"That sounds oddly familiar."

"Why do you say that?"

"When mom wasn't dreaming about her and my dad's retirement days, she would zone in on my life. She never wanted me to become a Forensic Pathologist. She'd always say I should do something fun that I'm passionate about like publishing a magazine so I could rub elbows with the rich and famous."

Jova flashed a wide smile with tears streaming at the same time. "That's my Brenda."

"You needed me?" Yoana walked inside the bedroom with wild eyes.

"Yes, she doesn't believe what I said about her parents. Tell her."

"What kind of people do you think we are?" The way Yoana eyeballed me; I should be in a fighting stance. "My sister isn't a liar. None of us are liars, and we sure wouldn't drive six hours to lie to someone we hardly know. You're Daphne's daughter. Your father is Alessandro Arevalo. Daphne is married to Richard Conner. They have two daughters and a son. They live in Scarborough. Alessandro is widowed with three sons. He lives in Caster."

My mouth went dry. "I matched with his name too, and Ricardo, Mateo, and Marino. Who are they?"

"They're Alessandro's sons and your brothers."

"This is too much." My mind was blown. This was more than I expected. All I wanted to do was meet a few family members. I didn't want to have my childhood ripped from under my feet. I kind of felt like Daniel Kaluuya in the movie Get Out when the mom sent him freefalling into an oblivion of darkness. I was falling and there was no bottom.

"Yeah, I agree. I couldn't imagine being in your shoes," Jova tried her best to comfort me.

"Please don't try to sympathize with me. You have no idea how I'm feeling." I ran out of there to find my girls. They were outside sitting on the front porch.

"What happened to you?" Brooklyn ran to my side, wrapping her arms around me, wiping my tears away.

"No, please don't hug me right now. I need air."

The girls backed off without qualm. Tammy fanned me and Lorraine did her best to coach me into getting my frantic breathing under control.

"What the hell is going on? Should I ask them to go?" Tammy asked with her hands on her hips like the superwoman she was.

"My life is a damn joke."

"Use your words. What the heck is going on?" Brooklyn asked.

"She's not making sense. I'll go find out." Tammy stormed away.

"Everything will be okay, Iris. Stay calm. Tammy's crazy but she'll get to the bottom of whatever's going on."

Lorraine gave up on comforting me. The betrayal tasted like rotten eggs. I'd been mourning complete strangers.

"Oh my God." Tammy walked outside wearing the same expression as I did when I learned the dark secret.

"Would someone tell us what's going on?" Brooklyn slapped her leg in a huff.

"Iris, do you want to tell them or would you like me to tell them."

I couldn't speak. I simply waved her on.

"Respectfully, to make a long story short, Iris found out her parents are actually her aunt and uncle."

"I don't understand." Lorraine scratched her head.

"Yeah, I don't either. What are you talking about? I met her parents before they died," Brooklyn explained.

"I asked Jova why Iris looked like she'd seen a ghost and she told me everything," Tammy divulged. "Daphne is one of the sisters, and she is Iris's birth mother. She gave her away to Brenda because she was only sixteen when she had her."

"So you're adopted too?" Brooklyn gasped. "Daphne? That's not one of the aunts in the house, is it?"

"No, she's not here." I regained my voice. "Jova told me she was afraid to face me in fear of what I'd do or say to her." I scratched my head. "She made the right decision."

"Oh come on, Iris. Show a little grace. Daphne was only sixteen. If Brenda was in a better position to take care of you financially, she made the best decision," Tammy gave her two cents.

"How was leaving me in the dark about all of this the best decision?"

"Yeah, why'd she give her away to her sister without ever looking back? There's nothing upstanding about that," Lorraine yelped.

I jumped to my feet. "Lorraine's right. I should've asked why Daphne handed me over like a used scarf and went on with her life. I should've asked why my parents left me in the dark. Why was I isolated from everyone? This has only given me more questions."

"Go back in there and get the answers," Lorraine urged.

"Every time I get answers, more questions are raised. What's the point? It's a bottomless pit of deceitfulness."

"I don't care what questions are raised. Keep going until you get them all answered."

I took a deep breath and marched back inside with an even bigger fire growing in my belly. Yoana and Jova were still inside my parents' bedroom looking around and crying. But she agreed to tell me everything. Mourning or not, I was going to make sure she kept her word. "Something's bugging me." I walked inside and shut the door behind me. "If everything you've said is true, then where have you all been? Why abandon us if my mom did the right thing by stepping up to raise me? It's a selfless act of love. Why ostracize her for it?"

"Daphne wanted you to know she was your mother, but Brenda wouldn't hear of it. So by the time you turned one-years-old, Brenda and Raymond cut all contact. They moved away and changed their phone numbers. Raymond even legally changed you guys last name to Reid as his mother's surname. His last name was originally Hurst. We couldn't find them."

"Do you know my dad's family?"

"Your father was an only child. His parents died years ago. They didn't attend their funerals. I always figured their absence was because they didn't want any run-ins with us. I mean, I completely understand because that's exactly why I was in attendance. I wanted to see them."

"Are your parents still living?" I asked.

"Yes, and they're excited to meet you. They're old but their minds are in pristine condition." Yoana touched my arm.

"How do they feel about me? They are the reason for all this muddle."

Yoana stuck her chest out. "My parents were already over-the-hill when Daphne got pregnant. You're an adult. Think about it," she explained. "Some people cannot deal with a newborn baby at that age."

"It's not like they were going to have to raise me until I moved away to college. Daphne would've been of age in two years. So again, how do they feel about me?"

"Nobody is perfect, Iris," Yoana said with scrunched eyebrows. "Making that decision doesn't mean they didn't love you. They made sure you went to Brenda and Raymond because they loved you. If they would've put you up for adoption into some unknown family, I'd understand your hesitation to believe they care about you. But that's not what they did. Give them a break."

I hated to admit it, but she was right. Although I wasn't ready to let her know I agreed with her. I walked over to the window and looked outside at the callery pear tree mom and dad helped me plant when I was nine-years-old. There were so many wonderful memories around the house that wouldn't allow me to be upset with my parents. I wanted to be alone. I was afraid of spreading my bad energy. A ticking time bomb had nothing on me. I was angry. I was vulnerable. I was confused. Every emotion known to man, I embodied it. "I'm not ready to make a commitment to meet them. I need time to take this all in."

"That's understandable," Jova sympathized. "We'll be here for two more days. Then we're heading back to Caster. Maybe it's best we call it a night. We all have a lot to think about. We could pick this up tomorrow for dinner. Are we still on?"

"I can't say right now. I'll think about it."

"That's fair," Jova replied, resting her hand on Yoana's arm. "We'll give you a call tomorrow."

Being the fireball she was, Yoana pulled away to speak her peace. "I canceled a lot of business affairs to be here. That should show you how much this means to me. We want to get to know you. Don't push us away. That's the same thing Brenda did. Now she's gone." No one could silence her. Not even Jova. It would've been nice had she spoken up to my parents before they wrapped me up and ran off in the middle of the night.

"Who asked you to cancel your business affairs? My world has been turned upside down, so you'll have to excuse me for needing a little time to come to terms with this life-changing revelation."

"Come on Yoana. It's been a long night. Let's round the crew up and give her a little space for the night."

I walked them to the living room. We said our goodbyes the best we could with our raw emotions. I sat on the porch with the girls and watched my family disappear down the street. We sat in complete silence until my phone rang.

"How did everything go with your family?" Rodney asked.

"I promise I'm in the Twilight Zone." I walked away from the girls with the phone stuck to my ear.

"Talk to me," Rodney fast-talked.

"I met two aunts, two uncles, and two cousins. There's another aunt, and it turns out she's my birth mother."

"Wait, I don't think I heard you correctly. Repeat that."

"Oh no, you heard me right. My mom and dad aren't my biological parents. My birth mother's name is Daphne and my father's name is Alessandro. I have five siblings. Daphne has two daughters and a son. Alessandro has three boys."

"Unbelievable," Rodney sighed. "How are you taking all this in?"

"I'm crushed. I don't like being lied to, especially by people who claim to love me unconditionally."

"Do you believe this to be true?" he asked.

"Of course I have to take their words at face value for now. But it explains so much. I never knew any family outside of my mom and dad. No one ever visited us. We didn't visit them. There were no phone calls. We were out here on our own. It never made sense to me."

"How'd they manage to keep this from you for so long?"

"According to Jova, my parents cut all contact with the family before I turned one-years-old. They changed our last names. No one could find us. They went out of their way to make sure I never learned the truth."

"Your family will be there for two more days right?" Rodney asked.

"Yes, why?"

"Would you like me to bring Junior there to meet them? Are you going to meet your birth parents?"

"No, this isn't the right time for him to meet them. I'm still processing everything, and like you said, we don't know what's true. I don't know these people," I never took a breath. "Daphne didn't come because she was afraid of what I would do or say to her. I don't want to expose my son to this mess."

"I get it. Calm down," Rodney replied. "What do you think you'd say if you met her?"

"I have no idea."

"What I'm about to say is not meant to hurt you," Rodney explained. "Did you ever know who you were? Wasn't that the point of this trip? To find yourself? Put the pieces together? Daphne and Alessandro are the two biggest pieces of the mess of a puzzle you call your life. You can't complete it without them. The least you could do is hear them out. Then you could finally make peace and truly get to know yourself for the first time in your life."

"That's easy for you to say. You're not the one dealing with all the bullshit."

"You know what, you're right," Rodney backed down. "I'm not the one dealing with this. But I am a co-parent to our child, so if it affects him, it affects me. With that said, I'm making arrangements to get there. I'll leave Junior with my parents. You can introduce him at a later time."

"No Rodney, you don't have to come here."

"I know I don't have to. I want to be there—with you," he clarified. "You've got your girls. But they aren't all you've got. I'll see you soon." He ended the call before I could talk him out of it.

The girls had gone back inside the house. I could see them busily cleaning the kitchen through the window. For a moment, I drifted back in time. I envisioned my mom moving about the kitchen while dad worked in the yard. They were great parents. I never wanted for anything. But I couldn't help but wonder how different my life would've been if we were a part of a tribe instead of the three amigos against the world.

I crept through the house to avoid the girls bombarding me with more questions than I had the answers. They mean well, but there's only so many, *"how are you feelings"* I can stomach. I walked inside the study and quietly closed the door. Surely there had to be something in here to connect the dots. There was nothing. My parents had covered all their steps.

But there was one place they never allowed me to go—the attic. Said it was too dangerous. I high-tailed it down the hallway and pulled the ladder down. It was covered in dust and cobwebs. Boxes were stacked almost to the ceiling.

"Iris, are you up there?" Brooklyn called out.

"Yes."

Within seconds, the girls climbed up to join me.

"What are you looking for?" Tammy asked, swiping her hands together to clean the dust off from an old box she'd touched.

"Answers," I replied. "There has to be something in all of this."

"We'll help you." Lorraine grabbed a box.

For the next couple of hours we poured through the boxes, looking for anything to corroborate Jova's story. We found old photos of my parents with their respective families. My aunt and uncles were younger, but I could tell it was them.

"None of this makes any sense," I mumbled.

"Umm, Iris, this is addressed to you." Tammy passed me a sealed envelope.

"It's my mom's handwriting." I ripped it open without thought. I didn't care what she'd written. I was already drowning in the deep end of lies. What else could there possibly be?

Tammy and Lorraine stood on either side of me with Brooklyn behind me. They all had their hands on my shoulders and back. They held me up with their energy and love.

"You know what? I think I want to go to my parent's room to read this."

"Are you sure you want to do this alone?" Brooklyn asked with the saddest eyes.

"Yeah, I'm sure. I have a lunch date with Derek tomorrow. So after I read this I'm going to call it a night." I held a stack of photos and the letter to my chest.

"You still want to have lunch with him after all this?" Brooklyn asked.

"I haven't seen Derek in years. I want to spend some time with him. Plus he's a good distraction."

"Okay," alas Brooklyn backed off. "Go ahead and read your letter. We'll put this stuff away."

14
THE LETTER

After I got away from the girls I went to my parent's bedroom and grabbed my mom and dad's picture and sat it on the bedside table so they would be near me while reading the letter. My hands trembled as I opened the letter. A picture fell out. It was my mom and dad with a woman holding a baby. They were standing outside of our old house. She'd penned on the back, *Brenda, Raymond, Daphne, and baby Iris.* Seeing her face while reading her words felt all the more real.

My sweet Iris,

If you've found this letter, that means you've been in the attic. Which also means, we're gone by now. I wonder how old you are. Isn't that something? The date is, January 25th 1999. You're sixteen-years-old, and actually in your bedroom with Bianca, playing music and talking about boys. Yes, I know you talk about boys. Derek in particular. He's a sweet young man. I love how considerate he is of you and respectful he is of your father and me. If you haven't gotten married as of this letter or in love with a significant other, remember those characteristics and don't accept anything less. You are worthy of it and so much more.

You've been an amazing daughter. You never give us any problems. You're simply perfect. I'm sure by the time you find this letter you'll have done amazing things in your life. But there is something very important I need to tell you. I hate to cop out and write it in a letter, but your father hasn't given me much of a choice in the matter. If he finds out I'm telling you this, I'm afraid it will be the end of him and I.

I'm sure you've noticed the lack of family outside of the three of us. No summers enjoying family gatherings. There haven't been weekends with grandparents. I'm truly sorry about that. I accept my part in keeping you away from everyone. I can only pray it hasn't ruined your outlook on life and family. So, I guess I'll stop stalling.

When you turned one, we severed ties and moved away from everyone who knew us. The reason is because of my sister, Daphne. She would visit you around the clock, and when she wasn't with you she'd call to check on you. She became an emotional wreck, and it's all because she terribly missed you and she missed you because she's your birth mother.

Please don't stop reading. Allow me to explain.

Daphne was only sixteen when she became pregnant with you. Mom and dad thought it would be best that your father and I raise you because we were married and already well-established. We'd recently learned we would never have children of our own due to a childhood injury your father suffered. We knew we wanted to be parents, so making the decision to raise you as our own was easy.

I remember the day we got the call from my parents. They'd gotten older and couldn't see themselves raising another child. Little did they know, God answered our prayers because that meant we'd finally complete our family.

Who knows what will happen over the years. Maybe your father will have a change of heart and we will tell you ourselves. But I don't see that happening. He's so afraid we'll lose you if you learn the truth. He believes in his heart of hearts that you'll run into the arms of Daphne and Alessandro and forget about us. I've told him a thousand times you'll love us the same and to have a little trust in you. But in the words of your father, "there is no need to complicate something that's already so beautiful."

If this is your first time hearing the truth, I beg for your forgiveness for the both of us. I've always let your father run the show to my own detriment. I hope this is a trait you won't pick up from me.

I wish I was sitting next to you right now. I'm sure you have a ton of questions. You have the right to be upset with us. But all I ask is that you won't hate us but understand. We didn't want to lose you. I say we because I selfishly went along with your father's decision. I miss my family terribly. We were so close, especially Jova and me. I never in a million years would've thought I'd be separated from them in this way. I feel like we're stranded on an island. I wish you could've gotten to know them. They're really good people. Maybe one day you'll find them.

If you do, please be open to meeting them and establishing a relationship with them. They're loyal people who will shower you with love and support. Jova, Yoana, Mateo, Matias, and lastly but not least, your mother, Daphne.

I love you with my entire heart and soul. It's not our intention to hurt you. We love you immensely.

Fingers crossed I will be able to tell you all these things face to face, so we can talk about it. The thought of you learning these things without us being there tears me apart inside. But right now seeing your innocent sixteen-year-old beautiful face has driven me to write this letter to make sure you know the truth. God forbid you never find out.

Now I'm about to come and bust up your girl time.
XoXo Love Mom XoXo

I closed the letter and screamed, "Guys, please come here."

It's like they were waiting outside the door because they ran inside the bedroom like the three stooges, Larry, Moe, and Curley, tripping over each other.

"Read it." I passed the letter to Brooklyn. Lorraine and Tammy stood on either side of her to read along. Their eyes darted from left to right. Their sighs and gasps let me know how far they'd gotten in the letter.

"So your mom wanted to make sure you knew the truth. That's good, right?" Brooklyn asked.

"Yes and no, she should've told me herself. She knew the letter was a cop out."

"I agree," Tammy wagged her finger. "It would have been better to make sure she could help you through your emotions upon finding out. To leave this letter and let you process it without them or family seems cold."

"Bingo," I replied.

"That's a bit harsh," Lorraine chimed in. "If I couldn't have children and I adopted Violet, I don't know if I'd want her to know either. You hear stories about this all the time. When the kid finds out they are adopted, sometimes they abandon their adoptive parents for their biological family, leaving them heartbroken and alone."

"But look what their secrets have done to me. As a parent you should be able to step outside of your own feelings and do what's best for your kid."

"You have to get beyond your own selfish feelings when you're a parent. You have a duty to do what's best for your children and quite frankly I don't believe my parents made the best decision. They failed me," I cried. "After reading the letter, I can no longer say Daphne gave me away without ever looking back. She took it the hardest. She also had no say in the matter. She was a sixteen-year-old kid. How was she going to take care of a child on her own without the help of her parents? But Alessandro is still a mystery. He was never mentioned in the letter. Did he care? Did it affect him in any way? Was he happy I was out of sight out of mind?"

"That's why you should speak with them. Put this to rest once and for all," Tammy said.

"Every time I learn a truth another lie is uncovered. When will it end?"

"I know this was all from my doing, but I think you should leave it alone," Lorraine said.

"Too late, trouble maker. The truth is already out." Brooklyn exclaimed.

We spent the rest of the night throwing out different scenarios of what could happen if I reached out to my birth parents or if I put all this behind me and carry on with my life. But I'm not someone who operates well with unanswered questions. Stuffing this in a box and going on as if it never happened would be impossible. There was finally a clear path for the journey of me finding myself, and I needed to take it.

15

CAN OLD FLAMES STILL
BURN HOT?

Derek arrived at noon the next day with three dozen yellow roses for the girls and one dozen red roses for me. *He remembered.*

When we dated in high school, Derek would buy me red roses every Friday. That's what my mother referred to in the letter. I'd open my locker and there would be roses with a silly note saying something like, *can't wait to squeeze your butt at lunch.*

Romantic, huh?

Derek and I shared a wonderful connection. But it was puppy love. Relationships are different when you become an adult. You have to consider all the responsibilities that come with adulting like kids, bills, work, and constantly be open to compromising and communicating.

I needed to get to know the adult Derek. Sure, he looked good with his fresh haircut and crisply ironed navy button down shirt, jeans, and brown dress shoes. If I passed him on the street, I'd give him a second look. But what's in his heart? Who is he these days?

"Wow, you look fantastic," he said with a toothy smile, admiring my short yellow ruffled dress. "I bought roses for you and your friends."

"I like him." Tammy took the three dozen yellow roses. "We appreciate your thoughtfulness."

Lorraine and Brooklyn ran over to claim their roses. "Thank you." They snatched them from Tammy's grip.

"Where are you taking our dear Iris for lunch?" Brooklyn asked.

"Red Chops Bottle and Bites." He kissed me on the cheek and passed me my roses. His mustache tickled my face. I had to get used to this grown-up Derek. Back in high school he couldn't grow a strand of facial hair. Now he walked around with a full mustache and a five o'clock shadow. I also wasn't used to seeing him so buff. Time had been good to him. I was enjoying the view.

"A steakhouse?" Tammy asked.

"Yes," Derek turned to me. "Are you okay with steaks? You haven't gone vegan on me, have you?"

"Slow down," I touched his chest. "I love steak." I turned to Tammy. "See what you do? You scare people." I passed my roses to Brooklyn. "The vases are in the kitchen cabinet near the door that leads to the driveway. I'll see you guys later to start dinner for the second round tonight."

"What's the second round mean?" Derek asked as we walked out of the house.

"I'll tell you later." I slid inside Derek's Mercedes G Wagon. The seats were already heated. The last time we were in Pinemoor I rented a sports car for the weekend. Loved it so much I bought one the moment we were back home. Now Derek made me consider a G Wagon. I've got a cute coin. I could make it happen.

He'd changed in many ways. But one thing remained the same. He was still a neat freak. I wondered if he kept a hand held vacuum in his car like he did back in high school. If we tracked dirt or spilled anything he'd go bananas. It didn't matter where we were. He'd pull over to vacuum his car. My friends hated riding with him. But they didn't have a car, so beggars couldn't be choosers.

"I love your car."

"Thanks, but it's not a car. It's a G Wagon," he corrected me.

"Ooh, I stand corrected. What year?"

"2023," he replied. "I can't believe you're here. You left us in the wind after," he paused.

"My parents died—is that what you were going to say?"

"Something to that effect. Why did you disappear?"

"I wanted no parts of my old life. I couldn't deal with anything that reminded me of my past because then I'd have to deal with the fact that my parents were gone and actually confront my grief."

"Why are you back now?"

"It's a long story," I huffed.

"Good thing we're having lunch. We have time to talk." Derek hopped out and raced to open my door. Then he did it. He pulled out his handheld vacuum to go over the floor mats. It took everything inside me not to hurl over in laughter.

"I can't believe you still do that."

"Cleanliness is next to godliness."

It appeared Red Chops Bottle and Bites still held the title of being the hottest spot in town. But it had a complete facelift. Thankfully so because half of the tables and chairs were hanging on by glue and a prayer.

Props to the owner.

"If it isn't Iris Reid. What brings you to town?" My high school nemesis asked with judgment in her eyes. "You two just can't seem to get enough of each other."

Jasmine Carter. She made my life a living hell in high school. She was in the group of "*it*" girls. They taunted anyone who didn't worship them. But for some reason, Jasmine focused more on me. Especially when it came to Derek.

"Oh but you sure tried to stop it, didn't you." I replied with hell in my veins. "Don't think I forgot." Derek pulled me away before we went into a place of potentially causing us both to regret this lunch date.

"I have reservations for two," he explained. "If you could seat us, that'd be great."

"Follow me." Jasmine never walked like that. If she swung her hips any harder she'd pop her spinal cord. "Here you are, almost the best seat in the house. Peace offering?" She stuck her hand out.

I begrudgingly accepted. We were much too old to continue fighting like teenagers. Besides, I had bigger fish to fry. I didn't need any more problems.

"Great, it's high time we leave the past in the past. I'm actually happy to see you looking so well. My condolences for the loss of your parents."

Could it be? She actually has a heart now. "Thank you. That was nice of you."

"You're welcome." She smiled. "Your waitress will be with you soon."

"Now see, you two can play nice," Derek chimed in.

"I should be upset with you," I replied. "You were my boyfriend, but you were riding her around town like it was nobody's business."

"Oh, for the love of God. We were partnered for a project. We had to gather supplies. I've told you that a million times.

You were territorial and wouldn't listen to anyone but that voice in your head."

A perky woman arrived at our table with a big smile. "Hello, my name is Jennifer. I'll be your waitress today. What could I start you with?"

"A cabernet sauvignon would be great," Derek ordered. "You were about to tell me what brought you back into town after all these years."

"My friends and I took ancestry tests. Brooklyn is adopted, and well, you know my story. So we decided to go on a journey to connect with our family."

"Have you met any of them?"

"Yes, they're lovely people. But they dropped a major bomb on me."

He sat his glass down to give me his undivided attention. I loved that about him. He knows how to effectively communicate. "What happened?"

"It's too heavy. Thinking about it makes me lose my appetite. I only came because I wanted to see you and get out of the house to clear my mind."

"This must be major?"

"What's bigger than major?" I couldn't hold back my tears any longer. They came in full force. Before I knew it, I'd turned into a full-on mess.

Derek gave me a hug and a kiss on my forehead before I completely fell apart. "Hey, hey, talk to me."

"Go back to your seat," I ordered, wiping my eyes. "I don't want Jasmine to get excited because she thinks we're fighting. You know how she is."

"Okay, but tell me what's going on. I'm in the dark here."

"I met my aunts yesterday, and by meeting them I learned my parents aren't my biological parents."

Derek gasped. No words. Just animated sounds.

"Tell me about it," I validated his disbelief. "They also told me one of my aunts is my birth mother."

"Do you believe them?" He asked with raised eyebrows.

"I wanted answers. So, me and my friends searched through the boxes in the attic. I knew I'd find answers there because that space was off limits to me per my parents."

"Well?" He urged almost climbing over the table in anticipation.

"I found a letter my mother wrote to me when I was sixteen. It confirmed they never intended on me finding out about this until they were dead and gone."

"How do you know their intentions?"

"She admitted it in the letter, Derek. Keep up," I snapped. "My biological mother was sixteen in high school when she got pregnant with me. So her older sister who I thought was my mother all these years took me in and raised me as her child."

"Call me biased because I loved your parents, but I'm sure they had good reasons for severing ties with their family."

"Not so fast. My mom pretty much threw my dad under the bus, saying my dad was afraid they'd lose me if I learned the truth. They thought I'd gravitate towards my birth parents and forget about them. But I've missed out on thirty-eight years of having them in my life. There's no way they could do that with good intentions."

"Put yourself in their shoes. They never meant to hurt you. They loved you."

"I have major issues that stem from not knowing my family. When I had my parents, it didn't bother me as much. But after they died, I was alone. I had no family to lean on, and after a while I got used to being alone until I met my best friend, Brooklyn. She's the reason I'm friends with Tammy and Lorraine. Otherwise, I never would've been open to befriending them."

"Damn, I never thought about you being alone. I knew you didn't know your family but it never dawned on me when I heard about your parents passing."

"You of all people didn't wonder if I had anyone to help me get through the most traumatic time in my life."

"I thought about you often, but I had no way to contact you."

"Okay big time private investigator."

Derek held his hands up in a surrendering position. "Ah, see that's where you're wrong. I was a college kid. A broke one at that."

"You're right, you're right," I surrendered. "I'm a little on edge. I need to remember you're my friend and not my enemy." I sighed.

"Hello," the waitress towered over our table with perfect timing. "Are you two ready to order?"

"Ladies first," Derek said with a nod.

I ordered a Caesar salad. My stomach couldn't hold much and I didn't desire food. This journey was taking a lot out of me, and with that went my appetite.

Lunch with Derek gave me a much-needed break from the girls going on about my family drama. This unraveling mystery had already taken a mental toll on me. I put on a good enough front to keep people from worrying about me, but I wasn't sleeping. I didn't have an appetite. I could only do my best to exist.

"If you ask me, I'd say leave it alone. Like I said, your parents were great. Trust their reasons for cutting ties and move on."

"You know me better than that. I want to know why," I explained. "Besides, the door is already open. I've met them, and my mom encouraged me to be open to meeting my family. She said they're good people."

"Wow," he whispered. "If you want, I can put my skills to work and get your bio parent's addresses for you."

"You'd do that for me?" I could feel myself lighting up. It felt much better than being held prisoner in the darkness.

"I don't think it's a good idea. But I'll do it if that's what you need in order to feel whole," he said with a half-smile. People are placed into our lives for a reason. I hadn't seen Derek since we graduated high school. Running into him wasn't a coincidence. I needed him to help me along this journey.

"Thank you. Thank you. I'll text you their names and where they live. We'll be here four more days. If you find their addresses, and I have the nerve, I'll plan a trip to meet them."

"I remember when you'd tell me how you wished you had siblings and cousins. Now you have five. This is life-changing. Something you've always wanted. But that doesn't necessarily mean it's a good thing. Too many personalities could come with a lot of drama."

"It already has. Learning about this secret comes with knowing my parents may have lied to me my entire life. They cheated me from having the experience of growing up with siblings and cousins. How could they have ever loved me knowing they were keeping those things from me? I'll never get that time back."

"Everything I'm saying must be going in one ear and out the other." He gulped his wine. "This doesn't automatically mean your parents didn't love you. It could be the exact opposite. They could have loved you so much they wanted to protect you from those people."

"I don't believe that for one second. I told you my mom said they were good people. Their reasoning was selfish," I replied, on the cusp of becoming irritated. "What's funny is you and my dad were always at odds. Now look at you taking up for him."

"Well, no matter what happened, they gave you a great life. You were a spoiled rich kid who went on to college with your tuition paid in full. The rest of us are still paying off student loans." Derek's face twisted in angst.

"You're right." I finished the last of my salad. Derek had a lot more to go with his slab of ribs. Seeing them made my stomach turn. "But I still want these so-called bio parent's addresses. I have questions and they have the answers." I rested my hand on top of his.

Derek smiled from ear to ear with red cheeks. Sitting there with him made it impossible not to think about the past. The first time Derek came to my house, dad wouldn't allow me to answer the door. He stood tall in all his six-foot six glory. I thought Derek would run away screaming. But he stood tall as he could at a mere five feet seven with his chest stuck out.

Dad talked with him for almost an hour before I ever had a chance to see him. When I did come out, he handed me a dozen red roses. Some of the stems were broken from Derek squeezing them so tightly. But I loved the gesture. So it warmed my heart to see after all these years Derek still remembered to buy me roses.

"What are you thinking about over there?" He asked.

"You."

"Oh yeah?"

"The first time you came to my house," I laughed.

"Please don't remind me." He rubbed his head turning red as vampire blood. "Your dad told me I better keep my hands to myself or he'd put his hands on me."

"Is that why you never held my hand or even hugged me goodbye that day?"

"Hell yeah," he screeched. "Do you remember how big your dad was? I knew I had a good chance to outrun him. But I didn't want to find out because I wanted to see you again outside of school."

I laughed so hard the wine almost spewed from my nose. "Dad never told me he said that. But I should've known. He was so overprotective."

"He loved you."

"Yeah, he did. They both did." My heart smiled about my parents for the first time since I learned the truth. My parents were human. They deserved some grace. It's the least I could do after all they'd given me. "Thank you for dinner and the kind words. You always knew how to make me feel better."

After Derek paid, we held hands and walked out of the restaurant. But before he opened my car door he looked into my eyes and said, "I don't want to play it cool with you. We're way past that. You stole my heart back in the day and you still have the same effect on me. Would it be too presumptuous of me to think you feel the same way?"

"I don't believe feelings for a first love ever go away."

"Would you stay the night with me?" He asked, gently brushing his fingers through my hair.

"Absolutely not," I bellowed. "We haven't been in each other's lives for years. I don't know who you are these days. I wouldn't feel comfortable staying with you."

"That's the point. I want to get to know the woman who stands before me now. I appreciate the few hours you've given me here and there. But soon we'll be going our separate ways. I'd like more uninterrupted time with you."

"Blame it on me being a Forensic Pathologist. But I don't feel comfortable being alone with you. People thought they knew Dexter. But that didn't stop him from being a serial killer with a fridge full of blood samples."

"Oh man, that used to be our favorite show."

"I'm sorry," I laughed. "I had to do it. But, I'll make a deal with you if you're interested."

"I'll take anything you give me," Derek said with raised eyebrows.

"If you want, you could stay the night at my parent's house with me and the girls."

"Deal," he yelped without thought. "Mind if I stop by the hotel to grab a few things?"

"I'll wait in the car," I replied.

I knew the odds were low that Derek had become a serial killer. Though after hearing stories from the family and friends of the people I've autopsied, you learn not to operate on blind trust.

The conversation reminded me of a case. A twenty-six-year-old woman reconnected with an ex-boyfriend she dated at nineteen. They essentially broke up because he was too controlling. Years later she let him back into her life after he promised he'd changed only for him to end up taking her life. Sometimes second chances can be deadly when it comes to love or at least what you believe to be love.

I must've rubbed off on the girls because after I explained why Derek would be crashing on the sofa, they took a picture of him upon our arrival. When he asked why they took his picture, Tammy responded, *"If the police ask for an updated photo, this is what they'll get."* She shook the camera phone with a menacing glare.

Proud was an understatement.

Derek and I stayed up until dawn sharing details about our lives since we graduated high school. We even shared a kiss. He's a good prospect. He ticks all the boxes off my checklist of the kind of perfect mate.

Lucrative career ✔

Financially stable ✔
Present father ✔
Owns property ✔
Well-traveled ✔
Except, I didn't feel anything when we kissed. *Damn it.*

16

SECRETS NEVER STOP AT
JUST ONE

The next morning, Derek woke up before me and the girls. So, he ran out to buy muffins, kolaches, and coffee. He didn't forget my red roses. I never shared with Derek that my dad told me how much of himself he saw in Derek. As long as I could remember, dad would buy mom flowers every Friday. There wasn't a day our house didn't have a vase of fresh flowers.

I could make those same special memories with a man like Derek. The little things are what matter to me. You could date or marry a guy with all the money in the world. But if he doesn't care to learn your love language, none of what he does will add up to a hill of beans. When you have a significant other, you should take the time to learn how they receive love. Derek had a good idea of my love language although it has expanded since becoming an adult. He knew how to ask the pertinent questions, and then put his knowledge in action. That's nothing to scoff about.

"I have something for you." Derek hid his hands behind his back.

"What is it?" I tried to reach around him.

After a few minutes of him laughing at the sight of me struggling, he handed me a piece of paper. He'd gotten Daphne and Alessandro's addresses. I thought things had gotten real when I read my mother's letter. This small torn piece of paper made things real.

"When did you have time to do this? We talked all night."

"It's what I do." He waved his hands as proud as a peacock.

I held the paper in my hand and collapsed onto the sofa. I couldn't pinpoint an exact emotion. I felt excitement, anger, nervousness, and curiosity all wrapped up into one.

"Hey, hey, are you okay?" Derek rubbed my shoulder. "I thought this is what you wanted."

"It is," I replied. "I think. I mean I'm conflicted. I want to talk to them. Then again, I don't want to hear what they have to say. I'm afraid of how it'll affect my willingness to move forward."

"You don't have to endure all this confusion. You've made something of your life. Focus on your son and yourself. The past happened. Now it's over."

"Excuse me, I'm sorry for interrupting," Brooklyn stood near us. "Did I hear you tell Iris to forget about all this?" She asked.

"I don't believe any of this is worth her peace of mind. Do you see the toll it's taking on her? She's not sleeping. She's not eating. She's a ball of nerves."

"Have you told him everything?" Brooklyn looked at me.

"Yes," I replied.

"Then you know she should see this through or she will always have questions. Iris has been operating at 40%. This could help her operate at full capacity and truly know herself to live a better life. She is extremely deserving of that life."

"Honestly, Iris is the only person who should make this

decision. All I'll say is, I've known you since we were teenagers. You know how to look a challenge square in the eyes and make it your bitch," Derek laughed. "Whatever you decide, I know you'll take it and make the best of the situation."

I fell into Derek's arms, thankful for his reassurance even though he didn't completely agree. He was right. I have no idea which way this could go. It could leave me scarred for the rest of my life.

"Do you hear yourself?" Brooklyn asked. "Her parents weren't her birth parents, and you expect her to freaking forget about it. That's ludacris."

"Yeah," Lorraine came racing inside the living room to offer her two cents. "If you say you'd forget it and move on, you're a liar. A person can't live thirty-seven years only to find out everything they knew and loved wasn't the exact truth."

"Call me selfish, but I'm thinking about her mental and emotional well-being," Derek explained, squeezing me tighter.

"How are you thinking about her well-being if she doesn't see this through?" Brooklyn posed the question with her hands on her hips. I knew that pose all too well. She wasn't playing nice anymore. "The stakes are too high."

"Okay you guys," I waved a white pillow in the air in place of a white flag. "I'll figure this out, and once I make my decision, trust that I've thought of every outcome."

"I know that better than anyone. I'm adopted," Brooklyn replied with her hand on my cheek. "I dreamed about my family all my life. Now that I've met them, a huge weight has been lifted off my shoulders. I'm free."

Derek placed his hands on either side of my face. We stared into each other's eyes for what felt like a million years until the doorbell broke our trance.

"I'll get it." Tammy ran off.

"No matter what, I'll only be a phone call away." Derek assured me before taking a seat.

"Surprise." Rodney pranced inside the living room, holding his bags showcasing a goofy smile.

"What are you doing here?" I hugged him.

"I told you I was coming. Who's this?" He pointed to Derek. "I thought it was just you and the girls?"

"This is Derek. He's an old friend from high school," I explained. "Derek, this is my son's father, Rodney."

"Nice to meet you. So what's on the agenda today? When is your family coming over?" Rodney asked, never allowing Derek to speak.

In true to form fashion, Tammy wisecracked. "Well this isn't awkward at all."

"Why should it be awkward? What am I missing?" Rodney shrugged with a baffled expression.

"Tammy's being a smart ass because Derek and I were high school sweethearts."

"Oh, so that's why the place looks like a floral shop." Rodney looked around.

"He likes to buy me roses." I smiled.

"Yeah, and he bought us flowers too. He's a gentleman," Tammy piped up. She loved Rodney as a co-parent for me, but not as a mate. Said he's too much of a flake. He'd only lead me on until I pulled the plug.

"Hush it and come with us." Lorraine pulled Tammy away by her arm.

"What's the big deal? Are you two in a relationship or something?" Derek asked.

"Yes," Rodney replied.

"He's joking," I quickly explained. "We aren't in a relationship outside of co-parenting."

"But we do have a relationship outside of Junior. We're

friends. So, I'm here for moral support."

"Right, we'll always be friends," I explained. "To answer your question, my family should be here this afternoon. We'll have a little lunch, and then they'll be on their way. But in the meantime, Derek found the address to my bio parents." I waved the paper at Rodney.

"That's amazing." The girls ran out of the kitchen. "Are you going to see them?"

"That's the quandary. What if they don't want to see me?"

"The only way you'll find out is if you go." Rodney grabbed my hand.

"Look how easy it was for me to find them. Don't you think it could've been just as easy for them to find you?" Derek said.

"In their defense, they aren't private investigators and my parents changed our last names," Brooklyn replied.

"Private investigator, huh," Rodney reiterated. Swarming Derek the same way buzzards swarm dead carcasses.

"Yes, that's right," Derek replied. "And speaking of, I need to run. I'm scheduled to meet with a client this morning." He glanced at his watch.

"Oh cool, what kind of case is it?" Rodney asked with inquisitive eyes.

"A money chase to locate missing funds."

"I guess the perks of traveling makes up for the monotony of the business."

You'd think Rodney and Derek would form a friendlier disposition with Derek having a career as a private investigator and Rodney's career in Cyber Security.

"I guess it would for some. I'm getting pretty old now," he laughed, turning to me. "Will I see you before you go?" Derek turned to me, holding my hand.

"I'd like that." We hugged long enough for Rodney to clear

his throat. At that moment, he reminded me of my dad. It was almost like old times in this familiar place.

"Good to meet you." Rodney shook Derek's hand, and then walked over to the sofa. His eyes followed Derek until he was long gone from the house, and then he turned those eyes on me. "He had an overnight bag. Does that mean he stayed the night?"

"Does that make you jealous?"

"Actually, it does," he replied. "Now answer the question."

"Yes," I replied eager to see where this was going. For a man who didn't want to start up again, he sure was invested in knowing the details of my romantic life.

Rodney's face twisted in angst. But he remained as calm as the day. "Did you have sex with him?"

"No."

"Good." His shoulders dropped.

"What do you mean *good*?"

He massaged his temples. "We have conversations ever so often about us getting back together. But, I avoid it because I feel guilty for destroying your trust in me. I may no longer deserve a place in your life beyond being the father of our child. But it hurts to think about you being in the arms of another man."

"It's good to know you still care." I avoided the conversation all together. I already had enough on my mind. Adding me and Rodney's issues to it would be catastrophic. "Are you hungry? Derek bought muffins and kolaches."

"Great, he buys breakfast too."

"Let it go." I pulled him up from the sofa to drag him into the kitchen.

The girls were already eating. All that remained was one pitiful kolache. Rodney did the chivalrous thing and offered it to me. After the girls left, we came up with a game plan to go see my parents without it being an ambush.

* * *

My family arrived at the house at noon and Rodney was the star of the show. I never expected anything less. His personality easily captivated people. They fawned over him and his corny jokes.

"We made lunch if you guys want to follow us into the dining room." Lorraine announced.

Jova grabbed my arm. "Could I talk to you alone for a moment?"

"Sure."

"I thought about you all night. I shouldn't have told you anything until I was sure you were ready to receive it. We'd just met. I was out of place and I apologize."

"I accept your apology. Thank you for acknowledging that."

"How have you been?"

"What do you think? You told me my parents weren't my birth parents."

Jova rubbed the side of her face. "I feel horrible."

"It's not your fault. I asked you to be honest and you were."

Jova intertwined her arm in mine and gave me a kiss on the cheek. "Even still, I apologize. I wish we could've met under different circumstances."

"Me too," I exhaled. "There's one more thing I'd like to ask of you."

"Anything?" Her eyebrows nearly touched her hairline.

"Would you give me Daphne and Alessandro's addresses? I'd like to see them before I go home."

"I'm not sure about that," she paused. "Well, at least when it comes to your mother."

"What's the issue?"

"Your mother wasn't happy about us coming here to see you. I should talk to her before you go there. See where her head is at."

"Call her now. I'm only here for a few more days," I urged.

"Fine," Jova took out her phone and walked away. I moved closer, but I couldn't make out her whispers.

I'd resorted to pacing. The conversation went on longer than I anticipated. You'd think a mother who allegedly didn't want to give up her child would be excited to meet me. This lady had some nerves.

"Okay," Jova pushed her phone inside her back pocket. "She's not ready to meet you right now."

"Oh, is that so?"

I wasn't going to let Jova in on the fact that I already had Daphne's address. She'd only warn her of me popping up. No way, this stayed with me and Rodney. Not even the girls would know.

The plan was to drop them off at the airport, and then Rodney and I would catch a flight to Scarborough to see Daphne. Then we'd drive to Castor to see Alessandro.

They owed me a face to face, and it was going to happen whether they liked it or not.

17
PUT ON YOUR BIG GIRL PANTIES

We saw the girls off the next morning. I told them I'd be taking a later flight. But my plan with Rodney was still on.

I knew keeping this from the girls would eventually bite me in the butt sooner rather than later. Be that as it may, I needed to do this without them. I loved my girls, and I appreciated them wanting to hold me up during this time, but they had a way of taking over, and right now, I needed answers.

The shock of learning about my parents still weighed on me heavily. Sleep abandoned me days ago. My brain downloaded new questions every second. My understanding of how people go mad became clear because I stood on the edge.

Rodney knew me so well, he could tell I was struggling. So, he held me in his arms the entire flight and thankfully he gave me a break on asking questions about Derek. It didn't help that Derek stopped by the house before we left with more red roses and a coffee. Rodney huffed and rolled his eyes in detest. I knew it killed him not to talk about it. But another one of his greatest characteristics was his tactfulness. He didn't burden me with unnecessary drama.

Frankly, I never knew how much Rodney still cared until Derek came back into my life. Though honestly, it should never take another man to show interest for Rodney to express his feelings. But it's way too much to unpack when I have more important things to focus on.

Once our flight landed, we picked up a rental car and headed straight to Daphne's address. We had to stop twice because my blueberry muffin tried to climb back up. The navigation system alerted us we were approaching our destination in less than a mile. I'd never experienced hyperventilation before that moment.

"Hey, hey." Rodney parked, gently rubbing my back. "Take a deep breath and slowly release it. I'll turn around right now if you can't handle it. Just say the word."

"I don't know," I shouted. "I don't know what I want anymore."

"Then don't force it if you're not sure. Think it through and come back another time."

"No, no," I said. "I need to do this now. Putting things off is never good. I'd be no better than all the players in this mess."

"Well, Daphne's house right there," he pointed. "So what's it going to be?"

"Is this real?"

"As real as it gets," Rodney replied, squinting his eyes.

A red Mercedes Benz and a black Range Rover were in the driveway of the modern two-story white brick home. A mass of large windows decorated with black shutters covered the walls with green shrubs. Talk about the grass being greener. This was the kind of house you'd see on the cover of a House & Garden magazine.

"It looks like your mom has done well for herself."

"Sure does..."

I sat in the car for a moment before trudging to the house. A little girl bolted outside, blowing bubbles and running into them. A few moments later three women joined her. The two younger women hugged the older woman, and then they drove away in the red Mercedes Benz. Me and Rodney ducked down as they passed by to avoid being seen. The older woman stayed behind with the little girl.

She stood at about 5'5", petite with silver hair dressed in a blue and tan kaftan dress. I knew without a doubt the older woman was Daphne. The pictures I'd seen were a younger version of her, but not much had changed.

She blew bubbles into the air while the little girl excitedly ran into the blister of clouds. I could hear the little girl giggling without a care in the world.

The sight was something to treasure. As teens, we rushed to get older. But once we're on our own in the world with a mass of responsibilities on our shoulders we learn to appreciate those days of our lives. Watching her play with the little girl birthed more questions about my life with these people and exactly where I'd fit in.

"Here goes nothing." I stepped out of the car and hiked up the driveway. Daphne had such a keen focus on the little girl, she didn't notice me until I was standing there with them. "Hello, Daphne," I said.

She drew the little girl to her side under her arm. "Do I know you?"

"Technically, yes," I replied. "I'm Iris Reid, but you may know me as Hurst or Cabello."

The color drained from Daphne's face. She froze without emotion. She'd turned into a statue right in front of my eyes. But she snapped out of it the moment I began to walk closer.

"No, you stay right there." Daphne sent the little girl inside the house.

She couldn't stop me. Nothing or no one could. I walked close enough to smell her perfume. It was a playful mix of fruits and jasmine.

"You can't be here." Daphne backed away, holding the palms of her hands up at me.

"I'm not here to cause you trouble. I only want to talk. Please," I begged.

"No, you need to go before I call the police."

"The police," I repeated, totally baffled as to why she'd taken such an extreme reaction to my presence. "You'd call the police on your own daughter?"

"You need to go now." She looked around as if she expected someone to drive up at any moment.

"Wait, please take my card. If this is a bad time, I'll be in town for a couple of days. Call me when you're able to talk. Just tell me when and where."

She took the card and hastily ran inside. I threw my head back and looked up to the sky, encouraging my tears to go away. Rodney stood outside the car. I ran into his arms and the tears fell. He'd become my safe place.

"What did she say?" He asked.

"She told me she'd call the police if I didn't go," I cried. "She treated me like I was begging for change."

"I'm sorry, sweetheart. Maybe, just maybe, your father will be willing to talk," he explained. "Unless you've changed your mind about seeing him?"

I wiped the tears away, cursing myself for allowing Daphne to treat me like a red-headed step child.

"Come on, I'll buy you a drink." Rodney kissed my cheek and helped me inside the car.

I couldn't bring myself to look at Daphne's house as we drove away. I felt ashamed, unwanted, and confused. I can see the bill for my therapy sessions now. It's going to blow Tammy's mind. I'm not big on, I told you so. But this was a can of worms that should never have been opened.

I thought about all the years I encouraged Brooklyn to get out of her head.

How stupid was I?

It's intrusive and downright insensitive to tell a person how they should feel when you have no idea what that person is going through. For that alone, I owe my sister an apology.

"Iris." Rodney tapped my leg. "Your phone is ringing, dear."

"Oh." I dug through my messy purse only to see Jova calling. "Hello?"

"Hi Iris, I thought I told you Daphne wasn't ready to see you. How did you get her address? Why would you do that?"

I wanted to end the call without saying a word to her. But I wasn't a coward. I didn't owe her an explanation why I wanted to see the woman who's supposed to be my mother. "It doesn't matter how I got her address. What matters is how she treated me."

"What happened?"

"She threatened to call the police if I didn't leave."

"No she didn't," Jova gasped. "There are things you don't know. I need you to trust me when I say, give her time."

"She's on my time now." I ended the call. "Take me to Caster. I want to see Alessandro."

"Let's do it." Rodney set the navigation and got onto the highway. "We should be there around four-thirty."

"Perfect, I've had enough of tiptoeing around this bullshit. Someone is going to give me answers and acknowledge my damn existence. I'm a real person with feelings."

"I believe Alessandro will be the key to unlocking all of this."

"Why?" I asked.

"They are two different people. We react to circumstances in different ways. Daphne reacted in her way–a negative one at that. I have faith Alessandro will react in a positive way. Someone has to balance things out."

"What if they both react the same way?"

"Then fuck them."

I jumped with my hand over my heart. "Where did that come from?"

"From my damn gut," he replied. "If they can't own up to their truth and make this right for their daughter, then fuck them. Say it with me."

"Fuck them," I shouted.

"That's my girl. Fuck them."

It's a shame me and Rodney haven't figured out our romantic relationship. We make a damn good team when it comes to everything except fighting for us. I've never been a fan of missed opportunities. Though perhaps I should brace myself to experience it when it comes to Rodney and me.

We called Junior on the drive to Caster. We could hardly get a word in. He was on cloud nine after making the basketball team. He and Rodney had been practicing for months. Junior opted out on spending the last two summers running free with his friends to attend basketball camp. A page he'd taken out of Brooklyn's boys pages. His dedication would pay off in the long run of him learning life lessons. You have to work for what you want. It doesn't always come to you.

How a person could stop looking for their child is beyond me. I'd move mountains for my son. I'd swim oceans to get to him. I'd search until I couldn't physically search anymore. Being away from Junior hasn't been easy. I couldn't imagine living thirty-seven years without him. From the moment I carried him in my tummy he'd been a part of my very soul.

Derek's name glowed on my phone screen. I leaned away from Rodney to read the text message. He'd made it safely to Common Cove. Despite his modest answer to Rodney about his career, it's quite the opposite. Derek worked closely with many police departments and was sought by families who needed answers about their deceased loved ones. We bonded over stories about our cases the night he stayed over. We had a lot in common growing up. But as adults we have even more commonalities. Derek would be the wise choice as a partner. However, Rodney and I shared a child and a special bond. You can't have more in common than that.

"Was that your boyfriend?" Rodney asked.

"What's going on with you? When we were in La Isleta, I asked you about rekindling our relationship and you were dead set against it. So, why do you care now?"

Rodney shook his finger. "Actually I said I don't think you'd ever trust me again after I cheated."

"Whatever," I huffed, rolling my eyes. "I tried to talk to you about us trying again more than a few times and every time you shut me down. So why does Derek bother you so much?"

"It makes me crazy to see you moving on. The thought of you being in another man's arms almost brings me to tears. I want to give you everything you want and need in a mate. But I made a huge mistake. I don't even know why I did what I did because I love you. Even still, I messed up. People don't forget heartbreak. You could say you forgive me. But you'll always make me pay for it."

"Basically you're saying I'm not capable of forgiveness. Good to know how you really feel about me."

"Fine, here's the deal," Rodney declared. "I feel like a damn fool. I kick myself every day for wrecking what we had. Me saying you would never forgive me is a crock of shit. I can't forgive myself."

"I don't know what to say." Rodney wasn't the vulnerable or transparent type when it came to our failed relationship. Now all of a sudden he's in touch with his feelings and willing to share them. It threw me for a loop. Everything was out of control and unfamiliar. I was existing in a new dimension from the moment I swabbed my mouth.

Fine time for him to be a perfect man now that I had a potential relationship on the horizon. Over the years, I wondered what kind of man Derek had grown into. Was he happily married? Did he have children? Was he happy? If we'd found each other again would the love still be there?

Derek wasn't the type of man I could shrug off. I needed to explore the hell out of him until I knew exactly what I wanted to do. Otherwise I'd be left with regrets, questioning if I made the right decision. I had my heart set on Danny Hampton in college. But those feelings eventually faded away. This thing with Derek had spanned over decades. Perhaps it's my unfulfilling relationships that caused my mind to wander back to the one man that made sense. But it was puppy love. We hadn't experienced life. We had no responsibilities outside of school and house chores. We were kids.

Rodney and I have a child together. We bought a house together. We established a daily routine with our child, careers, and financial responsibilities. We were a well-oiled machine. Then it all fell apart. Part of me expected it. I'm used to doing life alone. It's been my greatest strength and biggest fault to date. But I'd do whatever it takes to make sure it doesn't become my downfall.

"I don't want you to move on unless it's with me. But I know it's insensitive and it's not how life works. I hate to say it, but Derek seems like a nice guy." He shrugged with an expression of tension.

"Don't walk me and Derek down the aisle just yet. He's

great. Always has been. But his job will keep him away the majority of the time. I can recognize I'm much too selfish for that," I chuckled. "I want someone who will be there to cook together, watch movies, go on dates. I want to make love without distance being an issue. I know I can't have those things with Derek on a consistent basis."

"You do know you described the life we had together, right?"

"I know." I smiled. "I loved doing life with you."

"Until I ruined everything." He heaved a heavy sigh with regret written over his face.

"Stop the pity party and figure out why you broke us in the first place. You have an issue with commitment. Have you ever thought about seeking therapy?"

"Often," he responded candidly. "How about we go to counseling together? Put everything out on the table and work on us," Rodney proposed. "We don't have to jump back into a relationship. We could work on getting there with a professional."

"No, sweetheart." I rested my hand on his knee. "You need to go on your own. You have issues beyond us. You cheated after I asked you to make a decision about us getting married or ending our stagnant relationship. Until you can figure out your commitment issues, we will never be."

Rodney went silent. He looked straight ahead with glassy eyes as if tears would pour from his hazel eyes at any moment. Any other time I'd fold and console him, making promises that weren't in my heart or my values to make him feel better. But in this instance, pain was his best teacher.

Pain had a way of making a person put things into perspective. My absence made him long for me. Moving on taught him what he should and could do to be a better man. Giving in would only undo all these lessons he'd learned.

"Don't get quiet on me. You would pull away from me every time I mentioned marriage. Then you committed the ultimate sin—you cheated on me. I deserve better." I explained almost to the point of tears. I was feeling too many emotions. This wasn't the best time to talk about our failed relationship. Truth be told, if it were any other day before all this, I'd jump on the couple's counseling. But not now.

The only way one will learn about their standards in mates, you must experience everything that comes with the joys and disappointments that come in relationships.

"I agree. You deserve much better. I'm willing to do anything to show you I want us to be together. So, I'll go to counseling on my own. If you're still available after the work is done, I'd love the opportunity to try again with marriage as our goal."

"I'd love that. But make sure you're doing it for yourself to become a better man. Only then will you take it seriously and put in the work."

"I'll do it for myself. But I'd be lying if I said I wasn't doing it for you too. I love you, Iris. I don't have commitment issues. I was committed to you. I wanted to grow old with you. I don't know, I just got scared. I can't apologize enough for hurting you. I wish you could forgive me and leave it in the past so we could repair our relationship."

"I forgave you a long time ago."

"Thank you for saying that," he replied with a smile.

We zoomed past the welcome sign as we entered the city limits of Caster and rolled onto a tall bridge over the lake where boats and jet skis glided over the waters. I lowered my window to feel the warm breeze of air over my face. Unfortunately I was met with the repugnant smell of gasoline and algae.

"Alessandro's house should be on the lake here." Rodney pointed, slowing down to not pass by the address.

"I hope he's home. It looks like the whole town is at the lake."

"Actually, it looks like the whole town is at Alessandro's house," Rodney pointed out, stopping on the street directly in front of the house. "He must be having a dinner party. What should we do?" Rodney stopped in the middle of the street.

We sat in the car, watching people move about the house through the large window. Everyone of them had a crazed smile; laughing and schmoozing with one another. Alessandro must be the man on Shevale Lake. It was a punch in the gut.

"I don't want to be rude and drop this in his lap with so many people around. But then again, why should I care about being polite after he practically abandoned me."

"I never tell you what to do. If you go in there right now, I'll support you. But remember, to every action there is a reaction. Daphne's already being difficult. Do you want to have the same outcome with Alessandro as you did with her?"

"I hate it when you're right," I sighed. "Let's go get something to eat and find a hotel. We'll try again tomorrow."

"You got it," Rodney punched the gas. "What are you in the mood to eat?"

"I'm too stressed to care. I only eat to nourish my body these days."

"It's a good thing I know you better than you know yourself. Relax, I've got you."

I peered outside the window once again before we drove away. A wave of emotions hit me. I wondered if his other children were in there having the time of their lives, making more memories with him. I wondered how they interacted with each other? Did they joke? Were they the serious types? Did they have intellectual conversations about life?

See you tomorrow, Mr. Big Shot.

18

THREE GUYS AND A CHEF

M y rampant thoughts kept me up most of the night.
After only a few hours of sleep, I woke at sunrise. I
toyed with different scenarios of how I'd introduce myself to
Alessandro. The last thing I wanted was the same reaction as
Diabolical Daphne. But it was hard to focus with Rodney
sawing wood in the bed next to mine the entire night.

Perhaps my family woes must have been wearing the poor
man out more than I realized. In all our years of sleeping
together, his snoring had never been so elevated. Then again,
it's been so long since Rodney and I slept in the same bed I may
have forgotten.

"Rodney, it's time." I shook him awake since the rising sun
wasn't doing the job.

He turned over with a growl. "What time is it?"

"It's nine o'clock," I replied. "I'm ready to meet
Alessandro."

"Do you want me to go with you or do you want to take the
car?"

"Please come with me. You're good with people and if things veer off, you'll know how to get us back on track."

"Okay, I'll get dressed now." He sat on the side of the bed, rubbing his head before going to a shower. "Care to join me?"

"Rodney." I rolled my eyes in a huff.

"I know, I know," he laughed. "It was only a joke. Laugh a little."

I knew he wasn't joking. Rodney was testing the waters. But there are hurricane waters between us, and I don't think they'd calm anytime soon.

I returned a missed call I'd gotten from Derek while Rodney was in the shower. "Good morning, is this a good time to talk?"

"It's always a good time to talk when it comes to you. How are you this morning?"

"I'm not too happy. I went to see my alleged birth mother and she threatened to call the police on me as soon as I told her my name."

"Wait, hold on," Derek said. "When did you go see her?"

"Yesterday," I replied. "It was weird. If she never wanted to give me away, why shun me after finally reuniting with me?"

"Yeah, something deeper is going on. Did you talk to your aunt about it?"

"She called me before we could get out of the neighborhood. Acted like I went over there and started a fight with Daphne. My life has become unrecognizable."

"Okay, so this isn't the ideal outcome. But I remember when we were teenagers, and you'd talk about how you wanted to find your family one day. Since you're there, it's time to put your emotions in check and do what needs to be done. Then only after you've gotten the answers, you deal with your feelings on how to move forward."

His words reignited me. Daphne almost accomplished

what she set out to do to make me go crawling back home to hide from the world. But I was willing to give Alessandro a chance to rectify all this mess.

I stood in front of the mirror, dressed in a long peach maxi dress and sandals. I touched my rose ring. It reminded me that my girls were there with me in spirit. Their strength combined with mine and Rodney's charm gave me high hopes.

* * *

We arrived at Alessandro's house where two cars were parked in the driveway. Good sign. He wasn't having a party this time.

Rodney killed the engine and turned towards me. "I want you to go into this with a positive attitude. Be relentless for the truth and open to hear what he has to say. Get all the facts without being impetuous. I will be right by your side should you need me." He kissed both my hands. I loved when Rodney did that. He made me feel like a princess. Sadly he also knew how to make me feel like I wasn't enough. I'd deal with that at a later time.

"I got it, thank you," I acknowledged with a nod. I stepped out of the car and marched up the pebbled sidewalk to ring Alessandro's doorbell.

A salt and pepper haired gentleman opened the door with an enthusiastic smile. "Hi there, how can I help you?"

He was so polite and welcoming. I almost fell for his good guy act. How could he be a good person if he gave his child away without ever looking back?

"Hello, my name is Iris Reid. You may know me as Iris Cabello or Hurst. This is my friend Rodney Carghill."

His smile flipped upside down and silver tears saturated his face. His tall shoulders hung low. "Were your parents Raymond and Brenda Hurst?"

I nodded without words.

"Oh my God, you're my daughter. You look exactly like your mother." He didn't need convincing. "I tried my damnedest to find you but Brenda and Raymond didn't make it easy. I can't believe you're here."

"Are you saying you didn't know where I've been this entire time?"

"I knew where you were up until you turned one-years-old," he explained. "Where are Brenda and Raymond? They owe me a conversation."

Rodney grabbed my arm and quickly took over the conversation, "Umm, they passed away in a car accident years ago."

Alessandro dropped his head with a series of scratches. "I didn't know. My condolences. But it doesn't change the wrong they did. Come inside. We have a lot to talk about." He held the door open. "Could I get you two anything to drink? Coffee, tea, soda, water?"

"No, thank you," Rodney and I replied simultaneously.

"It's obvious you came here for answers. Am I right?"

"Yes," I replied, trying my best not to look like a lost puppy. Unfortunately I was miserably failing.

"Okay, I'll start from the beginning." He clasped his hands together. "I met your mother, Daphne when we were fourteen-years-old. She was born into a well-to-do family. Do you know about them?"

"No."

"Well, your grandfather Alexander Cabello was a prominent attorney and your grandmother Elenor Cabello was a dentist. They both had their own practices. So, their kids were destined for greatness and nothing less would be acceptable." He huffed. "You could only imagine how your grandparents took the news of their sixteen-year-old daughter's pregnancy.

Now add to her being pregnant by someone your grandparents deemed as low class. Their words, not mine."

"That's terrible," Rodney huffed.

"Somehow they came to the conclusion you should go to Brenda and Raymond for them to raise you as their child. But my parents didn't take it lying down." He paced with his hands on his hips recalling the past details blow by blow. "They tried to reason with your grandparents. Even offered to take you in. But your grandparents already made up their minds."

"So they gave up?" I asked.

"Not exactly," Alessandro replied. "For the next couple of weeks after that my parents became indefatigable. But when my father threatened to take them to court, they sent Daphne away until after you were born. She wasn't the same Daphne who loved to make people laugh. She used to smile twenty-four-seven. That's what I loved about her. She made you feel good whenever you were in her presence. But all of that changed. I asked her what happened to the baby, and if I could see a picture of you. She never spoke to me again. Then like I said, after you turned one-years-old, they vanished sight unseen."

"Why would they do that?"

"From what I've heard, they had challenges having children of their own. She and Raymond were afraid of losing you if you discovered the truth. At least, that's what Daphne told me. Boy do I wish I could speak my piece to them."

"You said you knew where we were. How did you find me?"

"I was about seventeen when I hired an investigator to help me find you. I saved two cheks just to hire the man. Once he found you I tried to reach out to Daphne before going to the address. But she'd gotten married and had her first child with her husband. She didn't want to have anything to do with me.

She stonewalled me and told me to never come back to her home."

"At least she didn't threaten to call the police on you."

"Come again," he said with fire in his eyes. "I can't believe that woman. It's sad enough she didn't fight to get you back but to threaten to call the police." Alessandro stewed in his seat. "I told you the man I hired found you. At the time, you guys lived in Forton."

"Yes, Forton is on my birth certificate."

"Right, I flew there to speak with Brenda and Raymond. You were about a year old at the time. I watched Brenda parade you around from afar for two days. After that, I finally got up the nerve to go to their house and confront them."

"What happened," I gasped in anticipation of his story.

"Brenda called the police and told them I was a strange man hanging around her house."

"I guess that runs in the family."

He chuckled, "Bear in mind, me and Daphne were sixteen-year-olds when we got pregnant with you. Brenda and Raymond were listed as your parents on your birth certificate. I'm sure they had legal documents drawn up thanks to your grandfather." Alessandro drifted from one decade to another without taking a breath in between. "I had to get out of there to avoid being arrested. I went back home and decided I'd come back, make a plan, and then go back in a couple of months when cooler heads prevailed. Except when I returned, Brenda and Raymond had vanished without a trace. The next time I searched, I couldn't find them. Where have you been? Where did you grow up? How was your life, my sweet daughter?" He moved closer to me.

"My sweet daughter," I repeated. "You call me that but where have you been? I truly don't get it. I have a son and I would move mountains to get to him."

"Could you move those mountains at sixteen?" He calmly asked.

"Maybe I wouldn't be able to move them but I surely would never give up."

"I didn't give up. I kept running into a brick wall and now I know why; they changed all your names. I'm sorry for making you feel like I gave up. It actually breaks my heart. You and your mother were my first loves. When I learned Daphne was pregnant with you I was so excited. I'd stay up all night dreaming about our lives as a family. Then it was all snatched away from me. Brenda and Raymond were the cause for the brokenness of this family. Why can't you see that?"

"You think I don't see it?" I asked. I could feel the hot tears on the rims of my eyes. "I can't be upset with them because there will never be a resolution. But you're here in the flesh and I have to get all of this out of me and make sense of it."

Alessandro walked over to me. "Would it be okay if I hugged you right now?"

"I need a minute. I feel way too exposed." I took a few steps back.

"Okay, what can I do to help you through your emotions?"

"I just need you to be honest and patient with me while I work through it all."

"You've got it. I'm right here and I'm listening to you."

"I want to know the truth and get to know you. I want to be a part of your life if you're my biological father."

"I want the same things. So, does that mean you're open to getting to know me and me getting to know you?"

"Yes," I replied. "I grew up in Pinemoor, and then I went to the university there. My parents died while I was attending college. So, after I graduated, my best friend's parents graciously took me in until I was able to stand on my own two feet."

"That's wonderful. I'm so happy to know you have good people in your life. How are you feeling so far?"

"I'm okay." I glanced at Alessandro, and then at Rodney. His eyes are where I found strength and comfort. He gave me a nod to keep going. So, I gave Alessandro a rundown of my life. He clapped and praised me. It made me feel good. I hadn't smiled like that in days. With him, welcomed was an understatement.

"I wish Daphne would've responded to me this way."

"I'm sorry it didn't go well. Daphne is the same as her family these days. She wants to appear to have a perfect family image and a child at sixteen doesn't fit the bill. Daphne's husband is in politics. You coming back will only dampen their plans. Look him up." He waved. "His name is Richard Conner."

Rodney's fingers moved fast. "Yup, that's her right there." He showed me and Alessandro his phone screen.

"Why didn't we think to google her name?"

Rodney shrugged.

"Yes, that's Daphne. A shell of what she could've been." He stood. "What can I do to make this up to you?"

"You've already given me what I needed–acknowledgement. I'm on a journey to learn who I am and where I come from. My parents raised me as an only child and outside of them, there was no other family."

"How did you find me?"

I dreaded having to say his name in Rodney's presence because I didn't want to talk about our relationship later. "I did an ancestry test with my girlfriends. After I received my matches I reached out. Jova, Yoana, Mateo, and Matias drove to Pinemoor to meet me and that's how I found out about you and Daphne."

"Oh, you've met Jova and Yoana."

"Why do you say it like that?" I inquired.

"They're carbon copies of their parents and they tell their siblings what to do. Whatever they say goes. I'll bet you a million dollars Jova is the reason why she stonewalled you. She has some kind of control over her siblings in a way I could never fully understand. Brenda is the only one who got away. Kind of ironic." He paced. "How was your life? How did Brenda and Raymond treat you?"

"They were the best. Mom was nothing like her parents from the way you described them. There was no illusion of a perfect family. They made sure I had everything I wanted and needed. My dad bought me a car at sixteen. We lived in a nice neighborhood. I had lots of friends. We even took family vacations. They also made sure my college tuition was paid in full. They were the best," I explained with a smile. Like it or not, my parents did what he and Daphne couldn't do and never did. He should be thanking them. "What do you do?" I asked in an attempt to change the subject. Alessandro held resentment towards my parents. He's entitled to feel the way he feels, but I didn't want to hear it.

"I own a bakery downtown. It's grown quite a bit."

"That's cool. Do you bake or just give orders?"

"Both," he chuckled. "I can make anything. If you're the same way, you get that from me."

"Oh, she can cook," Rodney butted in, rubbing his stomach.

"How about I make you guys lunch. Do you have time for that?"

Rodney and I looked at each other and shrugged. "I don't see why not."

"Good." Alessandro scratched his head. "Here's the big ask. You can say no if you want and it won't upset me. Would you like to meet your brothers?"

"Oh." I hesitated. "Could I talk to Rodney alone for a second?"

"By all means, take as long as you need. I'll be in the kitchen. Come join me afterwards." He left us to talk.

I paced the eclectic living room with my hands on my hips. I could tell Alessandro traveled the world and everywhere he traveled he bought something to commemorate the memory. "Do you think it's a good idea to meet his sons? How do you think they'll react to me being here?"

"It doesn't matter what I think. Get out of your head and follow your heart." Rodney drove his pointer finger into my chest. "Do you want to meet them?"

"Yes, I do. But I don't want to be attacked or disregarded."

"This is not a situation where you worry about the unknown. I know I'm not the best person to preach about this given our situation. But this is beyond a romantic connection. This is about your biological family. Now tell me again, what do you want to do?" He kissed my cheek.

"I want to meet them."

"And so you shall." He kissed me again. "Now, I'm going to go in there to see what Alessandro is cooking." He rubbed his hands together.

I sat in a green chair by a window that overlooked a beautiful purple wisteria tree. An iron bench sat underneath it. A sense of peace came over me at that moment. So, right then and there, I made my decision.

"I made my decision. I'm ready to meet my brothers." I stood in the doorway of the kitchen where Alessandro and Rodney were already becoming old pals.

"Maravilloso." Alessandro cleaned his hands with his apron and raced away to his phone.

Rodney scratched his head. "I couldn't help but overhear your conversation with your son. You told him to pick up his brother so they could come over to meet their sister. Is it safe to assume they already know about Iris?"

"They've always known about her." He turned to me. "Sweetheart, you're not a secret. Actually I have a picture of you the day I confronted Brenda. I'd already had a plan to take pictures of you. But once I realized she wasn't going to allow me time with you, I snapped it before she could say no." He walked away. I followed close behind. He pulled out a family album and flipped to pages, and there I was, a little baby wearing a yellow and white dress and matching headband.

"I can't believe you have this." I stared at the picture. The tears began to flow. I didn't stop them. I allowed myself to feel everything. On this short journey I'd learned I have to allow myself to go through the emotions, give myself grace, and then forgive everyone; including myself.

"That's all I have. I've shown this picture to your brothers a million times. They're excited to meet you."

By pure instincts, I held Rodney's hand. He kissed my forehead. I've incessantly felt protected by him. This moment, holding Rodney's hand gave me validation of why I chose to go on the rest of my journey with him.

"There's no way you move around the kitchen like this without formal training. Did you go to culinary school?" I asked.

"You're a smart cookie." He wiped his hands and pinched my cheeks. "I lived in Ven da Flores for two years while I was in culinary school."

"Ven da Flores," I repeated with wide eyes. "Impressive."

"Thank you, I worked at a small restaurant at night and went to culinary school during the day. That's where I met my late wife, Gloria. She and her girlfriend were having dinner. They laughed so loud I could hear them clear in the back. When I came out to introduce myself as the chef, her eyes beamed. I had her hook, line, and sinker. She stayed there until we closed just to have more time with me. I knew that night she'd be my wife."

"Sounds like a rom-com."

"No better way to describe it." In thirty minutes, Alessandro managed to cook pan-seared duck breasts with port wine sauce.

The doorbell rang while he set the table. Once again, I squeezed Rodney's hand when two buff men rounded the corner.

"Finally, we meet." The tall one drew me in for a long hug. "My name is Mateo."

The other one pushed Mateo out of the way to introduce himself, "My name is Marino, and I'm the oldest."

"You're only three seconds older than me. Let it go," Mateo said.

"Oh, you're twins. That's pretty cool. Good to meet you both."

The door slammed and another man walked inside the dining room. He looked like he came straight from the gym. The sweat under his armpits nearly made me lose my appetite. "Can't start the party without me. How are you?" He kissed my hand. "I'm sure Marino has already said he's the oldest twin. But I'm the oldest of them. Nice to meet you, sis. My name is Ricardo."

"Nice to meet you. I'm Iris, the oldest of you all."

Everyone exploded in laughter. Alessandro had the biggest smile on his face. He kept repeating how happy he was to finally have all of his children together. I could see the joy in his eyes. Rodney took the queue to have us pose for a picture.

Many years ago I'd given up on the idea of meeting them. Each time I resolved a broken connection with a family member I found another missing part of myself. It was an enlightening feeling.

My phone began to ring. "Would you all excuse me? I need to answer a call. Go ahead and start eating." I walked away. "Hello, Iris Reid speaking."

"Yes, Iris, this is Daphne."

"Oh," I replied. My energy instantly dropped.

"I'd like to apologize for the way I reacted. I was wrong and you didn't deserve it. Are you still in town?" Daphne asked.

"Yes," I lied, interested in seeing where this conversation was going.

"Okay, if you're available I'd like to invite you to lunch tomorrow?"

"I think I could do that. Where should we meet?"

"I'll send you the address," she quickly replied. "How about noon?"

"Sure, I'll see you then."

"Thank you for not holding my terrible manners against me. I'm really not that kind of person. I'll explain more tomorrow."

I ended the call with a deep sigh. Things were looking up and now I could enjoy lunch with Alessandro. We ate, drank, laughed, and learned everything we could about one other. We even made plans to see each other again before me and Rodney took off.

Being with Alessandro and my brothers made me understand why Brooklyn was considering relocating. After losing so much time, all you want to do is make up for it. I wanted to know everything about them and hear all their stories. I wanted to become a part of their lives.

Before we knew it, darkness covered the sky. The stars shone exceptionally bright in Caster. We sat in the backyard by the lake around the fire pit. I wasn't ready to go. But we'd have to get up early to drive back to Scarborough to meet with Daphne.

When Alessandro hugged me goodbye it felt as if we were already familiar with one another. No one hugged me like that since my parents. To feel that way in Alessando's arms put a lot into perspective. Perhaps he was my biological father.

Daphne, on the other hand, that's an entirely different beast.

19

YOU WANT ME TO DO WHAT?

I woke Rodney up bright and early without the need of an alarm clock. After all, my racing heart did the job just fine. But if we wanted to meet Daphne on time, we'd need to hit the road to get ahead of the traffic.

My curiosity had gotten the best of me. What could Daphne possibly need to say? She did everything but push me to the ground and throw dirt into my eyes.

After my shower I got dressed in a strapless olive midi corset dress with a snake print. I figured it was perfect for the occasion. Daphne was two negative actions away from me becoming Medusa and turning her into stone. If only I could manipulate my hair into a bed of snakes. I'm all for the dramatics when it comes to her. But I sucked in a belly of air and decided to take the high road.

Rodney strutted out of the bathroom with a towel wrapped around the lower half of his body. The sight of him in his natural state always sent chills through my body. I wasn't a fool. Rodney was trying to tempt me. He knows how I feel about his body. I'd scream those thoughts whenever we were together in that way. I'm no pillow princess. I don't find a sweet spot to lay in the bed and do nothing.

After he got dressed, we did a final sweep of our room to make sure we didn't forget anything, checked out, and set off to face Daphne for the second round. I sat in the passenger seat silently whispering prayers and taking in the city. We drove across a stone bridge over a massive still lake. Spanish Moss trees surrounded the edges of the lake. It was certainly a sight to behold.

Rodney bought me a stress ball on a pit stop at a gas station while on the drive to Scarborough. I had just about squeezed the foam out of the thing within minutes of it being in my possession. The drive seemed longer this time around. Perhaps I could blame it on my nerves because I didn't know what to expect from Daphne. She made it pretty clear she wanted nothing to do with me. What could've possibly changed overnight?

A thick layer of sweat covered my body. You'd think I'd run ten miles before the meet up. If I didn't calm my nerves, I'd slip right out of my dress. Then I'd really be in trouble. The woman would never take me seriously.

Once I snapped out of my momentary anxiety attack I did a double take of the restaurant Daphne invited us to, and she didn't strike me as the class of woman who'd patronize such a place. The old dilapidated building looked as if it'd collapse any moment. Three of the letters were burnt out on the neon sign. The paint had long faded and chipped away. I certainly wouldn't walk alone after dark in the seedy neighborhood.

"Why in the hell does she want to meet here? She better not flake on me or I will never speak to her again." I rambled.

"If she flakes, I'll drive you to her house and cause a scene myself." Rodney replied, looking around.

"You saw Daphne's neighborhood. We both know this isn't the type of place she frequents."

"When you have something to hide, you don't go to places where people know you," Rodney explained.

"You're right; I'm her dirty little secret." I wanted to tear up.

"Hey," Rodney grabbed my hand. "Don't ever say that again. You're not a dirty little secret. You're an extraordinary woman. She should be proud to have you as her daughter. She clearly has issues. Don't make them yours."

Rodney was right. Internalizing her issues would be a recipe for disaster. I had to figure out a way to face her without allowing her negative energy to impact my existence.

"Okay, let's do this." I stepped out of the car and paid careful attention not to break my ankle on the cracked asphalt.

The white square tables were straight out the eighties paired with worn green and pink leather chairs. Harsh sunlight shot through the windows, revealing the grit between the dingy tiled floors. I wanted to run out of there. Forget about Daphne and her games. Put them in the rearview mirror and do as my parents–forget I ever knew her name. But my curiosity got the best of me. I had to know why she wanted to see me again.

I sat in a booth near the door so I could see her the moment she entered this rundown greasy spoon palace. The palm of my hand stuck to the table in a glob of syrup. Things like this were the reason why I carried antibacterial wipes in my purse. A pool of orange juice rested beside me in the booth. I grabbed a handful of napkins to clean it up before it ruined my new dress.

I could smell the grease burning on the dirty grills so strongly I could taste it in my mouth. The stench soured my stomach. I wouldn't eat or drink anything from this place for a million bucks. The bacteria alone would kill me before the check cleared. If the table and chairs were dirty, one may as well assume the dinnerware was just as dirty. I mean for goodness sakes, I'd already stuck to the table like a gecko.

The place was pretty much empty aside from me, Rodney, and an older couple. Aside from the atmosphere they were kind of adorable. They read from the same book while sharing a shake. I hoped we wouldn't disturb them with our family drama.

Rodney sat in the corner of the small diner far away enough to give us privacy, but close enough to notice if I needed him. He gave me a wink when I looked back. I felt like a new kid in grade school watching my mom walk away to leave me amongst the wolves.

Ten minutes behind our agreed upon time Daphne entered the diner. She wasn't scoring any points from our last encounter. She didn't arrive alone. Another woman accompanied her who appeared to be as highfalutin as Daphne. They both wore big dark shades and scarves around their heads tied at the neck, Thelma and Louise style. I wondered who they were hiding from and if me and Rodney should be hiding too.

"Hello, Iris. Thank you for coming," Daphne greeted me with a pitiful smile, sliding in the booth. "This is my dear friend Rosalinda."

The woman waved with a smile and took a seat on the side with Daphne which was good because she wouldn't be able to run unless she climbed out of the thing.

"Rosalinda, this is Iris. The Forensic Pathologist I was telling you about." Daphne's voice wavered. But I was sure of what I heard. Forensic Pathologist, not daughter.

"Hello, thank you for coming," Rosalinda said. "When Daphne told me about you, I did a little research of my own. You have an impressive turnover with your cases. The majority if not all have been solved and closed. Which brings me to why I so badly wanted to meet with you today."

I cut my eyes at Daphne. She quickly looked away, pulling her purse closer. Even she didn't trust this place. "I'm listening," I replied, urging Rosalinda to get to the point.

"My daughter, Angelica Diaz was found dead in her high-rise apartment last month. I don't agree with their findings. Angelica had been seeing a guy she'd met online for a month before her death. He seemed nice and all, but as a mother I had a funny feeling about him. I believe in my gut he had something to do with her death. I'm willing to pay anything. No amount is too high. She was my only daughter and Daphne's Goddaughter. Are you a mother?"

"Yes." I nodded.

"Then you understand why I can't let this go. They're saying it was an accidental overdose. But my daughter doesn't do drugs. She was a Freelance Photographer, working towards her goal of becoming a Still Photographer on movie sets. She had already begun making great connections. She had too much to lose."

"We don't know everything our children do when they're away from us," I reminded her.

"No," she hit the table with the side of her fist.

Rodney swiftly jumped to his feet.

"I'm sorry, I'm sorry," she apologized and composed herself. "I'm telling you I know my daughter. She wouldn't do drugs."

Rodney retreated back to his seat. But he never took his eyes off us.

"Could I have a moment alone with Daphne?"

"Sure," she replied, standing to give us privacy.

"Is this why you wanted me to come here? I thought you wanted to talk about you being my birth mother, not use me."

"I'm not using you," Daphne insisted.

"You didn't introduce me as your daughter, so that tells me

she doesn't know my relation to you. Why are you keeping me a secret?"

"I'm not," she replied with scrunched eyebrows as if I was the problematic one.

"Then what is it?"

"When I saw your business card I knew you came into my life for a reason. Well, for more than one reason. But for a reason nonetheless."

"You're a piece of work," I hissed.

"If you do this, I promise I'll sit down with you and tell you everything."

"Wow, classic emotional abuse," I replied. "You can stuff it in a box and save it. Alessandro has already told me everything I need to know."

The color drained from her face and she swallowed hard. "You talked to Alessandro? When? Where?"

"It doesn't matter. I'm out of here. Good luck with your goddaughter."

Rosalinda raced over before I could get away. "Are you leaving? Please, don't go."

"Yes I'm leaving." I looked at Daphne. "Ask your friend why."

"I don't know what's going on between the two of you, and it's none of my business. But please, don't take it out on me or my daughter's justice. I need your help."

"I'm sure Scarborough has more than a few capable Forensic Pathologists who could provide you with the answers you need."

"Please, mother to mother," she pleaded with teary eyes. "I need your help. Isn't that what you're supposed to do–help."

Dammit if she didn't unlock my weakness. Rosalinda is a prime example of the people I took a vow to help. She's a mourning mother with questions about her child's death. I couldn't fathom the turmoil she's feeling. If something happened to my son, and I had questions, I'd want someone to help me too. Surely this was more important than my issues with Daphne—a woman I never knew existed a few weeks ago. Now she's dumping her baggage in my lap. The audacity.

"I'll do it for you. Not for her." I passed Rosalinda my card. "Go to the website and complete the necessary forms with our office to officially acquire our services. Once everything is complete, we'll request all the reports, photos, law enforcement documents, and medical records for our findings."

"Oh my God, thank you. I'll start working on this tonight. Thank you again." She hugged me. "I'm sorry, maybe you're not a hugger. But this means the world to me."

"I'll be in touch soon." I waved Rodney over. "Let's go."

"Is there anything I could do to thank you for helping my friend?" Daphne asked.

"No, I don't need anything from you anymore." I grabbed Rodney's hand and walked out of that tacky diner. I refused to cry. Daphne didn't deserve my tears. Jova's story about how hard it was for her to give me away was nothing but a fairytale. No mother who was ever forced to give away her child would act so selfishly as Daphne.

"Drive," I demanded.

The sooner we were away from Mommy Dearest, the sooner I could let the tears flow. I cried so loud Rodney covered his ears. This was the perfect time to visit a smash room. I needed an outlet, and Rodney's baby making stick wasn't the answer.

"What did she say?" Rodney asked.

"I'm washing my hands of that woman. She never wanted me. It's true, I'm her dirty secret."

Rodney parked in a busy parking lot. "Talk to me. Tell me what happened."

"That lady only asked me to lunch because she wanted me to help her friend get a second autopsy of her daughter. She googled me. I can't believe I fell for it."

Rodney rubbed the back of his head with a deep sigh. "Daphne may have given birth to you. But she's not your mother," he explained, wiping my tears away.

My damn tears, I shouldn't be wasting them on the likes of Daphne. My damn tears, I didn't understand. My damn tears of disappointment. My damn tears.

"You did what you needed to do," Rodney explained. "You know the truth. It's time to move on now. I can't have you breaking down mentally or emotionally. If later down the road Daphne reaches out to you, fine, so be it. Either you'll talk to her or you won't. No sweat off your back. You've done your part, okay?"

"Okay," I whimpered, hitting the dashboard. "Do you remember our old neighbor, Ashley?"

"Yeah, why?"

"I said we would never meet anyone as evil as her. Well, I stand corrected."

"I don't even want to think about Ashley," he sighed. "Do you want to drive back to Caster tonight or find a hotel and drive back early in the morning to see Alessandro?"

"Screw that. I need a drink now. We'll drive back in the morning."

"I knew you'd say that. I booked us a room at the Sapphire Hotel and Spa. They have a nice bar according to their website. I figured you'd need to unwind after meeting Daphne." Rodney fired up the engine and drove on two wheels until we reached Emerald Drive.

Traffic picked up the moment we arrived downtown. Pedestrians pounded the pavement along the sidewalks where tall buildings lined the streets. There were business professionals heading to meetings, shoppers juggling bags, friends heading into coffee shops, lovers strolling as if they were the only two people on the planet. For a mid-sized city, it was pretty busy. Charming nonetheless.

We entered the parking garage of the hotel. For a small boutique hotel, it appeared they were at capacity.

"Here we are." He killed the engine, taking a deep sigh.

"This is perfect. I'm not in the mood to be around a crowd of people."

"I told you, I've got you. Nobody knows you better than me. Well, maybe Brooklyn. But not Derek. He knows the teenage you. I know the woman." He winked, kissing my hand.

"That you do." I managed to crack a smile.

The small hotel had a total of seventeen rooms. Even still, it packed a punch with an indoor swimming pool, restaurant, rooftop bar, spa, and sauna.

Each of the seventeen rooms had its own theme. We rented the olive suite with a street view of downtown. The soft shade of green complimented the natural aspects throughout the room and smelled of vanilla beans. It helped calm my anxiety.

After we secured our luggage in the suite, we rode the panoramic glass elevator upstairs to the rooftop bar. On the way we were able to get a view of the Zen garden spa and hot tubs. They called my name. But they weren't louder than the bar. Nothing could be louder than the bar after what I'd just endured. I wanted to drink until I forgot this can of worms I'd opened.

We enjoyed the scenic views of the city from the rooftop. I closed my eyes to savor the first sip of my drink. I ordered a Dark & Stormy, the name alone was fitting for the day. But the rum, oh the rum, it extinguished the fires brewing within my soul. I thought, thank God I didn't inherit Daphne's personality, or did I?

She was bullheaded. So was I. She protected herself with a wall no one could get over. I do the same. As tacky as her actions were, she did it with her best friend in mind. I'd do anything for Brooklyn. So, I wondered if I was more like Daphne than I was willing to admit.

"Is there anything I can do?" Rodney asked, moving his chair closer to mine.

"You're doing enough just by being here with me."

"Are you sure? I feel like I could do more."

"Like what?" I asked as if I didn't already know where this was going.

"I don't know. I just feel like I could do more."

"I thought you were going to offer sex."

"I'm not a piece of meat, sweetheart." Rodney covered his chest with his hands. We laughed for the first time since the debacle with Daphne.

I wanted to take him up on his offer. But after the heavy conversation we had about our relationship, sex would only complicate things even more. Yet and still, my moments with Rodney were nothing to downplay. He knew exactly how to take my mind off the world and elevate me to another dimension.

"I apologize; I thought that's where you were going." I laid my head back and let out a sigh deep from within my soul. "I knew this would be an emotional journey, you know. But I never expected for Daphne to be so cold-hearted. I existed before her life she has now. Why shun me?"

"Her husband is a retired lawyer who moves heavily in the political world. He's helped develop community projects. He's worked closely with senators on passing city laws. His wife having a kid at sixteen and never being in her life would stain everything he's worked so hard to accomplish. But I say eff them." He held up his glass. "I'm proud of you. Usually you shy away from anything that could complicate your life. When you told me you decided to learn more about your family, I was shocked. I didn't think you'd see it through. Now look at you."

My heart fluttered and I couldn't stop smiling as he spoke.

"Yes, you've encountered some obstacles that you'll need some time to work through. But you've gained more insight about your past, family, and all the pieces have come together. What you do with it is what matters in the end." He tapped the side of his head with a nod.

I sat my third cocktail down, took hold of his hands, and looked into his eyes. "We've been through a lot together. But you never turned your back on me. I can always depend on you. We made a beautiful little boy and despite everything we've gone through, we stuck together as a family for him. It's more apparent than ever you're my family, Rodney. That's why I don't want to jump back into a relationship with you without first working on the things that tore us apart."

"You can't do the same things and expect different results," he whispered.

"Exactly." I squeezed his hands. "I love you with my whole heart. You mean the world to me. I don't want to lose you because who knows if we'll recover our friendship a second time around should things go bad."

"I respect your concerns, but I'm not giving up on us and I refuse to let dorky Derek win by default. I know without a shadow of a doubt, you're my person. I know I was the one who didn't want to try again. I was scared. But I want you to know I love you."

For the first time in five years, Rodney and I shared an intimate kiss. The tiny hairs on my arms stood at attention when he gently stroked my back. My heart fluttered and tears rolled down my face.

"Wow," Rodney said, lying back in his chair.

"Tell me about it," I replied. "But make no mistake. We're not having sex tonight."

We laughed and ordered another round of drinks. It'd be the last to avoid waking up in the morning to a trail of clothes on the floor and regret. A couple sat at a table over from us. They were in a deep conversation, two seconds away from one of them throwing a drink on the other. It snapped me back into reality. If things didn't work out between Rodney and me, we couldn't afford to hate each other. So we paid for our drinks, headed to our suite that consisted of two beds, and called it a night.

Sex with Rodney would be the same as putting a bandaid on a deep cut that needed stitches. It'd only do so much.

20
A WOMAN OF SCIENCE

Alessandro invited us to his bakery for breakfast the next morning so we could spend our last couple of hours with him before our flight back to Woodcrest. I could never get used to the traffic between Caster and Scarborough. It's heavy and hardly moved until we're at least forty minutes out of the city.

We woke up early to drive back to Caster. Our early morning conversation consisted of Daphne and how she blindsided me. I was officially over trying to have any kind of relationship with her. She hadn't shown an ounce of kindness, care, or concern for me as her so-called child.

We were stuck next to what appeared to be a well-to-do family in a gray Genesis GV80. The man drove while the woman sat in the passenger seat with three kids in the backseat —one in a baby seat. They sang and danced the entire time. I caught myself glancing at Rodney with contempt more than a few times.

As much as I wanted to say I'd forgiven him for destroying our family, I harbored resentment towards him for breaking our family. Perhaps a little therapy would serve me as much as it could serve him. When Rodney and I were together, we were the same as the family in the car–happy, dancing, and together. Sometimes I wondered if any of what we had in the past was real. It felt real in my heart. Rodney knew what to say, what to do to make me feel like I was on top of the world, and none of it consisted of sex. I wondered how he was so good for me and so bad at the same time.

The sunrise painted the sky in auburn and orange colors as it slowly made its grand appearance from the bed of big white clouds. My eyes welcomed the ball of fire in all its glory. I took a mental picture of it and closed my eyes for the rest of the drive to meditate on its beauty and manifest an even more beautiful day.

* * *

Alas, we arrived at Alessandro's bakery. He managed to bring Ven da Flores to Caster. The bakery sat alone a lot. Three of the walls were ceiling to floor windows except for the back exposed black brick wall.

The large window on the left side showcased four bakers who stood in front of their own gold tables, putting on a show for voyeurs and passersby to appreciate their baking skills in real time. We watched for a while before going inside. The bakers moved in sync as gracefully as a water acrobatic team as they knead, pulled, and tugged on the lumps of dough to form them into intricate shapes.

The exterior and interior of the bakery were trimmed in black and gold. Ivy plants grew along the black bricks of the exterior corners of the building. They almost reached the top of the roof near the sign—*Tiers of Joy*. I had to admit, Alessandro's shop added character to the otherwise common neighborhood.

At first sight I could tell he put a lot of thought into his menu. He incorporated local items with Ven da Flores recipes. There was a line of tall glass display cases of baked goods along the glass window that doubled as a wall with one long display case upfront where a smiling middle-aged woman took orders. Some of their items; psomi, pnika, lycabettus, mom bread, rizos, exarchose, miniature cheesecakes, pies, cannolis, cupcakes, cookies, macarons, cakes, and desserts in a glass jar. You name it or dream it, he had it.

The layout reminded me of a well-known bakery in Highsea. There were fifteen tables that only sat up to four people. All of the tables were taken and the line grew longer by the second. I was right when I said he was the man of the town. If they weren't at his house, they were at his bakery.

"Hey, hey, there's my girl," Alessandro sang as he raced from the back with his arms stretched out. "What do you think about the place?"

"I love it. You've done well for yourself."

"I was under the impression it was a small bakery. But this is magnificent," Rodney said.

"I appreciate it, but I can't take all the credit. My wife was the mastermind behind it all," Alessandro explained. "She designed it after her grandfather's bakery in Ven da Flores. All I did was sit back and allow her to take the lead." He put his hand on Rodney's shoulder and gave me a wink. "If you don't remember anything I say, remember that gem."

I took that as my cue to jump in. "Do you see what happens when you let the woman take the lead? You'll gain your very own oasis."

Rodney laughed and walked away to peruse the delicatessens.

"Hurry, come sit with me before this table is taken."

"How do you keep up with the demand?" I asked.

"I hire capable people," he laughed. "So you're leaving today, huh?"

"Yes, it's time for me to get back to my life."

He scratched his head. "Am I invited to be a part of your life going forward?"

"I'd like to get to that point," I replied with a nod. "Maybe we could start with the phone to get to know each other first."

"I understand. You can't be too careful." He scratched his head. "I wish it were the other way around with me finding you. But after so many years and me getting older," he sighed. "I can't apologize enough for not doing more. Honestly, I'm extremely embarrassed."

"I wished you would've found me. I would've loved to know all of this at a younger age."

"I was your father and I dropped the ball. I gave up. But I had no rights to you anymore. My hands were tied. Still, that's no excuse. All I can do is try to make up for it going forward."

"I do have one question."

"Lay it on me." Alessandro clapped and held his hands out to give me the floor.

"Why didn't my parents tell me about any of this? They left me without ever sitting me down to explain the ins and outs of our family. Why?" I don't know why I kept asking the question as if I hadn't heard the reason a thousand times. But, hearing it from different perspectives allowed me to make more sense of it.

He took my hands and said, "Sweetheart, you have a son, right?"

"Yes."

"Tell me how much you love him."

Alessandro had the sweetest green eyes. A million lines grew around them whenever he smiled. He'd gotten a fresh haircut. Perhaps it's presumptuous of me to think he spruced himself up in anticipation of seeing me. I felt special to think he may have.

"I can't put it into words," I replied.

"You would do anything to protect him, right?"

"Yes, I'd do anything for him."

"Well, Brenda and Raymond may have seen this as a way to protect you. Sure, there's a ton of selfishness if you ask me. But look at your life. You told me about all the great things you've accomplished. They poured values and wisdom into you. They loved you as if you were their God-given child. Who wouldn't be afraid to lose such a beautiful child you've raised from birth if the truth surfaced?"

"Fear is the beginning of wisdom."

"Indeed," he pointed with a smile. "It shouldn't have taken you this long to know the truth about your birth. I mean, I'm pretty amazing," he laughed. "But if Daphne raised you, do you think you would've been as accomplished?"

"I can't give you an answer to that. Daphne is a pill."

"She's dead wrong for treating you the way she did. But be open to hearing her reasoning for it. Then go from there. I don't know Daphne to be a vicious person. Losing you caused her trauma. You're an adult now, Iris. You know about trauma."

"Why haven't you talked to her? Why didn't you two join forces to fight for me?"

"I told you, when Daphne got married; she cut everyone off except for a few people."

"Let me guess," I said. "Yoana and Jova are the people she kept in her life."

"Bingo." He winked. "They never tell her when she's wrong. They protect her and go along with whatever she does. Daphne could blow up the world and they'd find a way to make her the victim."

"I have someone in my life like that. Her name is Brooklyn.

She's like a sister to me. I feel the same way about her," I sighed. "A lot has changed since we decided to go on this journey to reconnect with family. Now she's talking about moving to Marseau to be closer to her family."

"You don't sound too pleased about that."

"I hate it. Brooklyn was adopted. So she doesn't know anything about these people. Plus I'd lose her," I huffed. "I'm sorry, you probably don't care about all this. But it's really bothering me."

"If I had the chance to be closer to you, I would do it without hesitation. You're my daughter. I love you. So, keep that in mind when it comes to your friend."

"I wish my parents were here. They'd know exactly how to help me deal with this situation."

"*Parents,*" Alessandro repeated, rolling his eyes.

As a mother, I understood his frustration in me referring to Brenda and Raymond as my parents. But that's who they are, and nothing could change that fact. He should be thankful they took me in when they did. They gave me everything I needed in life to become a well-rounded person.

"Well, young lady, as promised, it's time for you to swab me." Alessandro stood with his cappuccino in hand. "Follow me to my office."

"Thank you for agreeing to do this. I'm a woman of science. So I need to see it in black and white before I'm able to fully comprehend everything."

Alessandro closed the door. "You don't owe me an explanation. I would've been surprised if you didn't ask me to do a DNA test. The only parents you've known for over thirty-seven years are Brenda and Raymond. Now you've been hit with a monkey wrench of learning about me and Daphne. That would blow anyone's mind. I don't know how you're still standing. It would've knocked me off my feet."

"You've got that right. I was thrown a major monkey wrench," I replied, reading the instructions. In my heart I believed Alessandro was my father. But the heart runs off of emotions. "Well, that's that. We should get the results back in five to seven business days after I mail it off. I'll let you know."

"Would it be too much of me to ask that you call me when you make it home and get settled in?"

"It's not too much to ask. I'll give you a call."

"Wonderful." Alessandro clapped. "Okay, I'm going to pack you and Rodney some good food to-go. You can fill your bellies up while you wait for your flight."

Alessandro jumped right into the role of a caring father. Although we'd never be able to eat all the food he packed, it's the thought that counts, and it meant the world to me. "I can't wait to try everything. It all looks so delicious."

"These are all my recipes. I especially want to know what you think of the rizos. I added a little twist to it."

"Ah, I see you've got a little rogue in you," I teased, tapping his shoulder.

"You know it," he laughed. "Go on honey. Be on your way before I start crying."

"You're a breath of fresh air. I'm so happy I met you. Thank you for opening your heart to me."

Alessandro placed his hand over his heart with an enduring smile. "I'll always remember this moment with you, my darling daughter. You may not believe me right now, but I love you more than you'll ever know. My only hope is I can show you how much I love you before my time is up."

None of this was expected. I thought I'd meet a few aunts, uncles, and cousins. To find out my parents weren't my birth parents crushed me the same as being run over by a Mack truck on a dark dirt road. My parents mean the world to me. They always will. I'm thankful for the life they gave me when they could've said no and carried on with their lives. So, I want my memories of my parents to remain intact in my heart.

Many nights my father would come home from work, and I'd sit with him in the kitchen while he ate dinner prepared by me and my grandma. She spent a lot of time teaching me how to cook. My dad would tell me how important it was for me to know myself and love my life. Up until this time in my life I thought I knew everything about myself.

I refused to trash the memories of my parents. I may not have known my roots, but I knew love because of my parents. They are my roots. They made so many sacrifices. My mother and father were talented dancers. That's how they met. But they gave up their dreams when I came along. That is what you call sacrifice. They took in a baby that wasn't theirs and they loved me and cared for me without boundaries. That is the ultimate expression of love.

"My sweet daughter." Alessandro placed his hand on the side of my face. "Take care of yourself. I hope to see you soon. Is it okay for me to hug you?"

"I'd like that."

He didn't want to let me go and there was a part of me that didn't want him to let go. The girls were right. These little pieces of the puzzle mattered. I never knew how much I was missing until I put it all together. For the first time in my life, I felt whole. It's unexplainable, but it's amazing. I wished I could bottle it up and use it whenever I'm down.

Rodney walked over to say his goodbyes to Alessandro. They slapped hands as if they were old buds with a long embrace. "It was nice to meet you Mr. Arevalo. I hope to see you soon."

"Can't be soon enough." He looked over at me with tears in his eyes. "Take care kiddos."

Rodney put his arm around me to walk me outside to the

car. Alessandro stood beside the door of the bakery, watching until we were no longer in sight. I never imagined I'd feel the separation after just meeting my father and brothers. But I did, and it wasn't a good feeling.

We had enough time to make a stop at the post office to mail the DNA results. The sooner the better. Then I'd finally know the truth. I couldn't help but wonder how lucky I was to have another chance in life to experience a father-daughter relationship once again. But boy were those shoes going to be hard to fill because my dad was more than amazing.

My chirping phone fought for my attention,

Daphne

"I know I'm the last person you want to hear from, and I can't say that I blame you. I didn't handle this the right way. I hope you will accept my apologies. When I found out I was pregnant with you, I was so happy. I can't remember ever being that happy in my life so far. Foolishly I thought my family would be happy too. That was my sixteen-year-old brain. Needless to say, it was the complete opposite. I was forced to give you away to my sister and her husband. Then they shut me out. After so long, it was as if it never happened. I know it sounds horrible. But it's the only way I could make something of my life without sitting in that hurt. Maybe one day I'll find the words. I was never the same. I went numb and I learned to live with the numbness. If you find it in your heart, please call me. I'd like to make this up to you for the both of us. Please."

I wasn't sure how to receive her words. I'd already given Daphne two chances. A third would be pushing it. But I didn't go on this journey for no reason. Like it or not, she's my birth mother. That alone is worth trying as many times as it takes to get it right.

2 1

HOME SWEET HOME

L ater that afternoon, the girls were hot on my heels the moment Rodney and I landed in Woodcrest. They were adamant about driving me home to get all the deets of my trip to meet my birth parents. I could hardly thank Rodney for being my wingman for the past few days before they whisked me away in Brooklyn's black Tahoe. They moved quicker than CIA agents and I was nothing more than a wanted fugitive of the state with nowhere to hide. The only thing missing was a blindfold and handcuffs. Though I'm sure Tammy had both in her purse. She considers them essentials.

Brooklyn rolled through the maze of the airport into civilization. Traffic didn't mean anything to her. Once the other drivers saw her big black truck barreling towards them, they parted like the Red Sea.

"We have a bone to pick with you," Tammy blurted out.

"Why? I've been sight unseen since you guys left Pinemoor."

"That's the problem," Tammy replied in haste.

"Yeah," Lorraine offered her two cents. "Why didn't you

tell us about your plans to meet your parents? We would've gone with you." She swatted my leg.

"We made a plan. We promised to stand by your side," Brooklyn said, veering into the left lane to pass a slow driver.

"You need to pay attention to the road before you kill us," I yelped, holding on to the overhead handle.

"I've got this," she replied, zooming back into the lane to her place in front of the lead of the slower car.

"You're all over the road," I reiterated. "In case you didn't know, those horns are honking at you."

"Nevermind them. Answer the question." Brooklyn honked back at the drivers.

"You know why she didn't tell us," Tammy said. "She went away with Rodney for three days. They were too busy slapping skins to call us." She clapped after every word. Her ability to turn every conversation sexual was a gift. Maybe not one to be proud about. But a gift nonetheless.

"Slapping skins," I repeated. "Have we gone back in time to the nineties?"

"I don't know, you tell me," Tammy said. "You had two fine men chasing you, and you didn't use them as a stress reliever. I'm disappointed in you."

"Why is your mind always in the gutter?" Lorraine asked.

"The gutter is fun and dirty. You should try it sometime. I see how tense you are most of the time. You, my girl, need a stress reliever."

"Sex doesn't fix everything." Lorraine rolled her eyes.

"Oh but it takes the edge off. I could smoke a cigarette just thinking about it." She puffed on an imaginary cigarette to further get under Lorraine's skin.

"If it helps, I thought about mounting Rodney several times. We had a dynamic sex life. But I had more important things to focus on. Besides, Rodney shared his feelings. Sex wouldn't do anything but complicate an already complicated situation. I don't want to ruin what we've got."

"Wait," Brooklyn said. "I want to know what deep feelings Rodney shared with you."

"Come on, Brooklyn. You were there when Rodney and Derek met. We all know what feelings he shared," Tammy explained before I could say anything. "The man almost had a brain aneurysm."

"You think you know everything," Lorraine said.

"No, she's right this time. Derek being there struck a nerve with Rodney. Now he realizes someone else wants me romantically, all of a sudden he had a breakthrough to share his feelings," I explained.

"Does he want to rekindle the relationship?" Brooklyn asked.

"Yes, but I'm not sure I want to go back down that road. I begged that man for years to make a commitment—to make our love official. Instead of stepping up, he slept with someone else. Who does that?" I quickly answered my own question, "a man afraid of commitment does that. It almost destroyed me when he broke my heart. I'd be stupid to trust him again, right? But I still love him. I won't lie about that." I looked around at the girls.

"Can't you find it in your heart to forgive him?" Lorraine asked.

"Believe me I've tried. He's the one who resisted until Derek came back into my life. But I'm happy he resisted because after going on this life-changing adventure with you ladies, I realized I was living in a land of make believe. We both have a lot of work to do emotionally and mentally. I'm going into therapy on dear ole Tammy's dime, and until Rodney seeks help to figure his shit out, he's off limits to me." I ran my hands over my body to remind the girls I am the prize. "Now if another woman is willing to put up with his shortcomings, that's on her. I don't want half of a man. I need him to be whole."

"That's my girl." Tammy high-fived me. "But I wasn't talking about a relationship. I was talking about back breaking sweaty sex."

"You're disgusting," Brooklyn said, switching lanes to pass an old station wagon that was more than likely about to break down any minute. "I'm on the fence. On one hand, I know Rodney's a good guy. On the other hand, I saw first-hand how he hurt you. Why give him another chance to break your heart again?"

"I don't know. I kind of want to see you two back together. You accomplished so much and you haven't been as happy without him," Lorraine confessed.

"You need to practice more self-love, Lorraine. That hopeless romantic ideology will leave you dazed and confused. You'll always be mending a broken heart," Tammy replied.

"Why do you always need to drag me for filth? Sometimes I wonder if you're even my friend." Lorraine pouted with her arms folded across her chest.

Those two argued so often I wondered the same thing. But, the moment it crosses my mind they'll do or say something to remind me their bond is as strong as Brooklyn and mine.

Tammy grabbed Lorraine's hand with a stern expression. "I love you so much I'm not willing to sit back and watch you live in la-la land. I want more for you, but most of all, I want you to want more for yourself."

"Thanks." Lorraine peered out the window. Tammy over and gave Lorraine a kiss on the cheek. "You're so annoying."

"But you love me." Tammy smiled.

Lorraine smiled back.

"Now that you two have kissed and made up, could we get back to my issues?" I said.

"My bad, go on," Tammy replied.

"Do you take pictures with your mom or dad?" Brooklyn asked.

"I took a few pictures with Alessandro and my brothers. But I don't have any with the She Devil better known as Daphne."

"What did Daphne do to earn that name?" Tammy asked.

I gave them a rundown of my experiences with Alessandro and Daphne for the rest of the drive. I even reminded Tammy of her offer to pay for my counseling sessions once again so she would know I meant business. I'd be making an appointment first thing in the morning. I told her I accept blank checks and that I'd give her a call with the appointment date so she could take me out for drinks as she promised. She didn't argue.

After Brooklyn dropped Lorraine and Tammy home, we stopped at Coffee Snobs for a one on one. Tammy and Lorraine are our girls, but my sisterhood with Brooklyn transcends beyond them. I felt safest with her than anyone else.

"Well hello there. It's good to see you gorgeous ladies safely back home from your trip around the world. How'd it go?" Gene ran from behind the counter to greet us with a hug.

"It's a long story. But the short version is, we met a lot of family. Figuring out how to move forward is the question."

"I'll say this and take it as you wish. Whenever there is an elephant in the room, you eat it one piece at a time," he simply explained. "I'll get your usual, but this time it's on the house."

"Thank you, Gene." I sighed, rubbing my temples as he walked away before I shared the details of my family woes with Brooklyn. "Daphne treated me like the dirt on the bottom of her Christian Louboutin heels. Yet she's the one who gave me away. Even if it was out of her control, why take it out on me?"

Brooklyn reached across the table to hold my hands. "I'm not saying this to take up for Daphne. I hate the way she treated you. But is it possible seeing you is a reminder of the worst time in her life? Think about it," she continued with her hypothesis. "You're a mother. Imagine getting pregnant with Junior when you were in high school and your parents forced you to give him away. You'd be enraged."

"Sure, I'd be enraged. But once I'm financially able to locate and reunite with my kid, all my rage would go out the window. I'd welcome my child with open arms the same way Alessandro welcomed me into his life."

"Everyone's not the same," Brooklyn replied, sipping her coffee. "I don't know what state I'd be in mentally after experiencing such a traumatic event."

"I hear you. But I'm on the receiving end, and it hurts like hell." I finally allowed myself to cry. "My parents took this secret to their graves. They didn't care if I had knowledge or closure from it," I sucked in a lungful of air. "I also wondered what type of person I'd be had I known the truth about my biological parents and keeping a connection with the family."

"I get it. My parents told me the truth about my adoption as soon as I was old enough to understand. Still, I had a ton of questions. So just because you didn't know doesn't mean you'd be any different. You're an amazing person. That's all that matters."

I looked down to see Jova calling. "Hello," I quickly answered.

"Hi sweetheart, I'd really like the opportunity to sit down and talk with you."

"What do we need to talk about? Alessandro told me everything."

"Then you know we had no contact with Brenda," she

explained. "Please, we need to sit down and talk. I'll come to you. Where are you?"

"I'm home in Woodcrest now."

"When did you leave?" She asked.

"Does it matter? I'm home, and honestly, I want to put all of this behind me."

"You mean you want to forget about everyone except Alessandro?"

"Actually, I'm on the fence with him too. I don't know how to move forward with any of you. I can't trust what you say because it comes with conditions. That isn't fair to me and the truth doesn't reside in conditions."

"I can't apologize enough. We love you. Daphne's behavior towards you may not have been the right way to go about this, but she loves you. Giving you to Brenda was the most difficult thing she's ever done in her life to date," Jova explained. "How about I fly to Woodcrest and we could meet at a nice restaurant if you're not comfortable with me coming to your home?"

"Let me think about it and get back to you." I ended the call. "Can you believe her? She may run their clan, but she doesn't run me."

"Are you sure you want to close the chapter completely? You have a unique opportunity to experience the parent-child relationship again. But this time with siblings, cousins, grandparents, aunts, and uncles. Do you really want to throw that away?"

"I'm not sure." I turned my cup up to drink the last drop. "Thank you for the coffee, Gene." We waved goodbye. "Rodney's bringing Junior home. It's been way too long since I've hugged my little man, and after this spider web of lies, I need it more than ever."

"Come on." Brooklyn put her arm around my shoulders. "Let's get you home, old woman."

"Hey, we reserve the old jokes for Tammy and Tammy only." I wagged my finger.

Laughter does the soul good, and we laughed all the way to my house. Brooklyn could pull me out of a funk with little to no effort. We came into each other's lives for a reason. When I saw Brooklyn sitting alone under the pavilion I was drawn to her like a magnet. I wanted to get to know her and be around her. It's like I needed her friendship and she needed mine.

We've gone through major life changes; her diagnoses of Huntington's disease, the loss of my parents, becoming mothers, and her getting married. Now meeting our extended family. She means the world to me. The thought of her moving gave me physical pain. Who will I be without her? It's a question I never wanted to learn the answer to.

"You're so deep in thought over there you can't hear your chirping phone."

"Oh crap." I dug through my messy purse.

Derek

Hello Iris, I miss the hell out of you. I have business in Highsea next month. I see that's about an hour away from Woodcrest. I was wondering if it would be okay if I come for a visit? Of course I'd stay in a hotel unless you'd be so gracious to have me as a house guest. I'll have a couple weeks off after the meeting in Highsea. Think about it and get back to me.

"Wow," I whispered, stuffing my phone back inside my purse.

"Is everything okay?"

"Derek wants to come to Woodcrest for a couple of weeks."

"That's good, right?" Brooklyn asked.

"I don't want him and Rodney to run into each other and it's way too soon for him to meet Junior."

"You're a single woman who's a workaholic who craves more in life. It wouldn't be a bad thing to have a familiar person

236

with a possible romantic connection to visit you. The purpose of our trip was to learn more about ourselves, change things we don't like, and open ourselves to family and friends. The work doesn't stop now that you're home."

Brooklyn's speech gave me a revelation. Sometimes I felt like Sara Winchester and her house. I'd keep building and building to keep people at bay. Perhaps it's time for me to approach life with a different mindset.

"You're right. I'll tell him to come. Besides, this old flame never burnt me. Maybe there's something still there."

"You never know." Brooklyn whipped the SUV into my driveway.

Rodney and Junior were already waiting for me inside the house. "Thank you for being you. I'll call you tomorrow." I raced inside. "Guess who's home?"

"Mom," Junior yelled, racing towards me with his arms out.

His hug powered up my positivity and drained my negativity. "This is just what I needed." I closed my eyes to feel every drop of emotion.

"You're going to break me," Junior squealed.

"Forgive me, honey. It's been way too long." I finally let go. "Where is your father?"

"He's right here." Rodney walked over with a smile. "Your wine cellar makes me want to move back in."

"Is that all it takes," I teased. "But seriously, there's something I need to talk to you about."

"Uh-oh, I'll be in the game room." Junior raced away.

"I love you son."

"Love you too mom." He waved his hand in the air, putting his headphones on for a serious match in Madden.

"What do you want to talk about?" Rodney asked.

"Let's go downstairs for this one."

"I'm almost scared to hear what you have to say."

"Oh come on, you opened my 2005 bottle of Château Duhart-Milon." I screamed, shaking the bottle.

"You have four of them. I thought it would be okay."

I rolled my eyes. "You could've at least called before doing it. Pour me a glass since it's already open," I huffed. "Okay, here's the deal. Derek wants to come for a visit for a couple of weeks."

Rodney clawed his chest. "Repeat what you said."

"You heard me. Derek is coming for a few days or a week," I replied.

"Is he staying here with our son?"

"You know me better than that. I'm telling you because Junior is going to stay with you while he's here."

"Are you trying to hurt me?"

"This is not about you. I need to step outside of my comfort zone. You remember telling me that, don't you?"

"I thought it would be with me. I love you. This guy may have dated you back in high school, but he doesn't know the woman you've become like I do."

"Jokes on you because I'm just learning more about myself as well. I thought you understood that Derek is in the picture for now."

"It doesn't mean I have to like it. I need to go." He turned his back to wipe his eyes.

"I didn't tell you to hurt you. I told you because I wanted to be honest with you. Would you rather it be a surprise?"

"You're right. I get it. Is there anything else?" He asked with his back to me.

"Yeah, I need you to confirm it's okay for Junior to stay with you for those two weeks?"

"What the hell. You went from a few days to a week, and now two weeks," he shrieked. "I poured my heart out to you. I've never done that with any other woman before. I know it's selfish of me to think you'd put your life on hold while I take the time to work on myself. I hope you won't forget about how much I love and adore you. I'll call you tomorrow."

Rodney made his way upstairs and out the door in a matter of seconds. He left me with a lot to think about. But tonight was all about me and Junior. So I shook it off and made snacks to join him in the game room. I didn't know the first thing about Madden. All I wanted to do was see his face and catch up with everything going on in his life. Thankfully one of my son's greatest strengths is multitasking.

"I come bearing snacks." I danced inside the game room.

"Thanks mom." He paused his game. "I'm happy you're home. How was it meeting your family?"

"Son, your mom is one pooped individual."

We talked about my vacation and the time he spent with his dad for the rest of the night. He even turned off his game. I had his undivided attention. The night was perfect and before I closed my eyes, I sent Derek a text to officially invite him to Woodcrest. Then I got the email confirming Rosalinda had completed the process to acquire a second autopsy of her daughter. Thankfully Derek wouldn't arrive until next month. So, instead of sleeping, I dug into Angelica's file.

"Well, Ms. Diaz, it's me and you for the rest of the night."

22

THE VISITOR

A month passed fairly quickly and Derek wasted no time traveling to Woodcrest. Thankfully I had enough time in between meeting my parents and Derek's arrival to come to terms with the DNA results. They confirmed Alessandro was my biological father. So, the truth had come to light.

I called him to give him the news. He wasn't surprised. He was happy I finally knew the truth. We talked on the phone for almost three hours. Since that day, he makes sure he calls me every morning and before he goes to bed. I appreciated how much of himself he extended to me. I know he would've been a wonderful father if he had the chance. But our journey took us on the path it was supposed to take us.

My therapist gave me homework to write a letter to mom and dad to address my anger and disappointment. But I also let them know I forgave them. Then the girls and I drove out to the lake to burn the letter and release it. I needed that closure in order to move forward with Daphne and Alessandro.

Derek arrived Friday evening with red roses in hand and a

big smile. I made a huge decision to welcome into my home and guest room.

Rodney picked up Junior Thursday for their boy's time. It actually worked out for the best because he asked for more time with Junior and this was a great time to appease him. But make no mistake, he fought to change my mind because he knew it meant I'd be alone with Derek for two weeks. He hated the thought of it and he made sure I knew exactly how he felt about it.

We stayed home the night he arrived and caught up. The next morning we ate breakfast in the park and watched the sunrise. Then, we took a stroll downtown by the canal. Derek said all the right things. He reminded me why I fell for him years ago. Having him in my life again conjured nostalgic memories of the old me pre-grief, and honestly, it did my heart and mind good.

At noon we attended a sensual yoga session for couples. We got closer than close. It's important for me to understand the adult Derek whose experienced life to see if it has changed him in a positive or negative way. Relationships never work when I move too fast without getting to know the person. I hit a wall, and most of the time it ends with me hurt and rejected. Been there done that, bought the t-shirt, and washed my car with it while promising myself I'd never do it again. Yet and still.

After yoga we went home to shower and relax for a few hours before going to Brooklyn and Kai's for dinner. They went all out. Romance was in the air from the sensual music, decorations, and romantic menu. They even hired a chef and a server for the night. Seems Brooklyn took a page from her family in Marseau. She'd stepped her dinner hosting game all the way up.

"You just can't stay away from our Iris, huh?" Brooklyn asked Derek.

"To be fair, she was my Iris before she was yours."

"I didn't know it was a competition." Brooklyn frowned.

"Hey, I'm waving the white flag," Derek replied, slowly backing out of the verbal swearing match.

"Peace offering?" Brooklyn stood next to Derek holding a bottle of wine.

He held up his glass with a cheesy smile. "I accept."

"Lyn told me you're a private investigator?" Kai attempted to change the subject. "I'm sure you have some interesting stories. I'd love to hear a few of them."

"Yes, and Iris told me you're a stockbroker," he replied. "I'll have to pick your brain on some stocks I've been eyeing after dinner."

"Perfect, I actually have a nice cognac and some Cuban cigars that'll end this dinner perfectly."

"Sounds like a damn good plan." Derek grabbed my hand with a smile. Perhaps Kai's invite gave Derek the acceptance he needed.

"Just go," Brooklyn urged.

"Thanks sweetheart." Kai kissed her on the cheek and disappeared with Derek in tow before either of us changed our minds.

I followed Brooklyn to the sitting room. "Now that we're alone, tell me how things are going with Derek."

"There's nothing to tell. We had dinner, we talked, he slept alone in the guest room, and I slept alone in my bedroom."

"No kissing? No sex?"

"Why are you smiling? What's going on with you?" I asked.

"Okay, the reason I had us come to the sitting room is because..." She paused to look out the window. Then at her watch.

"What are you up to?"

"Umm." She peaked out the window again. Then she

turned to me with a devious smile. "Oh there we are. I told Rodney you'd be here tonight and I'd sneak you away for a moment. He wants to talk to you."

"What? Why would you do that?" I asked, smoothing my hair.

"He said he needs to talk. Come on, Iris. It won't hurt to see what the man has to say."

"Do you remember when you cut me off for telling Tammy and Lorraine you had Huntington's disease?"

"You can't compare this to a fatal illness."

I stood for a moment. "Okay fine. But we're going to talk as soon as he's gone."

"Oh, that's a given. I want details. Now scoot." She slapped my butt and pushed me out the front door.

Rodney stood beside his car draped in a new outfit. "You look amazing."

"Thank you, but why are you here?"

"I needed to talk to you... alone."

"Is everything okay?" I asked.

Rodney held my hands. His eyes were sad. "I haven't told you, but I've been seeing a therapist. I'm learning a lot about myself."

"That's wonderful," I replied with a smile.

"I need to talk fast before your friend figures out I'm here," Rodney explained. "I've dated many women in my lifetime. But you are vastly different and in a league of your own. Your heart and your intelligence turned me on. It was hard for me to understand because look at you, you're freaking gorgeous. You have beautiful green eyes, full sun-kissed lips, a smoking figure —the full package. But as hot as you are on the outside, I was even more turned on by your intellect. After being in a relationship with you for years I knew I was in trouble because I knew you were the one." A tear rolled down his cheek. "It scared the hell out of me, and like a dumbass, I cheated. I thought nothing this good could be real, and nothing this good would end well. But here's the kicker," he continued. "I was terrified at the thought of you breaking my heart because I knew I would never survive it, and I was right. When you ended the relationship, it broke me. I put on a brave face because of my ego. I couldn't allow you to see how much it affected me. I was a coward. I'm ashamed of what I did. I hate myself for it. You were the best part of me. That's why I haven't dated anyone since we broke up. I know another woman could never measure up to you. I love you with every ounce of my being."

"I don't know what to say."

"You don't need to say anything. I didn't sleep last night because every time I closed my eyes I saw you and Derek kissing, touching, making love or God forbid, falling in love. I vomited at the thought." He inhaled. "I couldn't go through another night of you and him under the same roof without telling you how I felt. I need you to know how much I love you. He's not your only prospect. Please, don't forget about me."

Rodney appeared different. For the first time, I could see he was afraid of losing me. Some women would feel empowered to have a man pretty much grovel for them. But it made me sad for Rodney. At our age, he should know what he wants without being on the verge of losing it.

"Thank you for hearing me out. We'll talk soon." He kissed me on the cheek.

"Wait," I said. "Where is our son?"

"He's with my brother. I'm on my way to pick him up now. That's one thing you don't have to worry about when it comes to me. I love you."

"I never doubted your love for me. It's your commitment I questioned. With that said, I love you too," I said.

"Don't only hear me, feel me." He gently rested his hand on my chest, making my heart flutter uncontrollably.

"Being completely in committed love with me is a totally different ballgame. Are you ready for that?"

"I'm more than ready, and I'm going to make you a believer in me." He kissed my hand. "We'll talk soon."

I watched him drive away. In a matter of seconds, Brooklyn was hot on my tail for a play by play. I didn't leave out any details.

"You're the last person I thought would arrange this little meeting. You're the one who convinced me to invite Derek here because you said Rodney had his chance."

"I know, and I feel terrible for sneaking around with Derek here. But I've given it a lot of thought. If Rodney is in therapy and makes the necessary changes, you should be open to him. You're not committed to either of these men. Don't limit yourself." She paced. "This man will spend the rest of his life showing you how much you mean to him because he knows how it feels to lose you."

"See, that's where you're wrong my beautiful sister." I touched the side of her face. "Rodney has already proven his character to me. Giving him another chance would be reckless."

"We all know you're a strong woman who is willing to stand alone. But beyond being strong, you're smart. You'll know what's best for you." She sat across the room from me with her legs crossed. She may as well have said checkmate. "Rodney is the father of your child. Neither of you have been in a serious relationship since you split. So something is holding you back. What that is, I don't know. Perhaps you should explore this breakthrough with Rodney."

"I've been begging Rodney to try again. Now he's suddenly all in. It's madness."

"Okay, okay, fine. Just think about it," she said. "I want to show you this new account I'm working on. I think you'll find it quite interesting."

"Okay."

She took out a file and passed it to me. It was a new marketing campaign for a TV show to discover fashion stylists. It carried a prize of one hundred and fifty thousand and each designer will have their own personal seamstress.

"You were the first person I thought about when it came across my desk. You should audition for it. I know you'd kill it."

"I have a career and a child. I can't go away for four weeks."

"It's not until next year. Surely you could spare four weeks to live in the big city and compete with like-minded people to do what you love. The money is only icing on the cake compared to the experience."

"That would free up a huge chunk of money for Junior's college tuition."

"See, now you're thinking." She drilled her finger into my shoulder. "The benefit of having me as your friend is I get the inside scoops. You should look over the requirements and work on your audition. You have an entire year to perfect it."

"I don't know," I pondered.

"What do you know? You say you don't know about love. You don't know who you are anymore. Now you don't know if you want to explore an opportunity that could make you happy. Even if you don't win, the time you spend in this competition could enlighten you."

"How do you know that? It could be another thing that causes me stress. You know how competitive I am."

"If you're doing what you love, how could it be stressful?" Brooklyn asked. "I should know. Once I went full-throttle in marketing, I've found happiness outside of my family that fulfills me. I want the same for you."

"Ladies, how are we doing?" Kai and Derek invited themselves inside Brooklyn's office, wearing the smell of cigar and cognac.

We talked for a few more hours before calling it a night. Rodney's confession of love ran through my mind, daring to live rent free until I could come to a final decision to release him or make our relationship work. But I'm not sold on being with someone who is unable to recognize my worth from the beginning. Although, nobody is perfect.

23

SPECIAL OCCASION

Two weeks passed in the blink of an eye. Time does fly when you're having fun. We went on countless dates. We shopped until our feet and bank accounts hurt. I'd shown Derek every charming detail about the city, so my social battery was running extremely low.

Thankfully Derek planned a romantic Sunday dinner at home for us to commemorate his last night in Woodcrest. I decided on a sexy black lace dress. I'd only worn it one other time. Got a million compliments and a date. In my world, that makes it a good luck charm. Not that I needed or wanted the good luck. Derek is a wonderful man. But, turns out, he isn't the man for me.

He held my chair out. "Wow, you take my breath away. You look amazing."

"Thank you, and you're looking good yourself."

"Just trying to keep up with you," he joked. "Well, my time is coming to an end in Woodcrest. I truly appreciate you for being such a gracious hostess." He reached out to hold my hand. "So why have you been avoiding the conversation of us exploring a relationship?"

"It's not that I'm avoiding the conversation..."

"See, right there, you're doing it again." He interrupted. "I'll never forgive myself if I don't say this. I care about you. I always have. I want us to continue dating to see where this could go."

"I will always care about you, but..."

"Uh-oh," Derek interrupted. This was slowly becoming a thing with him. A thing I don't necessarily like. Interrupting is a poor characteristic and boils my blood. "That always leads to rejection. Are you still in love with your son's father?"

"Why did you go there?"

"I noticed his reaction when we met at your parent's house." Derek sipped his wine. "He has deep feelings for you. How deep those feelings go is unbeknownst to me. But I'm more interested in knowing how deep your feelings are for him."

"Oh my gosh," I sighed.

"Tell me the truth. I won't feel slighted. I realize I'm coming in the fourth quarter. I'd be a fool to think a woman of your caliber would be single with no prospects."

I took a huge bite of my strawberry ricotta bruschetta to buy myself a little more time. "Things are complicated with Rodney."

"You either do or you don't have feelings for him. It's okay if you do. The heart wants what the heart wants. I need to know if I have a chance in hell with you or if I need to take a step back."

"Here's the thing," I finally gave in with a deep sigh. "I fell in love with Rodney. It was the kind of love I've never experienced before or after, and that kind of love doesn't go away so easily."

"Ouch." Derek held his heart.

"I'm sorry, but you asked for it," I went on. "Rodney and I created the most perfect and handsome little boy. We bought this house together." I held my hands out like a Wheel of Fortune model. "We created a great life. But we weren't on the same page when it came to marriage."

"You deserve so much more. Any man should be proud to have you as his wife. Hell, I spent many nights dreaming about us being married one day. If my teenage brain knew you were wife material, his adult brain should've definitely known." He swallowed. "Truth be told, I've often wondered how our lives would've been if we ran off into the sunset after high school, gotten married, and had a few rugrats."

My heart sank. I made it a point not to lead Derek on to believe we could be more than friends. I'd even avoided sex. But maybe a kiss from me is more powerful than I thought. These lips were lethal. They have the power to drive a man insane.

Derek asked, "Am I pushing too hard?"

"No, I'm wondering if I've misled you to believe we're more than friends."

"No, it's not you. I'm stuck in the land of what-if. You were my first love and it wasn't easy getting over you."

"We were kids. We didn't know anything about love," I replied.

"You didn't love me?" He asked.

"Here's the thing about teen love vs. adult love. When we were teens, we had no real responsibilities outside of homework and a few house chores. Life was easy. So, it made love and infatuation come easy. We romanticized love. We could watch a chick flick and be head over heels for one another. There aren't many obstacles in the way. As adults with true responsibilities, love gets tricky. We come home after a grueling day with only a few hours to give to ourselves and to our partners. We're forced to overcome difficult situations and complications. Maintaining love takes work. So when I commit to someone and give them my heart, I don't take it lightly. I don't say it in jest and I won't accept less than what I expect."

"Is that a nice way to tell me you're not interested in pursuing anything more than a friendship with me?"

"Why are you in such a rush?" I asked.

"Let's take a step back," Derek replied, moving his chair closer to me. "The last thing I want to do is piss you off and leave town on a bad note. You mean way too much to me. It's not my intention to rush or force you into anything romantically. So why don't we relax and enjoy each other's company for the rest of the night. Who knows when or if this will ever happen again."

"Now you're speaking my language." I raised my glass. "Here's to a good night of much-needed laughter and fun."

Derek didn't look as enthused anymore. I could actually see his heart break right before my eyes. But what kind of woman would I be to lead him on? I had to figure out my crazy life before I gave my time and attention to another relationship.

We spent hours laughing and talking about the old days and new adventures. I enjoyed the mature version of Derek. He didn't lose his personality over the years. He practiced chivalry. If I stood, he stood. He showed consideration by asking about my comfort often.

But the night quickly changed when I received an email from my Aunt Jova. It burst my bubble and changed my mood to that of a dark one. Since Derek was the main reason I was able to contact Daphne, I shared the email with him.

Hello my beautiful niece,

I hope this email reaches you in good health and spirits. Your mother and I had a long talk recently. Well, it's one of many since I last spoke to you. I'm not sure where you stand with Daphne after everything that's happened between the two of you, but she seriously wants to make things right.

She's not as cold-hearted as you may think. It would be good for you two to sit down and have a meaningful conversation. If you're open to it, please give me a call. Daphne says she'll even travel to Woodcrest. That should show you how much she loves you and wants to make this right. She was caught off guard. Please give this one more shot for yourself, for her, your son, your siblings, and for our family. We want you to be a part of our lives, and we want to be a part of yours. I hope to hear from you soon.

Love you Lots,

Aunt Jova

"Well, what are you going to do?" Derek asked, passing my phone back to me with a concerned gaze.

I shrugged. "I want to hear what she has to say. But I'm afraid she'll hurt my feelings again."

"This has been traumatic for you. Everything has changed and I'm sure it hasn't been easy. I don't care how strong a person is, what has happened to you is soul-shaking."

"That's the perfect analogy," I pointed. "This has been soul-shaking. I didn't question my parents because I trusted them. I knew that if I couldn't trust anyone in this world, I could trust them. Now my guards are up even more and my parents aren't here to help me process it. I've lost ten pounds since this has all come about. My sleep pattern is off. I go to work, come home, sit up all night with little to no sleep. Then I do it all over again the next day."

"I didn't want to say anything because as a man, you don't

bring up a woman's weight. But you do look thinner since I last saw you." He reached over to touch my scrawny arm. "As much as I would love to give you all the right answers to your issues, I know I'm not equipped. Have you thought about seeing a therapist?"

"Do you remember my friend Tammy?"

"Yes, the wild card?" He chuckled. Tammy is pretty unforgettable. I love that about her. She's not afraid to be herself in any situation. What you see is what you get plus a lot more.

"Yup, that's her," I laughed. "I never wanted to take the ancestry test. I knew it would turn into a shit show full of secrets. But I never expected those secrets to be this huge," I sighed. "Tammy pushed me to no end to take the test. So, I told her if need be, she'd pay my counseling bill. I have therapy once a week now and I'm slowly getting back to myself. But it takes time."

"Good," he replied. "It also means you can agree to see your mother again because you already have a therapist on speed dial."

"As great as that sounds, I believe it'll be best for me to talk it over with my therapist before I pull the trigger."

"There you go, making things dark again." He downed the rest of his kiwi infused water. "I have my good eye on you."

"Oh my goodness," I giggled with my hand covering a wicked smile. "I promise I'm not coming unhinged. I don't know where these analogies are coming from."

"Right there." He poked my chest where my heart lay. "I really don't want to leave tomorrow. I haven't felt this alive in a long time. Thank you for that."

"No, thank you for being here with me. I know how busy you are with your career and being a father."

"It's crazy that we're both parents. Who would've thought

two wild teenagers who'd skip school and sneak out on week-ends would be parents to impressionable beings?"

"I pray our dirty dealings don't come back dressed in karma and bad intentions."

"Oh no." He winced. "Please don't say that. At least you have a son. I have a daughter."

"What is that supposed to mean?" I asked with my head tilted.

"You know what I mean. Girls bring babies home. They're vulnerable in a world full of wolves. Anything could happen to them."

It appeared his representative had taken a break and the real Derek was rearing his ugly head. "Are you kidding me? Please don't tell me you're one of those misogynistic assholes who thinks girls are inferior to boys so you would allow boys to run amuck while sheltering girls until they can legally give you their ass to kiss."

"Whoa, whoa," he replied, raising his hands in a surren-dering position. "I'm not that guy."

"No, I want to know where you stand on the subject."

"You're in a career that shows you exactly what I mean. I'm sure you've seen more female identified homicide victims than males."

"I wouldn't necessarily say that's true..."

Derek interrupted, "Oh be honest, Iris. There are more homicide cases for women than men."

"Forget my career. Let's go straight to the statistics." I logged into my MacBook to do a quick google. "According to the FBI statistics, 4,716 males were murdered and 1,857 females were murdered in 2019. That was the last time the chart was updated. Now, tell me again about your stance?"

"Fine, I give up. You say those are the statistics, then so be it. But I still believe we should take more precautions when it comes to girls rather than boys."

"Well, I have a son whom I protect with extreme caution. When it comes down to it, evil is lurking and preying on all of us. We should be as protective over our sons just as much as our daughters. You need to work on your misogynist views."

Derek's eyes widened two times their size. "Is that how I'm coming off?"

"That's exactly how you're coming off."

"I don't hate women. I love you all enough to want to protect you. I'm a man and I know my strength. I could overpower a woman with ease."

"Really?" I asked.

"You don't think so?"

"I can name three women who could beat you to a pulp."

"Oh yeah?" Derek turned to me. "Go for it."

"Bev Francis squats five hundred pounds and bench presses three hundred and thirty-five pounds. Chen Wei Ling deadlifts four hundred and thirty pounds and squats fifty-seven pounds. Iris Kyle holds a Guinness World Record in lifting up twelve adult men overhead in two minutes.

"That's cool, but they're the exception."

"You're a piece of work. But, I'll let it fly this time because I can hardly keep my eyes open."

"Are you going to bed already?" He checked the time.

"I'm no spring chicken and neither are you. Get some sleep. You have an early flight."

Derek stood to help me from the sofa. He kissed my hand and touched the side of my face. "I'll see you in the morning, beautiful. Good night."

"Good night."

I was way too sleepy to think about the sticky situation I'd found myself in with Derek and Rodney. They're both amazing men. I should be excited to have options. But with so much up in the air when it comes to my long lost family, I couldn't think of anything outside of them. A person can only give so much of their energy, and mine is already allocated.

Protect your energy at all costs.

24

A STORM COMES TO TOWN

I knew the day would be challenging when a thunderstorm woke me out of my sleep at five in the morning. My heart raced and my breath wavered. That or it could've been the thought of Daphne and Jova's plane landing later that afternoon. Meditation was needed.

Somehow Derek persuaded me into giving Daphne another shot to make things right. His exact words, *the can of worms have already popped. Now it's time to clean up the mess.*

I wanted to sit a bowl of coal out for Daphne as refreshments. But I allowed my higher self to take the lead and went with platters of fruit and veggies. But if she arrived with bad energy, I'd turn into Uncle Phil from Fresh Prince of Bel Air and throw her out.

The anticipation of their arrival wouldn't allow me to keep still. I could hear my mother's voice saying, *"Make sure the house is spick and span. You're a representation of me."*

My mother would never allow me to have any friends over until my room was spotless. That included vacuuming, dusting, laundry–the works. She took care of the rest of the house because my interpretation of clean could never measure up to hers especially when we were having visitors. She's what you would call a white glove inspector.

We all have our quirks.

I rested my hand over my chest to calm my heart when the doorbell rang. I took a deep breath, slapped on a smile, and welcomed them inside. "You made it safely."

Daphne opened her arms for a hug, but I resisted.

This wasn't the woman I met in Castor. She's smiling and seemingly filled with joy. Would the real Daphne please stand up?

"Let's see how this goes first," I replied.

Jova broke the weird silence, "Thank you for having us."

"I hope I won't regret it," I replied.

"You can let your guard down. I come in peace with endless apologies," Daphne explained.

She threw me a curveball with that one. "Let's make sure we keep it that way," I said. "Follow me, I have refreshments setup in the great room."

"You have a beautiful home," Daphne said, looking around. "Do you live here alone?"

"I mean, if you had given me the time of day in Caster you would know me and my thirteen-year-old son live here."

"I can't apologize enough for behaving the way I did. I'm not proud of it by any means. Is that my grandson?" She walked over, pointing at Junior's basketball portrait. He was so proud when he made the team. He worked extremely hard to improve his skills and maintain his A average. "He's quite handsome. Is he here? I'd love to meet him." She looked around.

"Thank you, but he's with his father. I don't believe this would be the best time for you to meet him until we hash out our differences."

Jova sighed, "That makes sense.."

"I'll start," Daphne spoke, downing half a glass of lemonade. "It's true that you're my daughter. I was only sixteen when I became pregnant with you. My parents threatened to disown me. I thought about running away with you and Alessandro. Then I thought about you and how you deserved so much better. At the time, it seemed like a no-brainer to let my big sister and brother-in-law take care of you until I was old enough and stable." She hung her head. "But it was all a lie."

"I'm listening," I replied, giving her my undivided attention. "Tell me your side."

"The plan was for Brenda and Raymond to take you in for the first three to four years of your life. By then Alessandro and I would be adults and we'd get you back and that would be that. But they reneged on the plan not even a year later. I was only seventeen and still in high school. My sister and Raymond came to the house with adoption papers. At first, I flat out refused and it turned into a screaming match. I wanted to rip Brenda's head off."

"She sure did. Luckily I was there to stop her," Jova whispered with hands in her lap.

"Why did you sign the papers?"

"I was seventeen in high school. I had nothing. I could never win with everyone against me. They forced my hand. Everything about me changed the moment I placed you in Brenda's arms. I knew I never stood a chance."

"You gave up?"

"No, I didn't give up. I tried to find you but I never had any luck. A person can only get their hopes up so many times. Even though my sister pretty much stole you from me, I knew you were in good hands. So I walked away from everyone. Then, at twenty-two, I met my husband. A year into our marriage I had my first child with him and we began growing our family. So, when you showed up out of nowhere I was confused. It was as if I was staring into the eyes of a ghost." She drank the rest of her lemonade. "I felt outraged, cheated, sad, and in endless love. I let you go a long time ago. I prayed that you were happy, healthy, and successful every single day. Imagine how it felt for me to see you standing there in front of me after all those years.."

"I guess I don't get it."

"Losing you caused me excruciating pain. You were a tiny part of my life but monumental. You lived in my heart. You shaped me. I deeply regret our first meeting. I need and want to make it right."

"Why now?" I asked the million dollar question.

"Because no matter what, my life will never be complete without you," Daphne simply explained. "You're my first born. Sure, me and Alessandro may have been a couple of irresponsible teenagers. But you were created in love and we deserve to know each other and love each other. I don't want to go another day without you knowing how deeply I fell in love with you the moment I learned you were growing inside me. It's time for me to let go of my anger. I want us to have a relationship. I want to be your mother." She walked over with her hands out. "Are you open to that?"

I wiped away the warm tears rolling down my hot cheeks and held her hands. She quickly pulled me in for an enduring hug, squeezing me with one arm, and gently cradling my head with the other. This was a mother's love. I recognized it all too well.

"Oh my God, it's about time," Jova cried out with her hands cupping her face.

"Thank you," Daphne said. "My darling daughter, I will gladly spend the rest of my life showing you how much I love you."

"This is all so inconceivable. I thought my days of having

parents were over. Boy, life can change in the blink of an eye," I cried.

"I brought you something." Daphne reached inside her purse to retrieve a small box.

I opened it to find a pair of tiny yellow crochet baby booties.

"I know it isn't much, but one day after school when I was only a few weeks along before anyone knew, Alessandro and I wandered inside a store and saw these. It was the first and only thing we ever bought for you. So, they've been very special to me as a reminder that you are here in this world somewhere."

I sat there, pressing the booties to my chest. Although it's a small token, it's an indication of her sincerity that I so terribly needed. "I'm sorry; I'm usually a woman of many words. But I have none. So, thank you."

"It looks like my sister did right by you. How was your childhood?"

"It was amazing. I was a little," I paused. "Well, I was totally spoiled. My parents gave me everything I wanted and needed. I followed in Dad's footsteps career-wise and it has allowed me to give my son a wonderful life."

"So, the guy who was with you is his dad? He looks just like him." Daphne said.

"Yes and he's the best father and co-parent I could've ever asked for."

"Perhaps this is a bit premature, but I need to know if you will forgive me for my absence in your life and for the way I treated you when you came to me?"

"Lucky for you I'm seeing a therapist. So, I understand your position of wanting to make sure I had a better life than you could give me. I would want to make sure my son has a good life too. But could I be selfless enough to allow someone else to give that to him, I'm not so sure," I sighed. "Then again, I couldn't imagine being pregnant at sixteen. Where would we live? How would I provide? Would I know the first thing about caring for a baby?"

Suddenly I understood Daphne's plight without judgment and anger. I felt compassion and sadness for her. But most of all, I was grateful. Falling in love with a child growing inside you only to have it ripped from you with only a promise to one day reunite. Then to be stabbed in the back by someone you trusted is painful. I could only cry, and that's when Daphne became my mother.

She rocked me in her arms as I let it all out. "There, there darling. We're together now. That's all that matters. We just need to do better with being open, honest, and caring with one another—me most of all."

"I've been alone for so many years. Mom and Dad died when I was in college. I'm thirty ..."

"Seven," Daphne interrupted. "You're thirty-seven." She kissed my forehead. "All this time you've been alone?"

"Not exactly," I went on to explain. "I didn't have any blood relatives. But I had a family. I met my best friend, Brooklyn in college. She was in my life before my parents died. So, when I got the news, she stepped up in a huge way—her and her parents and our other friends." I turned to Jova. "You met Brooklyn and the girls in Pinemoor."

"Oh yes, lovely women."

"Well, Brooklyn's parents allowed me to move in with them after Brooklyn and I graduated college. They became my stand-in parents when I lost mom and dad. It's because of them I was able to transition from college into my career."

"That's wonderful," Daphne said with an enduring smile. "I'd love to meet them and I want you to meet your sisters and brother."

The moment she mentioned my siblings, I couldn't help

but feel a twinge of jealousy. She raised them. They all share a lifetime of memories. But what do I have?

"You went silent. What are you thinking?"

"I don't have a connection with anyone. I'm afraid I'll be the oddball or blacksheep if you will."

"I've sat the kids and my husband down to tell them about you. They know why I'm here. They're excited to meet you."

"How does your husband feel about me?"

"I was blessed to marry a man who cares a great deal about my happiness and gives me his full support in whatever is going on in my life. It was my issues keeping me from searching for you. He's ready to embrace you with open arms. It's up to you at this point. We're ready to welcome you into our fold." She cleared her throat. "I spoke with Alessandro. He told me things went well with you two and you took a DNA test to make sure this was all true."

"I'm a woman of science. I had to see it in black and white."

"I understand," she replied. "You reached out to us, and now we're reaching back. It's finally time for us all to come together as a family. It's long overdue. Time is precious, you know."

"Tell me about it," I replied. "It's just that embracing all of you makes me feel like I'm losing my parents. I know what they did was wrong. But they raised me with so much love and I miss them terribly."

Daphne sucked her teeth. I'm aware of her hate for my mother and father. The same goes for Alessandro. But I'm stuck in the middle. I love them and I will never turn against them. If that's what she expects of me, it will never happen.

"You know what," Jova jumped in. "Let's focus on the present time. You have the opportunity to create a beautiful relationship as mother and daughter. Try not to lose focus on that."

"You're right," Daphne took a deep breath. "My sister isn't here to explain herself. She gave you love and support. She did a spectacular job raising you, and I'm grateful for that if nothing else."

"Thank you," I cried again. Letting go of all the pain I've carried through this journey to accept what's to come. "I'm going to call Rodney to tell him to bring Junior home. I'd love for him to meet his grandmother."

Daphne clutched her stomach. "Thank you, thank you, thank you."

I said a silent prayer before making the call to Rodney. We'd already talked about Junior possibly meeting Daphne if we worked things out. Now the time had come. He excitedly answered on the first ring.

I did it. I gave my son a family. It's the proudest I ever felt of myself. I'd grown mentally. I let people in. I faced my fear to release control. It's all like a dream come true.

25
FAMILY MEETING

The next week after reconciling with Daphne, Brooklyn called a family meeting at her house Sunday at six o'clock in the evening. Part of me wanted to immediately make an excuse not to attend because I knew she was announcing her relocation to Marseau.

Brooklyn and her parents filled a void in my life. It's because of them I still had a family dynamic all these years. They included me on all holidays. They remember every birthday. They've been a major part of my life. Now things were going to change, and I felt empty inside. But I've never left my sister hanging, so I pushed my feelings aside to be in attendance to hear the worst news of my life.

Kai greeted us with hugs and quickly whisked Junior to the designated area upstairs for the kids. I was the last to arrive, so I joined everyone in the living room and squeezed in between Tammy and Shelia on the sofa.

"Thank you all for coming," Kai said with a nervous smile, taking hold of Brooklyn's hand.

"I don't know how to say this, so I'll jump right into it," Brooklyn explained.

I rolled my eyes in detest. This was it. She was about to shoot a dagger to my heart.

"Last week the doctor informed me I've entered stage two of Huntington's," she explained.

Everyone gasped. You could hear a pin drop. Then suddenly our sobs filled the silence.

"Please, you guys are going to make me cry." Brooklyn and her mom tried their best to console us with hugs. But she wasn't done dropping major bombs. "I've also made the decision to move to Marseau. Mom and Dad will be moving with us. It's important that I get to know my family and build a relationship with them before I'm unable to enjoy them. I understand this will be a difficult change. I wish you all could move with us. But I need to do this for myself. Huntington's has done a number on my life. I've wasted so much time living in fear of this disease allowing it to control every decision I make. But not this time," she explained. "This time, I'm jumping ahead of it."

It was all too much to take in at one time. I couldn't slow my breathing. The room went dark.

"Hey, hey, Iris, wake up." Kai shook me. "Slow your breathing. Please."

I swallowed a belly full of air. Everything I'd feared since Brooklyn's diagnosis was happening. "There's no way in hell you and I should be separated when your illness is advancing. What about the promise we made?" I asked. "Do you even remember?"

"Of course I remember. But things have changed." Brooklyn hugged me tighter and kissed my cheek.

"Don't try to butter me up. I'm upset. I don't want you to leave. You belong here. This is your home."

"You've made amends with your bio parents. You guys talk

on the phone often. You're making plans to visit them soon and meet your grandparents."

"Yeah, so," I replied.

"I'm sure you want to make a deeper connection with them. You're finally getting to know yourself. I'm happy for you and I wish you would be happy for me too because I'm on the same journey."

I sighed, "I'm extremely happy for you. But you have a doctor who has you on a successful treatment plan. Look how you've thrived over the years." I turned to Sheila and Thomas. "How could you let her move away especially with her being in stage two? This time is so fragile."

"No, no, don't do that." Brooklyn touched Sheila's arm to encourage her silence. "My parents have gone above and beyond to ensure I have a fulfilled life."

"Is this really happening?" Tammy asked. "How could you consider leaving now that your illness has progressed?"

"That's exactly why I need to go. I've overcome every fear I've had since I was diagnosed with Huntington's. I fell in love. I got married. I had a kid. I wasn't able to adopt a child. It hurt for a while, but that's the way the cookie crumbled. At least I tried. You see, that's the key to life. You keep trying. I know I don't have much time left until I become a shell of myself. So, I need to try to build a relationship with my family," she explained. "Furthermore, I'd like you to finally do something for yourself. You followed your dad's career path. But that's not what you wanted to do. You're into fashion. You'd put on fashion shows for our dorm for goodness sakes. You're passionate about it. That's your true calling. It's not too late. I also want you to give your family a chance. Stop playing it safe with your happiness." Brooklyn was on a roll. She went down the line reading us our rights. "Tammy, you put on this act like you're some happy-go-lucky play girl. You want to be loved and you want to give love too. You're just scared because your marriage didn't work out. You need to explore that void and fix it."

"You don't know the half," Tammy mumbled.

"I know more than you think." She turned to Lorraine. "Now you, Missy, everything is not black and white. No one is perfect. Not even you. Stop living by what you think are the rules and enjoy life. Color outside the lines sometimes. Unlike Tammy, you need a one night stand," she laughed while Lorraine covered her blushing cheeks.

"I did have a one night stand," Lorraine confessed with red cheeks.

"With who?" We all asked simultaneously.

"Okay, hold on, that's our cue to get out of here and leave you girls to talk in private. I love you all," Sheila said, stuffing her purse under her arm. "Come Thomas."

"I want to hear about the one night stand," he teased.

Sheila grabbed him by the collar and forced him out the door. Kai followed suit and left us girls to our own vices.

"Okay now, tell us about your one night stand and don't be coy about it," Tammy urged, tugging on Lorraine's arm.

"I snuck out to see Keith one night after you all had gone to sleep. We talked over soft music and drank wine. Then one thing led to another."

"Unbelievable," Tammy squealed. "I'm so proud of you. It's about time you visited the wild side."

"All I want to know is if you were careful?" Brooklyn asked.

"Hey, I'm still Lorraine. I put the condom on myself."

We fell over in laughter. It was moments like this that made me furious at the thought of Brooklyn busting up our friendship with her upcoming move across the world. This kind of friendship only comes around once in a lifetime.

It took some time for us to get to this point. But over the

years, we had proven our love and loyalty to one another. We couldn't be more like sisters if we were blood. Why would she give this up for a group of strangers? Blood isn't always family. I know many people who are at war with their so-called blood relatives.

"Have you ever thought about what you'd do if you get to Marseau and they aren't as nice and welcoming as they were when you visited?" I asked.

"Enough is enough," Brooklyn said, sitting up from our pile up on the floor. "I thought we squashed all of this in Marseau. Now we're right back where we started. I'm getting really tired of your negativity. I'm not changing my mind."

"God forbid I show an ounce of concern," I replied. "I just don't think this move is warranted. You could visit and talk on the phone."

"You visit and talk on the phone with your family," she replied with scrunched eyebrows. "None of you know the time we have left on this earth. But unfortunately I know my time may be nearing an end in an able body. My next phase in this life may be me in a bed unable to speak, eat, think, or feel any emotions. So, back off."

"Hey, hey, guys," Lorraine put herself in between us. "I think me and Tammy's bickering has rubbed off on you two in a bad way. Maybe we should respect Brooklyn's decision and let her do what she feels is right for her life."

"Yeah, you think?" Brooklyn said.

I couldn't speak. I covered my face and let the tears flow. At that moment, I turned into a child who'd gotten her toy taken away and told it was bedtime, and I didn't care. I was tired of being the strong one and always in control. All I wanted to do was let the hurt out.

"You're driving me crazy." Brooklyn wrapped her arms around me while I continued to sob. "I don't want to leave you guys either. But I need to do this for myself. I wish I could be like you all. Then I'd visit my family and build from there. But my tomorrow may not look like today. I'm begging you, please understand."

"I understand," Lorraine folded her arms over her chest.

"You don't have to explain anything to me. I respect your decision." Tammy sat on the sofa.

"I now know what it feels like to have a sibling that you grow up with all your life only for them to pack up and move away to college and leave you behind. But it doesn't stop there. They move off to college and become a completely different person from who you knew. Then the relationship becomes unfamiliar," I explained.

"No, Iris, things don't always happen that way. It's up to those people to maintain their relationship. Distance doesn't mean the death of a relationship," Tammy did her best to smooth things over.

"She's right," Brooklyn piggy backed. "It's up to us to maintain our friendship. That's why I called you all over. We need to make a plan on how we can do that. Like maybe commiting to video chats and phone calls more than two times a week. You guys could visit me there and of course I'd come here. If we all make an effort the only thing that will change is the distance."

Tammy pulled out her phone. "I'll create a private group on Facebook for us. We could update each other on our day and share photos with each other."

"Oh, that's a good idea," Lorraine gushed. "But what about the time difference? How will we schedule video chats?"

"I think we should take turns on morning calls. One week you guys could do morning chats and the next week I could do morning chats."

"That sounds fair," Tammy agreed.

I sat on the sofa, filing my nails. I'd do whatever they say to keep the peace. The last thing I wanted to do was fight with Brooklyn. Especially now that she's moving away. It'd kill me if we were at war when she moves away. But I'd fly to Marseau to make up with her because she means that much to me.

"You're pretty quiet over here." Tammy brushed my shoulder with hers.

"I'm sorting out my emotions."

"Care to share it with us?" Brooklyn asked.

"You're moving away and my heart is shattering into a million little pieces."

Brooklyn put her arm around me and kissed me on the cheek while smoothing my flyaway hairs. That has always been her way of showing me she loves me and she's here for me. How was she going to show me that from across the world?

"You know you could have talked to me about this again if you were still having a hard time accepting it."

"I thought you would change your mind."

"Out of sight out of mind doesn't work with Huntington's disease. You know that as well as I do. You've been here since the beginning."

"I know," I replied, standing to get away from her. It's her energy that makes her so special. Now I've got to get used to being without it. "This is incredibly difficult. I wanted our kids to grow up together. Our sons are brothers."

"On the bright side, he has more family to build relationships with now. He will always have us." She kissed my forehead. "Okay, ladies, I think we should call it a night."

"Wait," Lorraine said. "Exactly when are you moving?"

"My grandmother wants us to move in with her."

"You're stalling," I said. "When is the move?"

"Next month. We listed the house today. Our careers allow us to work from anywhere."

Next month—those words rang in my head. I wanted to

react. But I couldn't hurt my sister. I had to put her happiness above mine. Whether I liked it or not, Brooklyn was right. She could be in perfect health today and tomorrow she could be bed bound. The time was now.

"Alright, I can't take it anymore." I gathered my things. "Good night, ladies. I love you all."

"Please don't go," Brooklyn grabbed my hand. Either I couldn't move or I didn't want to move. I wasn't sure which one it was, but I was still there and my ears were open.

"You guys go ahead and leave. I need to talk to Iris alone, if that's okay," Brooklyn explained to Tammy and Lorraine, still holding my hand.

"We love you guys." Tammy and Lorraine gave us kisses and hugs before they took off.

"Come with me." Brooklyn led me away, still holding my hand.

"Where are you taking me?"

"Just walk with me," she ordered, leading me to her office. "Look at this." She pulled a folder from her bag.

"What is this?"

"Read it," she demanded.

"These are your final wishes. Why in the world would you give this to me right now? I'm already emotionally depleted for the day." I was no longer in my body. I could float right out of there and it wouldn't alarm me.

Brooklyn took the folder and held me in her arms and we cried together. We cried for what seemed like hours. When there were no more tears, we picked right back up where we left off.

"This is your copy because you are a part of my last wishes. I need you to read it, accept it, and commit to it. Will you do that for me?"

"Yes," I cried. "I love you. I'm sorry for being a bitch. I just never imagined we'd have so much distance between us."

"We'll never be separated as long as we love and cherish this sisterhood we've built over the years. Nothing and I mean nothing will ever change the love I have for you. I need you in my life."

"You promise?"

"Yes, you have my word," she replied with an enduring hug. "There's something else I want to talk to you about."

"What more could there be?"

"In two weeks I'm sending you an invitation."

"What's going on?"

"Just be there and dress cute."

"What's the occasion? Is it your farewell party?"

"No, just dress cute and be on time. I love you." She called out for Junior. Good tactic because she knew I wouldn't make a big fuss in front of him. I do all that I can to shield him from the messiness of our adult drama. No point in stealing his childhood.

"Are we leaving already?" Junior asked out of breath.

"What do you mean already? It's been an hour. Now come on, it's time to go."

"But we were in the middle of a game. I was about to beat their best score."

"You can try again next time. Now get going." I playfully spanked his butt to give him a little push out the door.

After hugging Brooklyn goodbye, I joined Junior in the car.

"You've been crying," he said.

"Why do you say that?"

"I'm not blind, mom. I know when you've been crying. What's going on?"

I parked on the side of the road with my flashers on and turned to Junior. If I didn't tell him, he'd worry and I didn't want that. "Son, you're getting older. You'll be fourteen soon. So it's time for me to entrust you with details I'd usually keep from you," I explained. "You know Aunt Brooklyn has Huntington's disease?"

"Yes." He gave me a nod.

"Well, she's reached stage two." I kept my emotions in check to avoid scarring him for the rest of his life.

"Stage two means it's getting worse, doesn't it?" he asked with wide eyes. "Is that why you were crying?"

"Yes."

"I'm sorry, mom. Aunt Brooklyn means a lot to me too. What can I do to make you feel better?"

I smiled for the first time tonight. My thoughtful son would be the key factor in me getting through this entire ordeal with a sane mind.

"You don't need to do anything but be yourself. That's all I need." I kissed his forehead and rolled back onto the street to get us home.

The moon shone bold and high amongst the blanket of stars. Its sight provided a bit of much-needed peace. But nothing could take my mind off the folder sitting in the backseat. We'd reached that time in her life where she couldn't put off her last words. She was going to change. I wasn't ready to see her in that condition. Not by the least. So the backseat is where the folder would remain for the rest of the night. Maybe I'd get up the nerve to read it tomorrow or maybe the day after that. Until then, I was okay existing in intentional ignorance.

26

THE ENGAGEMENT

The day had arrived for Brooklyn's mysterious gathering at an unknown location. The day I've dreaded. I woke up with a knot in my stomach wondering exactly what Brooklyn had up her sleeve.

I'd already given Brooklyn enough grief about her decision to relocate. So tonight, I won't do that. It's time to preserve our relationship and support my friend even if it means breaking my heart. So, I put the perfect outfit together to wish her well on her new journey. I decided on a silk blush skirt pleated at the waist with a high side slit, silk white draped tank, and nude high heels. I didn't want to go so drastic as to look how I felt. Nothing is ever that oppressive.

I arrived at the address Brooklyn texted me at seven o'clock on the dot. Just as I suspected, it was a party. A waste of a cute outfit doing something I loathed. I sat in my car for a moment practicing a fake smile. I'll wish her well even though it stung. I'll keep my emotions in check, dance a little, nibble here and there with hugs and kisses. Fake it until you make it to the highest degree.

Walking towards the building almost felt like I was being forced to walk the plank to my death. It definitely felt that way. It's the death of life as I knew it. My close sisterhood with Brooklyn would change drastically. Will we drift apart and become strangers? Will the daily phone calls and text messages dwindle down to calls once in a blue moon? I'm not a blue moon type of woman. Now it hurts even more to bottle my feelings just to get through the night.

My hands were so sweaty my diamond clutch almost slipped away from me. The ulcer her news has given me made me physically ill. I thought about the passage I read about dread earlier. Dreading is a chance to overcome, reflect, and be at peace with change.

A tall slender woman greeted me upon entering the posh building and showed me to the room to join my party. I walked down the hallway with small steps to buy myself time. Diamond chandeliers hung from the oak wood paneled ceiling. Abstract framed art taller than me lined the walls. All of them with a color scheme of black, blush, blue, and orange. I stood for a moment to study the painting. It was signed, Lola. I could hear music when I looked at it.

Finally, I slid open the slatted doors and Brooklyn screamed, "It's the woman of the hour."

"What the hell is all this?" I asked.

Brooklyn ran over and pulled me to the other side of the room where Rodney was dressed in a teal tailored suit. Junior stood beside him with a huge smile. Thankfully styled differently from his old dad. It gave me hope the twin phase was over.

Rodney held his hands out for me to take hold of them. He cleared his throat and the room fell silent. "Iris, for the longest I've been running from my true feelings. You're beautiful, intelligent, and steadfast. There's no other woman like you. I love the way you smile. I love the sound of your laugh. I love how compassionate and intentional you are with our son. You are phenomenal."

Brooklyn took that as her queue to say, "A phenomenal woman she is."

Rodney carried on without a hitch, "I would like to ask you in front of all your family and friends for your hand in marriage. It would be my honor to spend the rest of my life showing you how much I love and adore you." He knelt on one knee and asked, "will you marry me?"

I was supposed to feel excited in a moment like this, but I didn't. My first thought was the pain he caused me when he broke my heart. Love isn't supposed to hurt before it feels good. Then I thought about him not wanting me–us, until Derek came into the picture. He's supposed to know he wants me without the threat of losing me.

Is this the love story I deserve?

These questions and issues clouded my head so much I almost forgot Rodney was still on one knee waiting for my answer. Then I looked at all the eyes on me, anticipating my answer. Could I hurt and embarrass him?

"Well," he said nervously. "Will you marry me?"

"We need to talk." I pulled Rodney by the hand and fled out into the hallway. "Why would you do this? You know we aren't in a place to consider marriage. You're still in counseling for God's sake."

"Iris, you're operating from fear. What does your heart say?" He gently touched my face.

"This is not fear talking. This is common sense. You never wanted to marry me or even be in a committed relationship until you saw another man wanted to have that with me. Why in the hell do you want to get married now?"

Once again he touched the side of my face. "Sweetheart,

you're missing the point. You're a force and any man in his right mind would want to be with you. I've always known your worth. I know you inside out. I know what drives you. I know how to be a rock for you when you're emotional. I'm there for you when you need me and even when you're unable to recognize you need me. You're more than your beauty to me. You're water. I need you to survive. I'm deeply in love with you."

"Those are beautiful words. But I need more time for you to show me you feel those things and it won't happen overnight."

Rodney dropped his head and his shoulders followed suit with no words.

"Hey," I touched his arm. "Give me the ring. I'll keep it in my jewelry box. When we both reach the last days of counseling, if we decide to move forward, I'll wear it and we'll plan the wedding of the decade. But should one of us make the decision to walk away, I'll give the ring back. Right now, I'm rediscovering myself. So we can't go into marriage as a work in progress and think it'll stand the test of time."

"So that's a no?" He asked with sad eyes.

"Are you even listening to me?" I huffed.

"I heard everything you said. You're rediscovering yourself and we both have work to do. It's a nice way to say no."

"Sweetheart," I rested my hand on his cheek. "I didn't say yes and I didn't say no. We will revisit it once we do the work. If you can't accept that, I understand. But that is all I can give you right this second."

"I'll take whatever you give me," Rodney said, reclaiming his dignity. "Would you at least wear the ring tonight so we don't have to explain your decision to everyone?"

"Yes, I'll wear it as long as you understand it's not a yes or a no."

"I get it, Iris. I get it," he replied, sliding the huge rock on my finger. "You see how much I love you. That red diamond in the middle of the white diamonds is my way of giving you your red rose, and I'll water it daily by doing the work and loving only you unconditionally for the rest of my life."

"It's beautiful," I replied, admiring the ring. It sat right next to the rose ring Brooklyn bought for us on vacation. Two important reminders on one hand. "How much did this ring cost?"

"It's priceless." He kissed my hand. "Now let's get back in there. There's more people you need to see."

"Who?"

"Come on," he gave me a gentle nudge.

"Well, what did you say? Are we having a wedding or not?" Brooklyn asked.

"With conditions," Rodney held my hand up. "If you know Iris, you understand."

"Yes, yes, yes," Brooklyn danced with Junior.

Everyone erupted in laughter. Their congratulations came quickly in abundance. But no one was happier than Junior. He smashed into me and wrapped me up in his arms. For the sake of my son, we had to get this right. But he'd need to learn about disappointment early in life if Rodney is a lost cause. I love my son and all, but I won't marry Rodney and omit my happiness for the sake of his.

Most people tend to see their parents as superheroes. Learning my parents weren't my biological parents, and meeting my family after being alone for so long sent my life in a tailspin. But thanks to my girls, I faced it all, and just as they promised, I gained so much more.

I was almost knocked out of my heels with shock when I saw Daphne and the two women who were outside her house standing in the corner with a stylish guy. Alessandro and my brothers stood next to them. Jova, Alisa, and Tiana schmoozed with everyone in the room.

279

"Congratulations sweetheart, I'm so happy for you." Daphne gave me a hug. "These three are about to burst, waiting to meet you."

"Oh hello there, I'm Iris," I introduced myself.

"My name is Nara," the upbeat brunette said with her arms stuck out for a hug.

"I'm Renta," a tall well-put-together woman followed the lead of Nara with a hug.

"It's nice to meet you both."

"My name is Elliott," the man smiled wide with blushing cheeks.

"These are your sisters and your brother," Daphne explained with a cheesy smile.

"Oh wow, it's wonderful to meet you guys. I have sisters and another brother," I squealed. They pulled me into a group hug.

They were total opposites. Nara sported an office attire style—a white ruffle blouse tucked inside black and white pinstripe pants with black high heels. I could tell she was all business and no play. Renta was dressed in a stylish boho blue floral print front pleated skirt with a matching shirt. She wore nude high heels with big curls swooped to the side. It was the entire look for me. She and I had one thing in common—fashion! Elliott was fluid with his style. He rocked a long black skirt, black mesh shirt, and a black blazer. He looked phenomenal and wore it with great confidence. I knew I could learn a lot from him.

"We have so much to catch up on," Nara said. "Wow, look at that ring. It's a beauty. Make sure you get it appraised and insured as soon as possible." I knew Nara was all business.

"I'll do that. Thank you. How long will you all be in town? We should spend the day together tomorrow," I offered.

"Oh yes, how's the shopping in Woodcrest?" Renta asked.

"Horrible, but we could drive to Highsea and really do some damage."

"I like you already." Elliott smiled.

"My children are together at last," Daphne said with a deep sigh. "Jova, come, come; take a picture of us."

"I'm on it." She ran over, pointing her phone to snap the picture. "Beautiful and handsome."

"Well lookie here, family reunited. I love to see it," Brooklyn said, joining us.

"Oh my goodness, I was so caught up in the moment I forgot to introduce you to my best friend who I consider my sister, Brooklyn." I pulled her close to my side.

"We've met, and I'm already in love with her," Renta said with a huge smile.

"Ah thank you, I love you guys too," Brooklyn replied, holding Renta's hand.

"Hey, you should come with us to..." she paused. "What's it called again?"

"Highsea," I said.

"Yeah, Highsea, we're going shopping tomorrow. We'd love for you to join us if you're not busy."

"If Iris is okay with me tagging along, I'd love to go."

"You're always welcomed." I kissed her cheek.

For the first time in many years, life made complete sense. Although I will always miss my parents on this earthly realm, I was thankful to know the truth and face it head on. I gained much more than I ever expected. I'm not a lone wolf. I have blood siblings who've welcomed me into their lives with open arms. I have living parents, grandparents, aunts, uncles, and cousins. I'm overjoyed and open to it all.

"Hey, hey, hey, do not take another picture without us." Alessandro said, dragging my brothers over with him.

By the end of the night, my cheeks were sore from smiling.

The only way to describe the night was a fairytale. My head spinned but I loved every moment of it. We ate good food, danced, laughed, hugged, shared life stories and connected on deeper levels.

Somehow I survived the total eclipse of my life and still managed to land a possible fiancé given we do the work. We as humans have a tendency to plan life without leaving much room for change. But it doesn't work that way. At least that's what I've learned. Even when I finally accepted my life for what it was, it still took me for one helluva ride.

Rodney had his shortcomings, but the man sure knew how to tap into the deepest part of my heart. Derek was a wonderful first love who opened my mind and heart to learn more about myself when in a romantic relationship. But on the other hand with Rodney, I learned how to navigate misunderstandings, trust even when it's broken, encouragement of growth and care, compromising, weaknesses, accepting what I can't fix or change, and being vulnerable enough to express my feelings.

Rodney gave me my forever roses. But, in that moment in time, I chose me.

BOOK CLUB QUESTIONS

1. Was there a moment when you disagreed with the protagonist's decisions? What would you have done differently?
2. Who was your favorite character? What character did you identify with the most? Were there any characters that you disliked? Why?
3. Which character did you feel the most sympathy for?
4. Did any part of this book strike a particular emotion in you? Which part and what emotion did the book make you feel?
5. How thought-provoking did you find the book? Did the book change your opinion about anything, or did you learn something new from it? If so, what?
6. Which part of the book resonated emotionally with you?
7. Did you find the ending of the book satisfying?
8. What do you think happens to the characters after the book ends?

9. If you could ask the author one question about the book, what would it be?
10. Would you read another book by this author? Why or why not?

ABOUT RIZE PRESS

RIZE publishes great stories and great writing across genres written by People of Color and other underrepresented groups. Our team consists of:

Lisa Diane Kastner, Founder and Executive Editor
Cody Sisco, Acquisitions Editor, RIZE
Benjamin White, Acquisition Editor, Running Wild
Peter A. Wright, Acquisition Editor, Running Wild
Resa Alboher, Editor
Angela Andrews, Editor
Sandra Bush, Editor
Ashley Crantas, Editor
Rebecca Dimyan, Editor
Abigail Efird, Editor
Aimee Hardy, Editor
Henry L. Herz, Editor
Cecilia Kennedy, Editor
Barbara Lockwood, Editor
Scott Schultz, Editor

Evangeline Estropia, Product Manager
Kimberly Ligutan, Product Manager
Lara Macaione, Marketing Director
Joelle Mitchell, Licensing and Strategy Lead
Pulp Art Studios, Cover Design
Standout Books, Interior Design
Polgarus Studios, Interior Design

Learn more about us and our stories at www.runningwildpress.com

Loved these stories and want more? Follow us at
www.runningwildpress.com, www.facebook.com/running wildpress,
on Twitter @lisadkastner @RunWildBooks @RIZERWP